PENGUIN BOOKS

LIFE *with an* IDIOT

Victor Erofeyev was born in 1947. The son of a high-ranking Soviet diplomat, he spent part of his childhood in Paris and later rebeled against Soviet high society's values. A literary critic and dissident writer, in 1979 he helped organize the collection *Metropol,* a literary magazine whose contents so outraged the authorities that Erofeyev was banned from Soviet print until the Gorbachev era. His publications include the novel *Russian Beauty* and numerous stories and essays. His writing has appeared in *The New Yorker, The New York Review of Books,* and *The Times Literary Supplement,* among other places. He lives in Moscow.

Andrew Reynolds is a professor of Slavic languages at the University of Wisconsin–Madison. Born in Swansea, Wales, he was educated at Dynevor School in Swansea and Merton College at Oxford. He was a research fellow at Queens' College, Cambridge, and a fellow and tutor at Selwyn College, Cambridge. He is the translator of Victor Erofeyev's novel *Russian Beauty* and joint editor (with Erofeyev) of *The Penguin Book of New Russian Writing.*

VICTOR EROFEYEV

TRANSLATED BY
ANDREW REYNOLDS

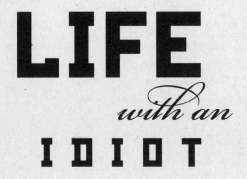

LIFE
with an
IDIOT

PENGUIN BOOKS

PENGUIN BOOKS

Published by the Penguin Group

Penguin Group (USA) Inc., 375 Hudson Street, New York, New York 10014, U.S.A.

Penguin Group (Canada), 10 Alcorn Avenue Toronto,
   Ontario, Canada M4V 3B2 (a division of Pearson Penguin Canada Inc.)

Penguin Books Ltd, 80 Strand, London WC2R 0RL, England

Penguin Ireland, 25 St Stephen's Green, Dublin 2, Ireland (a division of Penguin Books Ltd)

Penguin Group (Australia), 250 Camberwell Road, Camberwell,
   Victoria 3124, Australia (a division of Pearson Australia Group Pty Ltd)

Penguin Books India Pvt Ltd, 11 Community Centre, Panchsheel Park,
   New Delhi – 110 017, India

Penguin Group (NZ), cnr Airborne and Rosedale Roads, Albany,
   Auckland, New Zealand (a division of Pearson New Zealand Ltd)

Penguin Books (South Africa)(Pty) Ltd, 24 Sturdee Avenue, Rosebank,
   Johannesburg 2196, South Africa

Penguin Books Ltd, Registered Offices: 80 Strand, London WC2R 0RL, England

First published in Penguin Books 2004

10 9 8 7 6 5 4 3 2 1

Originally published in Russian (as a volume of fourteen stories) under the title
Zhizn's idiotom by Interbuk, Moscow, 1991.

PUBLISHER'S NOTE
These selections are works of fiction. Names, characters, places, and incidents either are the
product of the author's imagination or are used fictitiously, and any resemblance to actual
persons, living or dead, business establishments, events, or locales is entirely coincidental.

LIBRARY OF CONGRESS CATALOGING IN PUBLICATION DATA
Erofeev, V. V. (Viktor V.)
   [Zhizn's idiotom. English]
   Life with an idiot / Victor Erofeyev ; translated by Andrew Reynolds.
      p.   cm.
   Short stories.
   ISBN 0-14-023621-X
      I. Reynolds, Andrew.   II. Title.
PG3479.7.R58Z3613 2004
891.73'44—dc22   2004053393

Printed in the United States of America
Set in Scala / Designed by Lynn Newmark

# Acknowledgments

I should like to thank Kathryn Court, Sarah Manges and Caroline White for their generous support and helpful advice with regard to the English text, and David Vernikov, Victor Erofeyev himself and my wife, Olga Pobedinskaya, for their many useful suggestions concerning the Russian original.

—A. R.

ONTENTS

Translator's Introduction   ix

Life with an Idiot   1

A White Neutered Tomcat with the Eyes
   of a Beautiful Woman   28

Shit-Sucker   35

How We Murdered the Frenchman   46

The Maiden and Death   55

Anna's Body, or The End of the Russian Avant-garde   69

The Parakeet   75

Persian Lilac   91

Berdyaev   95

The End of Everything   123

Boldino Autumn   131

Letter to Mother   135

Three Meetings   147

Cotton Wool   159

Sweet Fanny Adams	170
Mother	179
The Girlfriends	191
Pocket Apocalypse	204
Notes	221

"East is East . . . ?"

VICTOR EROFEYEV AND THE POETICS/POLITICS OF IDIOCY

> To die from Gornfeld is as silly as to die from a bicycle or a
> parrot's beak. But a literary murderer can also be a parrot.
> —Osip Mandelstam, *Fourth Prose*

EVEN BY the idiosyncratic standards of Russian literature, the literary debut proper of Victor Erofeyev (the author's preferred trans-
literation) was one of the more striking confirmations of the
unofficial but popular Soviet self-definition that "we were born to
turn Kafka into real life," exemplifying as it did the various phe-
nomena of *samizdat, tamizdat,* censorship, repression, tragedy and
farce that in some combination or other inform the relationship
between state power, writer and reader in Russia. It is true that the
events surrounding Erofeyev's organization and "publication" in
1979 of an uncensored literary almanac, *Metropol,* did not reach
the level of absurdity epitomized by the "arrest" in 1960 not only of
Vasily Grossman's manuscript of *Life and Fate* but also of the author's typewriter, typewriter ribbons and carbon paper, to avoid any
chance that the work could be reconstituted; indeed, the fact that
the initial response of the authorities to the "*Metropol* affair" was to
close down the café where the book was to be launched under the

pretext that it was "infested with cockroaches" seems in retrospect to testify to how weak the Soviet Union had become under Leonid Brezhnev. This is not to say, however, that Erofeyev, Vasily Aksyonov, Evgeny Popov and the other *Metropol* writers were in no danger at that time: the book's *samizdat* publication (and promised publication in the West) truly outraged the authorities, and the main "conspirators" in particular faced the very real danger of being expelled from the country or falling victim to a KGB-arranged "accident," threats alluded to in a number of the stories in the present collection, and most notably by the unspecified crime for which the narrator of "Life with an Idiot" is punished. Thanks in no small part to a telegram of support sent by John Updike, Kurt Vonnegut, Edward Albee, William Styron and Arthur Miller, no such drastic fate befell the participants, but the authorities were able to enjoy a short-lived (though ultimately Pyrrhic) victory, in that a number of the contributors emigrated soon afterward. When the following year saw the Soviet invasion of Afghanistan, Andrei Sakharov's exile to Gorky and the end of détente, it seemed clear that whatever remained of Brezhnev's low, dishonest decades would offer no hope of change for the better.

Why did these writers feel the need to challenge the Soviet literary and political establishment in such a risky way? Why, in particular, should Victor Erofeyev, the son of a high-ranking Soviet diplomat who had been special assistant to Molotov and also worked as an interpreter for Joseph Stalin, have renounced his "birthright" as one of Soviet high society's golden youths and rebelled against its values? In Erofeyev's case, the fact that he had spent part of his childhood in Paris and enjoyed a privileged lifestyle undoubtedly helped him acquire an excellent knowledge of certain elements of twentieth-century culture not easily available to the average Soviet citizen, as well as to experience first-hand both the benefits and the costs of the Party elite's society within a society; and being like many writers a born rebel, heretic and contrarian, by the mid-1970s he was no longer willing to live the lies that the system demanded. Having graduated from the Philological Faculty of Moscow State University in 1970, in 1973 he completed postgraduate work at the Institute of World Literature in Moscow, and in 1975 he received his candidate's degree for his thesis on Dostoevsky and French existentialism. His first published works of literary criticism were on authors alien to the Soviet system—de Sade and Lev Shestov—and were scandalous enough in their own right.

Erofeyev was, of course, not alone in feeling, during the bleakest years of the "period of stagnation," that enough was enough. Stalin's death in 1953 had been followed by a series of political and cultural thaws and freezes, but after the removal of Nikita Khrushchev in 1964, and particularly after the invasion of Czechoslovakia in 1968, it became increasingly difficult for works that were not an "oath of abstinence from the truth" (Aleksandr Solzhenitsyn's definition of Socialist Realism) to be published in the Soviet Union. The system was powerful enough to deal successfully with dissident voices, but only at the cost of forcing into emigration many of the best minds of the generation; and the main consequence of the usually ham-fisted attempts to destroy these minds (both metaphorically and literally) was simply to confirm that the center of gravity of literature had indeed shifted to the diaspora. The 1970s saw the three central figures of Russian literature—Solzhenitsyn, Joseph Brodsky and Andrei Siniavsky—join Vladimir Nabokov in the West. Some major writers remained in the USSR and were able to publish, most notably Yuri Trifonov, Bitov and Valentin Rasputin; but any works that were thematically and formally provocative, and particularly those that revealed the darker side of Soviet existence, had little or no chance of being published. Writers who wanted to express themselves freely were faced with

stark choices: to write "for the desk drawer"; to risk the consequences that would come from publishing abroad; to follow certain of their predecessors in cultivating the genre of silence; or to
leave the country. Moreover, what was in fact the Soviet system's
loyal imitation of its leaders' senility appeared to many both within
the USSR and outside to be not stagnation but stability and strength;
and despite the pervasive corruption of the period, the benefits
brought by oil revenues and the regime's refusal to address the
underlying structure problems of the economy allowed the
regime to convince many that they had never had it so good. At
least the shops were full of sausage, that litmus test of the *dolce
vita* in Soviet times.

Metropol, which aimed to "provide a roof" for "homeless," out-
cast literature, almost inevitably became more than an expression
of the need for literary pluralism and a protest against the virtual
impossibility of getting works that were not Socialist Realist or Socialist Realist "lite" past the censorship. The *Metropol* stories were
not anti-Soviet, but as is always the case in Russia, works that appear to be apolitical have a political meaning, words have a tendency to become deeds and, as Erofeyev has noted, an attack on
the state's monopoly on the word, if not defeated, could have been
read as or encouraged an attack on its monopoly on power.
Though few critics have been particularly impressed by the literary qualities of *Metropol* as a whole, its significance in helping to
discredit further the Soviet system is not to be ignored; even if
Erofeyev exaggerates its importance when he claims that it
"buried Soviet literature" (which seemed to be doing the job well
enough itself), it was certainly one of the final nails in its coffin.

At the time, however, things looked rather different, as few
commentators foresaw the historic convulsions that lay ahead for
the USSR in the 1980s. After some initial hesitation, the authorities reverted to type: Erofeyev, who had just been accepted into the

Writers' Union, was immediately expelled from it, and there may have been a plan to expel him from the country too. Erofeyev's father, knowing that it would be the end of his distinguished career if his son refused to recant, nonetheless courageously supported his son (an episode that inspired part of Erofeyev's recently completed novel *The Good Stalin*, a modern reworking of the "fathers and sons" theme of Russian literature); and all the other conspirators behaved honorably and courageously too. Although the scandal meant that it was impossible for Erofeyev to publish his work in the Soviet Union until 1988, he believes that his "expulsion" from official literature was his salvation as a writer, as he no longer had to worry about either outer or inner censorship. Many of the stories collected here (as well as his novel *Russian Beauty*) circulated in manuscript and were read and discussed in the literary underground, in the so-called "kitchen culture" of the time; and with the advent of Gorbachev's *perestroika* and *glasnost*, Erofeyev was immediately recognized as one of Russia's most important postmodernist writers both by those Russian critics and readers for whom this is a term of praise and by those for whom it is a term of abuse.

It is as the author of the novel *Russian Beauty* that Erofeyev is best known in the West, the work being hailed as a "masterpiece" and "the book of its time" when it first appeared in English translation in 1992. One of Russia's leading essayists, literary critics and cultural commentators, and increasingly outspoken on political matters too, he is also a regular contributor of leading Western publications such as *The New Yorker*, the *International Herald Tribune*, *The New York Review of Books* and *The Times Literary Supplement*. The full extent of his talent, however, is still not sufficiently appreciated in the English-speaking world—among his many works still to be translated into English are a large number of short stories, the highly controversial novel *The Last Judgment*, a collection of literary essays *In the Labyrinth of Accursed Questions* and the following *sui generis* collections, *Five Rivers of Life, Encyclopedia of the Russian Soul, Men* and *God X,* as well as the already mentioned new novel *The Good Stalin.*

Like Martin Amis's 1995 novel *The Information,* Erofeyev's 1994 novel *The Last Judgment* can be read as in large part a variation on Pushkin's *Mozart and Salieri,* suggesting that, as is the case with most serious writers, Erofeyev's overriding concern is future fame and not, as his foes would claim, present wealth and popularity (or not just these things). His ongoing dialogue with the major works of Russian literature, and in particular his only partly resolved struggle with his namesake, Venedikt Erofeev (1938–1990), author of the masterpiece *Moscow to the End of the Line,* informs many of the stories collected here. Erofeyev's exaggerated revolt against certain of his literary precursors may be seen as a necessary overcoming, transformation and synthesis of the cultural heritage; as Elizabeth Rich has noted, his writing "represents a natural link...in the unnatural evolution of Russian literature." This is not how many of his critics see it, however: his polemical article of 1990 "Soviet Literature: In Memoriam" (*"Pominki po sovetskoi literature"*) provoked some 250 published articles, virtually all of them violently opposed to his argument that official Soviet literature and dissident literature alike no longer served any useful purpose. Erofeyev developed this argument further in his article "Russia's Fleurs du Mal" (*"Russkie tsvety zla"*), and the stories in *Life with an Idiot,* as well as those by most of the authors contained in our anthology *The Penguin Book of New Russian Writing,* are certainly representative of the "literature of evil" that is mainstream Russian postmodernism. The stories collected in *Life with an Idiot* were written in the period 1978–1990, and some critics felt that they would date quickly, not least because they seemed to be too closely linked with features of modern Soviet life that were already "history"; if anything, they now seem even more relevant to the concerns of Russia and indeed of the outside world than they did then, though this is not necessarily a cause for rejoicing.

Yet it should have been apparent that Erofeyev's ability to read the "Russian mind" was always his greatest strength, and the broader historical canvas on which he works is indicated by the fact that it is not easy to "date" these stories, because, as Mark Lipovetsky, among others, has noted, Erofeyev's "favorite narrative device is his idiosyncratic *skaz*, which binds together the locutions of different eras, weaving together paraphrases of classical texts with parodies of current *belles lettres*, superimposing naturalistic details on refined intertextual discourse." (The Russian literary term *skaz* may be defined as an attempt to mimic actual speech in writing, usually the speech acts of an unsophisticated narrator.) The story "The Parakeet," for example, one of his very best, is a symbolic distillation of all Russia's tyrants and all the subjects who have acquiesced in and assisted these tyrannies, and achieves its effects in part by allowing a Dostoevskian narrator to move freely between half a dozen linguistic registers, including those of Petrine times, nineteenth-century gentry speech and Soviet criminal jargon. Dostoevsky's polyphonic writing is taken to its logical (or illogical) extreme, so that the narrator speaks at once with the tongues of Porfiry Petrovich, Ivan Karamazov, the Grand Inquisitor, Smerdiakov and above all the sensualist Svidrigailov. Though some of these nuances cannot be conveyed in translation, one hopes that the parodic and exaggerated (yet also deadly serious) Dostoevskian tone comes through. At the same time a more academic metaliterary dimension is established as the story plays with the different definitions of *skaz* to be found in the work of Formalists like Eikhenbaum, on one hand, and Bakhtin, on the other. "Letter to Mother" describes a generalized period of *perestroika* that seems to take place simultaneously in the 1980s, 1917, and the nineteenth century, and many of the other stories disorient the reader in similar ways. Erofeyev rewrites and recombines the events of Russian and Soviet history and the classics of Russian and Soviet literature, and exploits Soviet discourse, in particular the Soviet equivalent of "pulp fiction," to give new life to language or unexpected connotations to ingrained habits of speech and thought.

Given that these stories were originally intended for the nation that, in a popular play on a favorite propaganda slogan, read the most *between the lines,* they may be baffling on a factual and conceptual level to a number of readers. If for many Russians the difficulties of language, style, narration and punctuation were no less disconcerting than the presence of explicit sex, violence, obscene language and the lack of clear moral purpose in Erofeyev's works, for Western readers the main difficulty is likely to be not the postmodern literary and linguistic games or the provocative subject matter, but a lack of detailed knowledge of the Russian world. I have therefore tried to assist the reader in a number of ways: by giving some general advice here and in the notes as to how to approach the stories; by glossing some points in the translations themselves when that was not too unnatural; and by providing for each story some brief remarks of both a factual and interpretative nature in the notes. If American life is well known to the outside world through film and TV, the unique features of life in the USSR are not nearly so familiar to Western readers; and it clearly was not feasible to provide here all the information about, for example, communal apartments, everyday life, Russian history, the Soviet literary scene, the politics of the last thirty years or the many other details that would be a given for an educated Russian reader. (If one were to recommend a few texts for background reading, however, they would include the "autobiographical" essays in Brodsky's *Less Than One*, Nadezhda Mandelstam's memoirs *Hope Against Hope* and *Hope Abandoned* and David Remnick's *Lenin's Tomb* and *Resurrection*.) Moreover, since the depictions of these realia usually possess what one critic called a "poetic exactitude," the careful reader should usually be able to put two and two together. In those cases where confusion still reigns, this is probably the point, and the Russian reader is doubtless in the same boat.

It should be stressed that Erofeyev is not an easy read in Russian, and to oversimplify him would be to do him a grave disservice. After all, perhaps Erofeyev was not being too presumptuous or pretentious when he said in an interview with Elizabeth Rich a few years ago: "I want Americans to know that I am a writer who will be better understood in the twenty-first century than he has been in the twentieth . . . In my prose . . . I attempt to create a kind of model relation between words, sentence, styles that in the present century still seems too fast, too swift, perhaps too hard to understand." Some of the difficulties stem from the fact that Erofeyev is exceptionally adroit at exploiting the Russian language's ability to create, through its tense system, word order and punctuation, considerable ambiguity about who is speaking, whether the speech is direct, indirect or a stream of consciousness, or even to what object, event, person or time a particular sentence or word refers to (or whether a number of these are referred to simultaneously). Even to those well attuned to postmodernist writing, Erofeyev's highly interactive, "multiple-choice" style may come as something of a shock.

What may be even more of a surprise to the Western reader,

however, and of most value, will be the ways in which this Russian's view of the Russian world and beyond both parallels and differs from many of our assumptions. Erofeyev has observed:

> You can say something universally valid only if you grapple with human problems in your own culture and language. Our own contribution has such a distinctively "Russian" feel to it only because our culture is so totally different from Western culture. Western civilization is largely determined by the mass media, commerce and so on. This produces a kind of leveling-out process with virtually no high point or low point. The only thing you can do with this concept is to do your job properly and make sure that society functions smoothly and that the streets are kept clean. But if you set out from the premise that life is an almost impenetrable complex of different realities, you'll find that Western culture isn't so well equipped to deal with it. In Russia there is virtually no civilization, we don't know how to keep the streets clean, but we have a deeper understanding of culture, at least in the spiritual sense. We live in a world caught midway between Europe and Asia. We don't know how to organize society—and so we have a more direct experience of life.

The new glamour of Moscow and St. Petersburg notwithstanding, much of this description still rings true. It may not appear, from a first glance at the title story, at least, that the Russians are in fact any better equipped to deal with life, though they may well be better equipped to deal with the consequences of living with idiots (even if they are partly or wholly to blame for the idiots in the first place). "Life with an Idiot" has already achieved some fame and indeed notoriety because it served as the basis for a libretto Erofeyev wrote for an Alfred Schnittke opera, first performed in Russian in Amsterdam and in English in London in the 1990s. Some felt that the opera merely (and crudely) argued that Lenin did to Russia what Vova does to the narrator and his wife. Certainly Erofeyev's text is partly responsible for the tendency to see the work as no more than an allegory of life under Communism; but irrespective of one's views on the work's artistic merits (Vladimir Sorokin has called it the "best short story of the twentieth-century," whereas others, less prone to hyperbole, perhaps, have been less generous), one has to admire the foolhardy, almost suicidal courage needed to write such a work. If Erofeyev's fellow postmodernist Sorokin could find himself in danger of losing his liberty for writing in a similar vein in 2002 (the pro-Putin youth organization Moving Together was behind a campaign that led to Sorokin being charged with distributing "pornography" in the form of his novel *Blue Lard,* particularly in its depiction of sex between Stalin and Khrushchev; Erofeyev, another of their main targets, wrote an open letter to President Putin protesting this attack on freedom of expression), it is hard to imagine what the powers that be would have felt about Vova-Lenin in 1980. For that matter, is it any easier to imagine the scandal in the U.S. or U.K. if George Washington or Winston Churchill were portrayed in print or on-stage in analogous fashion?

In "Life with an Idiot" the hero's choice of a "holy fool" symbolizes choices made first and foremost by the Russians themselves, and the broader theme that we all have our own idiots is perhaps not fully realized. The work parodies the Russian idealization of the holy fool, both as embodied in particular texts (above all Dostoevsky's *The Idiot*) and in the culture as a whole; and this leads into an examination of other aspects of the Russian soul, in particular its idealization of kenoticism, its utopian tendencies and the wider belief of the (alleged and actual) benefits of Russian moral maximalism, the phenomenon D. H. Lawrence termed "sinning one's way to Jesus." The story may also be read as a study of whether an analogous idealization of the power of culture is implicated in the failure of twentieth-century civilization to resist barbarism and tyranny. If the most important theme of the work is indeed, as Erofeyev claims, that we all have our own idiots, then the main failings we have in common would seem to be that we are willing to believe the most utter nonsense if it can be made to fit our oversimplistic, preconceived, overidealized or self-serving views of the world; and that we naively assume that those whose myths, language, money and power control or would control our lives and minds have our best interests at heart. The idiots need not be political leaders—they can be the media, the multinational corporations, other economic powers, cultural movements, systems of belief, ideologues and ideologies of all varieties, and not forgetting our good selves, who deservedly or not end up in some madhouse or other. The story expresses amazement at how intelligent people can ignore the evidence discerned by their own eyes and ears to believe, blindly, idiotically, in the inherent wisdom or goodness of totemic figures who can't string an intelligent, original, honest sentence or thought together, and whose only utterance is "Ekh!" (the Russian "Oh!") or its equivalent.

As the notes make clear, many of the stories confess in their titles (to the Russian reader, at any rate) their palimpsestuous relationships with other texts, and the remaining stories are no less allusive and metaliterary, confirming the special role literature has played in Russian life. The general thrust of the stories should still be clear even without detailed knowledge of their intertexts, though the keen reader may wish to read or reread some of the works alluded to in order to appreciate better Erofeyev's texts. Even the grimmest tales here are more than simply attempts to shock the bourgeoisie, for beyond the morally and aesthetically somewhat dubious pleasures of these texts one may sense not only the aesthetic bliss that Nabokov viewed as the only justification for fiction, not only that Erofeyev is a "master game player" in an "orgy of wordplay" (Elizabeth Rich), but also that he is someone who "knows and loves his country deeply" (Sally Laird).

As should be clear by now, and as one would expect from a self-proclaimed disciple of Joyce and Nabokov, Erofeyev is a difficult writer both in Russian and in translation. Time and again Erofeyev's texts embody the Orwellian insight that "political language ... is designed to make lies sound truthful and murder respectable, and to give an appearance of solidity to pure wind," but they also show that the problem goes far beyond politics. Sometimes Erofeyev (and his translators) overdoes the deconstruction of words or clichés, for even if his parodies of the violence Soviet "newspeak" inflicted on language and thought help him reveal how language facilitates actual violence, and in his case at least is done in the service of a good cause, the reading experience that results is sometimes neither as pleasant nor as easy as some readers might wish. Yet without the puns, the layers of parody and irony, the literary allusions, the polystylistic play with various types of discourse and the various linguistic and stylistic registers, and with a smoothing over of the more jarring elements, far too much would be lost in translation. I hope, therefore, that in trying to stay true to Erofeyev's artistic vision I have more often than not achieved a balance between what the theorists call domesticating and foreignizing translations, preserving the original as accurately as possible, while giving it, I hope, its own English style, an approach that seemed to meet with the approval of most reviewers of *Russian Beauty*.

In the notes I have tried to point out the most salient points of reference while avoiding a crash course in Russian cultural his-

tory. Occasionally I have substituted an allusion to English literature where the Russian one would be obscure, where glossing it
would prove too clumsy, and yet where a reference is needed in
the text rather than in a footnote because it is desirable that the
reader sense that a text is being alluded to or played with. So, for
example, a single allusion to a Gogolian text in Erofeyev's text may
turn into a double-voiced allusion to Gogol and Shakespeare in
the translation. Sometimes I have added some allusions to com-
pensate for those I was unable to re-create in any appropriate way,
but I hope none of them is too arbitrary or intrusive and all aim to
be true to both the letter and the spirit of the original. And if, for
example, I have been unable to avoid in a story about a dead
parrot—alongside both expected and unexpected "alien speech"
from a Dostoevskian Spanish Inquisitor—certain Pythonesque
echoes, this too is not inappropriate, in that an author like Erofeyev
can be seen as fulfilling, for a Russian audience unused to surreal
and black comedy in the post-Stalin years (in art, if not in life), a
role analogous to that of the Monty Python team and their ilk.

Throughout these stories one senses the terrible truth of Martin Amis's remark in *Koba the Dread: Laughter and the Twenty Million* that "Hitler-Stalin tells us this, among other things: given
total power over another, the human being will find that his
thoughts turn to torture." Some, of course, would prefer to explain
the millions of victims of Communism as simply an inevitable result of Socialist ideology, or of the political and historical context;
while others, including many Russians, are eager to take the long
view and blame Ivan the Terrible or the Tartar yoke instead. In
Koba the Dread Amis quotes approvingly Erofeyev's aside that there
are "some grounds for saying" that "deep down, Russia has nothing in common with the West." There are certainly major differences, and books like *Life with an Idiot* help us in that centuries-long

struggle to understand the Russians better. But the chief strength of Erofeyev's writing is that it avoids simplistic, comforting answers, and his critiques of many aspects of Western civilization (especially in *The Last Judgment*), of the liberal wing of Russian intelligentsia and its Western allies or of the condescending attitudes of some Westerners to Russia are no less significant than his deconstruction of various Slavophile manifestations of the "Russian idea" and the "Russian soul." True, the stories in *Life with an Idiot* probably tell us more about Russian life than about whether life in general is merely a tale told by an idiot. But a more significant and truer expression of Erofeyev's views concerning the differences between Russia and the West is to be found in his anticipation, in the introduction to *The Penguin Book of New Russian Writing*, of the likely response of the Western reader to these texts:

> The Western reader can breathe a sigh of relief: thank goodness he doesn't live in Russia, where human life is so cheap and where there is so much barbarity. But in fact the problem isn't Russia. The true significance of the new Russian literature does not lie in its exposure of the country, but in its demonstration of the fact that beneath the thin veneer of civilization man is nothing more than an uncontrollable animal. It is just that the Russian example is at times more striking than most.

In other words, the stories in the anthology and in this collection are no less important in helping us to analyze what Gorbachev termed "universal human values," and their absence and distortion, than they are in laying bare versions and perversions of the "Russian idea." In allowing us to understand and appreciate a very significant Other, they show us not only that which is lost in translation between cultures, but also that which recognizes no borders and can be preserved and shared, words that may warm or warn. In an interview before the premiere of the opera of "Life with an Idiot" in Amsterdam, Erofeyev gave an interview to Wilhem Bruls in which he stated:

> Vova, the idiot in *Life with an Idiot,* is fairly mad, but it's as a result of his madness that he attracts people, who become enmeshed in the toils of his own world and who then behave differently themselves. Of course, it's also an allegory of Soviet society under Communism, but at the same time it's a general, existential problem.
>
> At the end of the story the idiot simply runs away. He disappears, but he's done everything that he could do, everything he wanted to do, and he's the winner. He's simply done his job murdering and destroying everything. But it was the people themselves who took him in. Each person chooses his or her own idiot, here and everywhere else. We've all got our aggressive instincts, which are never far beneath the surface...
>
> We can't live without idiots. Either he stays or we exchange him for another one. Just as the guards outside Lenin's Tomb are replaced every two hours. Maybe the next one will be less aggressive, less destructive than Vova, but I don't think he's disappeared for good. I'm no pessimist, but the idiot is our reality, our *condition humaine.*

In the mid-1990s Erofeyev still seemed to hope that Russian literature would cease to be "the conscience of the nation," but this hope presupposed a far greater normalization of that society than has come to pass since 1985 (or was ever likely to); and in the light of recent events it is not surprising that Erofeyev now not only affirms the high quality and diversity of contemporary Russian literature (and rightly so), but also implies that writers once again have an important role in describing and analyzing the search for the Russian identity. He now seems to realize that the renewed threats to free expression may prevent the marginalization of the Russian writer, and it is clear that irrespective of whether Russian writers do or do not question where Russia is heading, others will be trying to chart her course, with results that are potentially fraught with great peril for all. Some might argue that Erofeyev's recent claims that Russian literature will once again become the true opposition to the state are melodramatic, and Erofeyev himself is not one to make a fetish of the alleged benefits of suffering, as he fully realizes the terrible human cost of those periods when Russia becomes the world's best stage for matters tragical-comical-historical. Even when Russian history seems to repeat itself as farce, the end result is nearly always tragedy. But writers can be early warning systems, and it may therefore be proper to risk crying wolf, as Mandelstam did in his *Fourth Prose* in response to apparently insignificant problems, before it is too late.

It would therefore be wise for Western governments and the Western media to pay careful attention to Russia, and it would also be desirable for publishers to publish more translations of Russian literary works (and indeed more translations from all languages). If Erofeyev's field guide helps us in some way to identify the various gradations of idiot active at home and abroad, and above all within ourselves (as *The Onion* puts it in one of its incomparable headlines, "Osama Bin Laden found in every one of us"), then, despite Erofeyev's own earlier protests against the usefulness of literature, it will certainly have provided us with something no less valuable than Nabokov's "aesthetic bliss." Let us hope that Russian writers will be able to continue the Dostoevskian approach of investigating what it means to be human without falling into the dangerous ideological maximalism of too many of the previous manifestations of the "Russian idea." And let us hope that this can be achieved without "the ambivalent tribute of a savage vigilance" (George Steiner), the usual lot of the Russian writer in a nation which is full of exceptional human potential but which is also a country that still has to come to terms with its unpredictable past and which is still, as the Soviet formula always reminded us, one-sixth of the world's land surface. Watch this space.

LIFE
with an
IDIOT

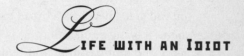 IFE WITH AN IDIOT

MY FRIENDS congratulated me on my idiot. Hey, that's *nothing,* they said. They embraced me, squeezed me, kissed me on the cheeks. I smiled vaguely, my head spun, hands and smiles flashed past; I kissed my friends on the cheeks, embraced them and squeezed them. The fumes of friendship were intoxicating. In the sweet steamy vapors my head was a balloon, and my body and legs a thread wound around a jacket button. I jumped up and down and twitched. A most strange feeling, I'll tell you. A revolting state of instability. That's how I remember myself being on the day of punishment.

My friends admitted that they'd feared the worst, that indeed there had been every reason to fear the worst. And suddenly there you have it: Life with an Idiot. A light punishment, far from onerous, indeed, one could even say that getting off so lightly is not a punishment at all. It depends, of course, on how one looks at it, and if one looks at it through the gaping hole of our disjointed times, then one can divine in such a punishment a secret form of trust (not all roads are closed to you after all!), a new form of existence, more of a command than a reprimand. In a word, a mission. The more so, my friends added, in that you have been given the chance to choose. *They* have condescended to grant you an indulgence . . . This put me on my guard. Surely it was my friends who were being condescending at my expense? Just for you to know, I said, life with an idiot is hardly going to be a bowl of cherries! I don't need anyone's indulgence!

As you will note, there was a broad hint here. Give me back my punishment. It is my punishment. It is for me to judge it, so you just squeeze and embrace me, and I shall squeeze and embrace you as well.

I was full of doubts and anxieties that winter, and the world toppled over into my paranoia, the boundaries between objects were eroded; sweetish fumes enveloped everything. My friends kissed me with new vigor, and I kissed them. So that's how we exchanged kisses.

Kissing me, my friends said: "Old man, there is good fortune in misfortune too. It has to be said, you could always have done with a hint more compassion: you're somewhat lacking"—my friends screwed up their eyes like true friends—"in that line of business, in that area . . ." And my unhappy wife also nodded: "Somewhat lacking!" "Well, thank God for that," I said with a show of emotion, "well, thank God for that! At long last I've understood why I've been punished: for not having just a hint more compassion."

Everyone laughed. We all took delight in my wit. We clinked glasses.

We ate lots of tasty food. Once we had quail in sour cream. That's how we ate them. And what was wrong with eating quail in sour cream? In sour cream they were superb, as if they were still alive.

I didn't argue with my friends. I didn't see the point. My ideal of an idiot was gestating inside me. I had no desire at all to take any old fool, some imbecile suffering from oligophrenia: a swollen, porous face, a spittle-drenched chin, the twitching of distorted hands, wet trousers. Cluttering up the living space and nothing more. I was dreaming of a totally different type of abnormality—of a blessed, holy fool type of abnormality, national in both form and content. I pictured to myself a crafty, staid *starets* with a little sharp eye the color of a faded sky. He holds lumps of sugar in his mouth to sweeten his tea, his visage is radiant and pure, but when the storm of madness breaks, it's as if the devil himself is stirring the waters. An ambivalent sort of wise old man. He wouldn't be too much bother, and he'd die soon anyway. But you just try coping with an imbecile, especially if the bastard decides to have a fit . . .

Well, perhaps my ideal was not totally my own—there were, of course, some influences, something old, something borrowed: the parvis of a Zagorsk monastery was there somewhere, and on top of that from childhood we all drink the same old literary milk—though naturally I wasn't planning to churn out the same old stuff to butter parsnips! I decided to pick an old man—since I'd been given a choice—not for the sake of experiment, and not for abstract study or a chemical analysis of the milk of our common wet-nurses (by the time of that memorable winter my passion for polemics had gone out of the window), in short, I was planning to choose a blessed simpleton not for the sake of diversion (in the Pascalian sense of the word, of course), but out of practical calculations intimately connected with the demands of one's inner life and one's gut feeling. For life is a tale told by an idiot, gentlemen! There you go—I'm bringing it all up again with a burp! My most humble apologies.

I had a newish and perfectly tolerable wife. My old wife had died. From scarlet fever. She was diagnosed incorrectly and treated incorrectly. She died. I am a widower. And the newish one died too. Unhappy woman! How she loved Proust! She'd have been happy just to read and reread Proust till blissful old age and prepare lovely mushroom juliennes for me. But she was brutally murdered. Sometimes I mix up my dead wives. Sometimes I shiver: wait a minute, surely the first one loved Proust? I'm seized by horror: it seems that they both loved Proust.

Vova, the idiot, leapt into the room, holding in his hand huge kitchen shears which my wife used—she'd brought the shears back from East Germany—to give short shrift to game birds. They were her favorite shears, but Vova developed the habit of cutting his toenails with them. No housewife can be expected to put up with that sort of thing. And so, just imagine, Vova leaps into the room, snapping the shears, while I sit, skinny and butt-naked, and drink tomato juice like a baby. Vova grabbed my wife by her hair, tipped her onto the soiled carpet and started to clip off her head. The expression on his face as he was doing this was instructive. I got so aroused, I got so aroused, I jumped up and down in the armchair so much that I spilled tomato juice all over myself. I banged my breast and shouted to Vova to cut off my inflamed organs. "Vova, cut them off! I can't stand it!" Vova was otherwise engaged and didn't even turn around.

"Oh!" he yelled at last and showed me his trophy with that instructive look on his face.

I sat there, soaked in tomato juice and cum. I was a widower once again.

Oh, Vova, Vova! Where are you now, Vova? Where? My weary heart senses that you are still alive. You'll outlive everyone, my dear little fool. What will become of you? Whose idiot are you now? How's work? You don't get beaten? Because I get beaten, Vova. He's a real bastard, you know. He says his name is Kraig Benson, but I think that he's a gypsy, he has a gold tooth, and he only got hold of me because he can really pull strings. He's mad, Vova. I know that for a fact. But what can he offer, a mere amateur, when put next to our proud, select group of professionals?! Adieu, Vova! This is me—your son.

And now, my dear reader, allow me to return to describing the events under description. I am a man of letters, I know my worth, and I'll stick up for my reader. I shall tell you about the good life.

Snow, sun, sea-blue shadows of aspens. Minus thirty-five degrees Celsius. The little corpses of frozen children. Silence. But from time to time, as if totally by chance, from the spreading bough of a royal fir, a contemporary of the Mongol raids on Old Russia, a fir-primogenetrix, a fir-mother and great fir-martyr, a fir-patroness and holy intercessor, whose roots have gone for all time into the native soil, from the bough will fall a fir-cone, to all intents and purposes looking, as any devoted naturalist will observe, like a brown sausage of dog shit; the fir-cone falls into the snow, and snowflakes scarcely visible to the naked eye, myriads of them, rise up, just as if a miraculous fairy visitor has sprinkled diamond dust in your eyes, sprinkled and then dissolved in the frosty haze, and you're left standing in total rapture, bewitched by this marvelous apparition, left without the strength to move even an inch, you stand and wait for the miracle to continue; while a flock of small songbirds, from the order of sparrows, is already, naturally, on the scene: the party twitters, its number conversing among themselves in their funny dialect incomprehensible to man, just as if they've flown in together for a meeting to discuss some business of great import to them all. The red-breasted, mustached cocks twitter, interrupting one another, look, it even seems as if over there two of them have had a quarrel of sorts, swinging their wings at one another, while the others seem to be laughing at them and take the bruisers to task—just as during a meeting in the director's office at a metal works two hotheads, two young bosses from the shop floor, will fly at one another, like fighting cocks, one shouts: "You're stopping me from fulfilling the plan!," while the other answers: "I don't have no intention to lie down my Party card on the table and resign just because of you!" But the director, who has seen many such scenes before, will tap on the table with his pencil, and the representative of the Party's district committee, sitting by the window in an austere outfit, will burst out laughing in her splendid little male bass, and lo and behold: these former fellow students, the favorites and pride of the factory, already regret that they'd got so worked up over this issue; and so, urged on by their comrades, they rush to each other with embarrassed, shamed faces. A purple flush spreads across their cheeks, and now they are already coupled in embraces, and the director is no longer able to control his emotions, he says: "You stupid devils!" and phones through to Moscow; and if you are an observant phenologist and not simply an unfortunate skier who has lost his way and is frozen to the marrow of his bones, and who dreams about only one thing, like a masturbator dreams about the figure of the vagina, about reaching the forest cutting as quickly as possible, the cutting leading to the bus stop, and getting on the bus which will take him to the city, as far away as possible from the forest miracles, then you will undoubtedly notice that the bullfinches too have their director who possesses an unassailable authority among the order of sparrows, and that he only has to make a cracking sound with his tongue for the fight to end, and then he'll have his say within the framework of this avian flying production meeting, so to speak: "So," he says, "and so, let's fly further," and the bullfinches will fly on, and with animated, virtually vernal faces they will glide down and peck out your rapturous, observant phenologist's eyes.

So my holy peasant Marei Mareich had to suffer as well. The idiot's rest period was over! I was oppressed and pursued by the image of the air balloon with the thread wound around the button of a checked jacket. Was I hankering after another tie?

Well, of course not everything here is that simple. Yes, I was intending to grind my old man, my blessed Simple Simon, in a mortar like a root of ginseng in order to make from him an elixir of life; but that certainly didn't mean that I wanted, once I'd got high, to leap with one bound onto the square of the Heavenly Jerusalem, where, as writes the Soviet poet with close links to the church:

THE RUSSIAN SOUL KISSES GOD ON THE LIPS...

A vile verse, it has to be said. No, an ecstatic theosexual encounter didn't appeal to me. Aesthetics, I suppose you'd say, were in revolt. Aesthetics sent me to the eye of the needle. I couldn't pass through, try as I might. I paid the poet a visit. "And how," I say, "did you pass through? Why," I say, "are you silent? Share the secret with your comrade; answer," I say, "the question." He simply laughs with the most stupid laugh: "Lend me," he says, "five rubles for our beloved drink." He and I drank the bottle, with Danube salad for *zakuski*. "My wife," I say to him, "died from scarlet fever. Will I ever," I say, "see my beloved wife Masha again?" "You'll see her again"—he laughs with the most stupid laugh— "you'll undoubtedly see her, no need to shit your pants." You'll never guess what happened next! My stomach tried to overcome the Danube salad. The Danube salad tried to overcome my stomach. A most unpleasant compromise was the result.

But I didn't mind at all going off my head, one can even say that I simply thirsted after going off my head, and in this sense I had laid great hopes on the old chap, I was betting on my Marei Mareich. I wanted to go mad, stark raving bonkers—and then we'd see.

And this is pretty much how it turned out, in accordance with my wish, desire and command. I went bananas and ended up sprawled on the floor. And how! So many loose screws went flying after my fall that I'm still picking up the pieces! Ha-ha-ha! But a big thank-you to dear Kraig. A big thank-you to his lessons. He is a harsh master. I'm now starting to wield a skillful pen again. I have drawn near to the truth. And I don't for one minute regret that I went flying and ended up on my back, on my back—it's both good and beautiful! No, I have no regrets. Well naturally, I have a few—I regret having my teeth knocked out, of course I feel sorry for the one who was killed brutally, no, her name's gone from my mind. Blanks. I'm getting ever closer to the truth, which is why there are these gaps in my memory. However, I remember, this I do remember, that Vova clipped off her head with some shears. This is like a beacon for a memory which has fled the nest. Vova and I stand in the rays of this beacon. Men naked and aroused, men who love each other. We are a monument.

Anyway, my newish wife was herself to blame for my picking Vova. She later said that if she had come with me, then she would have picked anyone but Vova, that she would never have taken Vova, that she'd have threatened me with hysterics if I'd tried to pick him. But she didn't go, just wouldn't start on account of the severe frost and strong wind blowing from the heart of the Arctic Ocean, and so I jumped in alongside the taxi driver and arrived at the place of election on my own.

The guard met me ungraciously, with a roulade of hung-over bad language.

"You should have come earlier, you motherfucker. I've already locked up."

I looked at my watch. It was nine-thirty in the morning. I was amazed.

"On the contrary, I thought that you wouldn't be open yet," I said with a polite grimace.

"You thought!" he snorted. "Don't think. Do as you're supposed to, and don't think!"

And he set off, crunching through the snow in his enormous black felt boots. A junior rank, with his roots among the common people. For some reason these upstarts always disliked me, for some reason my appearance always irritated them—I made them come over all twitchy and nauseous, as if I were a glass of *eau de cologne* or a full-blown Jew. I had got used to this and was not bitter, and I didn't try to suck up, as I had once tended to, as if to say, "Hey, brothers, what about me, then? Am I not one of 'us'? I'm a thoroughbred, one of us through and through, none of your motherfucking gentry blood here!" I simply shrugged my shoulders and rushed after the upstart, with the promise of a bottle peeping out of my pocket. He halted, somewhat undecided, weighing up which was sweeter: power over me or vodka. I hurriedly produced another half liter. His eyes even sparkled. And suddenly something came over me—not a fit of understanding or pity, no, nothing like that occurred—I was overcome with an intense hatred of other races. "That's something new," I thought, and I felt unwell. "Surely I can't have left things too late with my Marei Mareich?"

"Let's go!" said the former son of the soil morosely.

"Let's go!" answered the whoreson morosely.

And we set off.

It was a large underground chamber, flooded with a dull red light. On the benches along the walls sat numerous idiots. Others strutted around the room, parting the choking hot air with their foreheads. Each was preoccupied with his own business, his own thoughts, and no one paid the slightest attention to the guard or to me. All in all there were about a hundred of them.

"Well, then, which one will you take?" asked the guard impatiently.

"Wait a sec," I said and, without hurrying, set off along the benches, struggling against the stuffiness. Gathered here were different folks: youngsters and old men, bags of bones out of

Belsen and bruisers built like brick shithouses, crestfallen, flabby cowards, choleric fidgets, petrified, rough-hewn, heavyweight statues. Some muttered, others howled, some sang, others slept, some gobbled some slime from a bowl, others smiled, staring straight ahead, while others whimpered, played up, turning their lips inside out, others again hunted fleas, some dribbled as they wanked, others, bound, lay in the corner and were being punished. In the center of the hall the two young stocky shop-floor bosses—my friends from my Homeric simile—were noiselessly waltzing, staring deep into one another's eyes, not tearing their eyes away even for a second. Their eyes held a heavy feeling of otherworldly pleasure. I was struck dumb by this hallucination and began worrying. The sooner I got out of this place, the better!

"How about this one?" asked the guard, who had caught up with me. He was holding by the hand a fidgety great lump with a mad convulsive face. On this face were projected, one frame quickly replacing another, pictures of self-satisfaction (well, just like *Il Duce!*), despair, fear, submission, tenderness and God knows what else. The guard guffawed hoarsely. He had, in all probability, been joking.

"But do you have any holy fools?" I asked, greeting the joke with an understanding smile.

"But the whole lot of them are wholly fools," said the guard, extremely surprised.

"What I really need, you know, is some sort of blessed simpleton . . ."

"What, pissing here, you bastard!" roared the guard and gave the offender a quick pummeling. I set off to search for the holy simpleton, but whether the caustic reddish lighting, which intensified the ugliness of the faces, was to blame, or whether it was that the physical diversity of imbecility distracted me, or whether, simply, I had become stupefied as a result of the stuffiness, but whatever: at any rate, my Marei Mareich wasn't anywhere to be found... My gaze fell on a tall lad about thirty years old. He was sitting on the bench, with his arms akimbo, and he was singing in a mocking falsetto:

> *A birch was standing in a field,*
> *Was standing leafy in a field.*
> *Hey-ho, hey-ho, was standing.*

Red hair was falling in front of his eyes. For some reason I thought that he was blind, but he burst out laughing when he caught my gaze:

> *Hey-ho, hey-ho, was standing...*

He had a thin, completely human face; only his protruding ears spoiled the picture which had taken shape in my mind.

"Don't pick that one!" barked the guard from a distance.

"Why not?" I said, losing my temper, and becoming all the more determined to help the lad out.

"He bites!" explained the guard.

"That's nothing!" I countered in an icy tone. I was beginning to sense that this guard was a foe.

"Ow! Ow! Ow!" That's me shouting. The lad darted lizardlike down from the bench and, on reaching me, bit me in the calf.

"Ow! Ow! Ow!" I shout. Tears fly from my eyes. I collapsed into the guard's embrace, who took me in his arms and neutralized the lad by dealing him a crippling kick in the pit of the stomach. The madmen gathered around us and with great sympathy looked at me: they were clearly overacting, because they were madmen and had no sense of proportion.

"To your places!" commanded the guard, and they dispersed.

The lad lay on the floor and, clutching his stomach with both hands, sang about the birch tree.

"I told you he bites," growled the guard, taking me away from the crime scene.

"You've got a trying job," I said, limping badly on my bitten leg, and the thought struck me: I have been punished, and will have to live with an idiot, but *he* lives with a whole hundred of them. For what sins? For what salary?

"They are afraid of me," smiled the guard with the self-important smile of a lower ranker.

Vova was pacing around the room, his arms twisted behind his back and all ruffled: five steps forward, a sharp turn on his heel, five steps back—and another turn. He was wearing worn-out slippers and therefore he was shuffling his feet, but he had a watch and tie, and his small neat beard, in conjunction with his small mustache, gave him the appearance of a lecturer in a provincial institute of higher education who had recently passed his fiftieth birthday. There's a certain type of teacher, the secret martyrs of their own fantasies, ready to hang themselves for the sake of an idea. They are a dying breed, and they are being replaced by ignoramuses and failures. They squeeze out the martyrs of fantasies— the failures triumph, with their motto of ASH AND DANDRUFF—and thus it was that Vova had been driven into this cellar, under the wing of a lower rank. I gazed at him with interest. He did not reciprocate. He was engrossed in his dispute with an imaginary opponent, who irritated him with a supranonsensical string of vulgar banality, a supravulgar assortment of nonsense, and the prominent forehead of the polemicist was lit up by a blazing dream.

"How could you have picked him? You must be mad!" said my newish wife in horror. "He has the skull of a degenerate."

"His skull has been flattened by the sheer force of his fantasies," I objected. "His skull's rather Socratic, I'm sure."

"What is he, a Bashkir?" asked my wife with typical female squeamishness. "He's no Russian, that's for sure," she announced in disgust.

"He'll hear you and take offense," I said, looking in the direction of the kitchen; behind the glass door Vova was getting through a ham sandwich.

"I hate him," said my wife. "Trade him in for someone else . . . I beseech you: exchange him."

It was as if she had had a presentiment that ultimately Vova would clip off her head with the shears. I simply spread my hands helplessly.

"Open wide!" ordered the guard.

Vova stopped and readily opened his mouth.

"Obliging," nodded the guard approvingly. "Obliging and bright."

"How can you tell?" I asked and also looked the dreamer in the mouth.

"How can I tell? Nothing could be simpler. You see, he did open his mouth."

"What's your name and patronymic?" I asked the dreamer politely.

"Oh!" sighed the dreamer, as if he were complaining about the trials of life in the dull-red light of his world. He was enchantingly bald.

"OK, so a chap's forgotten his name," the guard said, sticking up for him. "He's forgotten it, he'll remember it again later. Doesn't it happen to everyone? The chap's forgotten it . . ."

"Oh!" sighed the dreamer once again.

"He doesn't say a lot," I pointed out to the guard.

"He will once he warms up," promised the guard. "I know him. Sometimes he comes out with such speeches. About higher matters. It makes you marvel."

Well, what a crafty old sod the guard was! He knew how to hook me! Well, what a crafty old sod!...I headed for the exit, spreading my legs wide, like a sailor, so as not to fall over from dizziness. We emerged from that hellhole into the light of day. Only then did a most interesting detail make itself known: the remaining hairs, the mustache and the beard of the dreamer turned out to be reddish. A redhead! What luck! We stood on the threshold of a new life. I signed for him in a school exercise book, small and well thumbed, and paid the guard off with a nice fat tip.

"What should I give him to eat?" I inquired anxiously, as if I were a boy who's just bought a goldfish in a pet shop.

"Shit!" screamed the guard with laugher.

We parted friends. If I had known...But no! I will be the pattern of all patience. I will say nothing! I loved you, people. Report from the gallows—it's happened before. Vova, joy of my life, light of my life, where are you? The blood-dimmed tide is loosed, Vova, the ceremony of innocence drowned.

That's how Vova became mine.

Now, my dearest reader, I shall tell of how I became his.

It didn't all happen at once, it didn't happen suddenly, but only after a long floral siege. In the beginning Vova was very quiet: he merely shuffled his slippers and built himself up. He loved having a bottle of drinking yogurt for breakfast and liked eating cottage cheese. He would sit modestly in our little kitchen and feed, then he would shuffle his slippers around the room a bit—five steps forward, five back—and once more into the kitchen, where he might peck at some sausage, or treat himself to ham. When he ate, his look would become evil, feline, but he didn't take anything without our permission, and he didn't raid the fridge. The guard had duped me. Vova didn't open up. He was a real silentiary, he was unwilling to speak out, and didn't use any words other than

"Oh!" I tried more than once to strike up a conversation with him, I set about questioning him about who he was and where he was from, what he had taught and where—by now I'd utterly convinced myself that he was a professor. I even spread out a map of the USSR before him, so that he could show me his native lands, but Vova merely ran his finger meaninglessly over the map, sighing quietly and mumbling quietly. Driven to despair, I didn't pester him any more, and he retired into himself completely. But something was, clearly, ripening within him, some thoughts, some dreams were draining him. He moaned at night, woke up frequently and, on occasions, he would sit in the dark on the ottoman for hours on end, narrowing his already slitty eyes and propping up his little tuft of a beard with his fist.

"Why aren't you asleep?" I would ask, poking my head out of the adjoining room.

"Oh!" Vova would answer dreamily. "Oh!"

I dreamed about entering his dreams. In the evenings, to stop Vova from suffering from insomnia, we would go for a stroll through the snow-covered lanes. Vova would look piercingly at the passersby. They would be frightened of him for some reason, they stood aside, and then they would turn around and look back at him. Perplexed or even, I would say, panic-stricken faces. What was the matter? What was it about Vova that unnerved the casual evening townsman? I couldn't put my finger on it. Weeks passed. Everything was as before: an uneasy, newish wife, a quiet Vova and I—a fine lad, in essence . . .

Once, on returning home, I chanced upon the following scene: Vova is sitting on the kitchen floor in a large puddle of milk, surrounded by foodstuffs he has just thrown out of the fridge; he sits there and gobbles everything in turn. One minute he's biting off a lump of cheese, the next he's shoving his hand into a jar of vegetable salad, then he crunches a wafer, and then he fancies a frankfurter, and then I see that he's spread red whortle-berry jam all along the frankfurter. He sits there, cheerful and pleased with life. I gave him a scalding—he frowned, lay down on the ottoman and without any sign of repentance quickly fell asleep. My wife was a bundle of nerves.

"I just knew it!" she said tearfully with a certain somber *Schadenfreude.* "I just knew it!"

I phoned my friends. They were distressed. They were indignant. They kissed me down the telephone and said: "Stand firm!" They asked me to drop in and try a pizza. "I've swapped my bird for a pizza!" droned a friend's voice. I laughed terribly. A few days later Vova tore into the books. He ripped up a good half of the library which I had put together so lovingly; scraps of pages dear to me clogged up the bath and the lavatory pan. And it wasn't just the lavatory pan! The whole apartment was strewn with this sacrilegious confetti.

"What did you do that for?" I roared in despair.

"Oh!" said Vova mournfully. But I saw how happy he was, I could tell by his eyes, by his impudent red eyes.

"Idiot..." I moaned.

He nodded his degenerate's skull understandingly.

"If you understand that you're an idiot," I said maliciously, "then that means that you're not an idiot, but an arrant knave."

"Let's tie him up," suggested my wife. She was inconsolable: Vova had ripped up all of Proust! "Let's tie the bastard up."

Vova gave a terrified howl.

"No, let's kill him instead," I suggested in a cold-blooded voice.

Vova gave an even more terrified howl. The suggestion terrified my wife also. All three of us were terrified and didn't know what to do.

I declared martial law. I instituted the strictest surveillance of Vova. He grew somewhat quieter, but didn't give in: he was wrecking and sabotaging things on the sly. Suddenly objects started mysteriously vanishing: shirts were lifted and disappeared, shoes went for a walk, toothbrushes, kitchen utensils. Suddenly, one fine day, he dumped a huge pile in the middle of the room and from then on things really took off: he smeared feces on the wallpaper, he ripped the wallpaper, he urinated in the fridge, he took a knife to the parquet floor and to the furniture. He farted and committed unforgivable crimes. He stripped right off, he paced around the apartment butt-naked, five steps forward, five steps back, his ginger groin gleaming, and something totally unthinkable raised its head: a gigantic claret-veined worm twitched on his scorched autumn grass . . . He turned out to be a strong one, this Vova, and he couldn't have given a toss for the martial law which had been declared against him. In fact he had declared martial law against us. Against me, a totally peacefully person, a convinced pacifist—I'd last fought when I was fourteen, in the seventh grade, or perhaps when I was twelve—and against my brand-new wife, the lover of Proust and of the innocent pleasures of married life, in comparison with which the claret-veined vision grew into a crisis of Sodomitic proportions.

Vova sat on the telephone and crushed it. The link with the outside world was cut. We barricaded ourselves up in the adjoining room and went into hiding; but my wife and I were at odds. We were at each other's throats. Instead of making us close ranks, misfortune tore us apart. My wife was becoming less and less bearable. I too was a shadow of my former self. I just couldn't put my finger on it. Why had Vova become so impudent? Why had he exploded now, like a delayed-action mine? Or was it that there, in the underground, they trained idiots to become torturers? Or was it my misfortune, my bad luck—just a random catastrophe?! Surely it couldn't just be pure chance? . . .

"How could you have picked him?" my wife kept repeating. Vova was running riot on the other side of the wall.

But why was it, then, that the passersby knew more than I did, why did they tremble so on meeting Vova, as if his mug were familiar to them, as if there were bad memories connected with that mug shot? I didn't understand anything.

A crash was heard. Breaking glass. The chandelier had fallen to its death.

"Lord, but why am I suffering *as well,* and *for what?*" implored my wife.

"So you also think that I'm to blame!" I yelled.

"You've ruined my life," she bristled. "I don't want this! I don't want this! No! You're a monster!"

"I'm a monster? Oh, what a bitch you are! How can you say that!"

But sometimes she said:

"Well, do something, then! Please, I'm begging you . . ."

And at long last I did something. At night Vova would drum on the door of our room and would howl, howl, howl. The stench of feces and sperm wafted under the door (recently Vova had been masturbating frenziedly, like an adolescent . . .). He grew hoarse. I leapt out of bed and jerked the door open. He was standing in front of me massaging seminal fluid into his red-haired chest.

"I'll kill you, bastard!" I yelled at the unshaven face, which was distorted by its obscene convulsions.

A huge sticky paw crashed down on my shoulder. Vova threw me to one side, like a toy poodle, and I smashed into the doorjamb and fell in a crumpled heap. He nimbly grabbed me by the legs and dragged me out of the bedroom. I was about to . . . The lock clicked shut.

I was smashing the door with my fists. In answer to my wife's cries I smashed my fists. Forgotten her name. How could I forget her name? Blanks . . . I ran into the kitchen to look for the bread knife, I kept stabbing it into the door—and kept hearing heart-rending howls, they kept growing—they were both howling, my wife and Vova, they howled heartrendingly, as if I were driving the knife into their flesh, and not into the door—that's how they were howling together, and suddenly all at once everything went quiet, everything went dead, and the deep unpeopled night ruled once more. I chucked the knife away and went into the bathroom to wash with cold water.

The next morning my wife came into the kitchen. A long orange dressing gown, toweling, with a hood. I looked at her pale, dismayed face.

"It's monstrous," she said, lowering herself onto a stool, and reached for a cigarette. The poor thing's hands were shaking.

I nodded and, unable to contain myself, burst out laughing.

Vova cleaned up his act a lot and hardly ever shat on the floor. He stopped going around naked, as he didn't see the need anymore, and in the mornings, whistling, he would shave his high cheekbones. My wife bought him a pink shirt and gave him her beige foulard. Vova wore a felt hat when he went out for his walks with my wife. Life was getting back to normal. I slept on the ottoman, with cotton wool stuffed in my ears. In the mornings I would be woken by the smell of coffee. My wife would prepare breakfast. A dressing gown with a hood. The three of us would drink coffee together. One day Vova presented me with a little bunch of violets. Spring had arrived. The pavings were shining. The shadows were black, and not sea-blue, as they had been in January. A little bunch of violets bought at no little expense at the market.

"That's sweet of you," I said, flattered by the attention.

"Oh!" yelled Vova, overjoyed.

For spring I got hold of a light overcoat for him, made abroad, in Hungary. Why shouldn't he show off a bit?! And I bought a load of Proust from a profiteer in books. A grateful wife buried herself in books when she had the chance.

Then Vova gave me tulips as a present.

"He's a dear, don't you think?" asked my wife.

Then some strange-looking flowers, resembling birds' heads. Then tulips once again, tulips. Lilac, red, yellow.

"But why does he give *you* flowers?"

"Jealous, eh?" I smiled.

Vova helped me hang a new chandelier. He was an efficient helpmate.

"Tell me, Vova," I asked him, "were you or weren't you a professor after all?"

"Don't offend him," said my wife. "Don't traumatize Vova."

Vova walked up to my wife and clipped her around the ear hole. I was pleased. That's how our male fellowship started to take shape. But at night they belonged to each other, and I would block my ears with cotton wool.

"Not more tulips!" said my wife, amazed.

"He's a sweet," I said.

"Watch out or he might screw you by mistake," joked my wife, somewhat aggrieved.

"Watch out or he might stop screwing you," I joked in return.

Outside it was May. Vova talked to me in tongues of flowers.

"I'm pregnant," said my wife. She was standing in her orange toweling dressing gown with the hood, and I thought: there's a type of flower, what on earth are they called, marrygolds or something . . . ? And once again her cigarette trembled in her fingers.

Vova was sleeping sprawled on the couch in happy languor.

"It's uncanny that I'm pregnant," said my wife confidentially.

"The thing is that Vova has his own proclivities. I've respected them and, I won't deny it, bent over backward to meet them. But pregnancy was therefore explicitly excluded! . . ."

"Life with an idiot is full of surprises!" I noted good-heartedly.

"He isn't an idiot!" exploded my wife. "You're the idiot! Yes, you! You! Idiot, with your irony, your friends, your callousness and arrogance . . . He's purer, more innocent, more spiritual than you! I feel like a woman with him, I shall feel like a mother with him. I want to have his baby! I love him. I'm keeping his baby. And don't you dare accept flowers from him! Don't you dare!"

She burst into tears.

"Ravings!" I said. "Incoherent, hysterical ravings. The ravings of a helpless fool who's off her head! You should listen to yourself! . . . Go on, then, have his baby! Go for it! See if I care!" I yelled. "Give him a child, good luck to you!"

In the evening I saw Vova stroking her belly tenderly. They billed and cooed and made plans. Then they screwed long and hard, all night long.

"Oh!" Vova yelled rampantly.

"Oh!" my wife echoed rampantly. I was intrigued. Which proclivities of Vova had my wife bent over backward to meet? How splendidly, I must say, she'd learned to yell, "Oh!" I thought, in my deliberations about proclivities, but I was slow on the uptake and chaste, like any intellectual, and I dozed off without finding out the answer to my question.

Then my wife had an abortion and returned home, shaken by the shamelessness and filth of the women who had undergone with her this operation which has quickly become a literary staple. "That is, you just can't imagine it!," to which I answered, "It's of no interest to me." But Vova didn't grasp straightaway that she'd had an abortion, and kept on stroking her empty scraped belly and

shaven haven, which looked like a new recruit, and this was very
funny, I simply rolled about with laughter. Then he realized what
had happened to his little baby, why it wasn't giving any signs of
life, it finally got through to the fool that the belly was empty, and,
flying into a rage, he battered her during the night. I woke up, despite the cotton wool in my ears. I lay there and listened to him
beating her. He was giving her a sound, thorough beating, using
his fists; she just yelped a little, like a faithful bitch, who understands that she's being given probably what she deserves. I felt
sorry for her.

The next morning Vova brought me an armful of carnations. I
was sitting in the bath with shampoo in my hair, reflecting on the
meaning of life. I didn't want to die. He threw the carnations into
the water. Cumbersome flowers past their prime, implanted on
web-footed little stalks, swam circles around me. I came over all
embarrassed and covered myself with my hand. Vova stroked me,
like a father, on my soapy head and, bending over, kissed me on
the shoulder. His little beard pricked me. It was ticklish and—not
at all what I expected. Overcome with bashful agitation, I said:

"OK, beat it."

But he didn't stir. The carnations were whirling around; they
weighted heavily on my heart. Having washed off the shampoo, I
started plucking them out of the water.

"Oh!" uttered Vova strangely, and suddenly, through the flowers, I caught sight of heavy, purple-veined outlines. They were repulsive, these outlines, they were so repulsive, rude and material
that they looked tempting, they held the allurement of wild thug-
gish strength, they held that which we seek in vain in women's
private, mingy, sacrificial nothingness—a feeling of dignity. One
felt like taking them in hand and taming them. Revulsion was in
need of some sort of revolutionary resmelting. The revulsion was

so material and dense, the beauty so fragile, unsteady and transparent, but this beauty was growing: as on a pile of rubbish a fire
takes hold, and its tender little tongues lick the rotten stinking
rags, they feed on carrion, they tremble in the wind; it is beautiful,
this flame, it gets stronger, it is stronger than abomination, it has
nothing to do with abomination; and the flame devours the rubbish
heap, an orange torch in the evening sky, the children run to it—
what a cause for celebration! Fire! Fire! Ding-dong! Ding-dong! It
brought back memories from childhood: a happy fairy tale, where
the beautiful princesses are nothing more than hags, stupid women
with titties and with mugs flushed in the public bathhouse—
remembrance of naked things past, lost, forgotten glimpses—and
where the proud men provoked one's greatest envy.

"OK, beat it."

But he kept on tarrying and didn't move, he was in no rush to
go, he just wouldn't be off, and tarried.

My Vova! My punishment!

O, orifice of croup! O, PAIN, eclipse of Europe . . .

Well, and now, scum-sucking reader, whoever you are, a friend
or a reptile or aesthete, a snob or from the mob, one of the black
masses or a scarlet guard, whatever life may lie ahead for you, or
whatever death may be waiting for you, remember this: I don't
care about your verdict; I've gorged myself on happiness, like a
glutton who's stuffed himself on pancakes and caviar, and your
judgment is that of a paupers' court, whereas my life's rich with
meaning, I'm a millionaire from the goldfields of the Lena River,
and my loads of money, rich inner life and warm fur coat keep out
the Siberian cold!

Vova and I lived in a state of harmony, tenderness and volup-
tuousness, giving each other modest presents: sweets, multicolored balloons, flowers, oranges and passionate kisses—as a son

lives with a father, when they are both Natural Born Poets by the Grace and Will of God, and there was no one in the whole wide world happier than us.

We made our home in the adjoining room, having put at my wife's disposal the expanse of the dining room, the ottoman and Proust, fraternal attention and fraternal unsullied love. Did we not get down on our knees before her, begging for a little tear of indulgence toward our happiness? Did we not surround her with filial respect? Were we not ready to bang our heads against a brick wall just in order to please her?

But she said, "No!"

No! No! and No!

She said, "You are a pair of scum-suckers, you are degenerates, you are slime and bastards, you are corrupters of each another and of the law."

She offended us, but we didn't say a single nasty word to her, we simply waddled out in single file: Vova first, with me bringing up the rear, we withdrew into the bedroom and, lying on the bed, grew dispirited.

"And you, Vova, are a particular bastard," shouted my wife from the other side of the door.

"Oh!" Vova threw his arms apart in despair and desperation.

"Oh!" I groaned.

Days passed. She was ruining everything and tearing everything up: she tore the curtains, Proust, my old love letters to her— we just shrugged our shoulders; she shat on the carpet, like an invalid—we pretended not to notice. We were above this, we didn't care about the stench. But even the gods' patience eventually snaps. So we beat her up, not very painfully, we stripped her clothes off for fun and beat her up, laughing loudly at her stupid titties, which bounced up and down friskily as we pounded her, but she lost consciousness nonetheless—and then her titties became totally ridiculous, and we even shed a few tears over their terminal stupidity.

She started starving us. She didn't grant us access to the food. We became emaciated from mutual love and from hunger. Hunger was arousing us. We were gigantic caryatids propping up an agitated sphincter. We were thin, happy men with bums turned inside out. But even the gods' patience eventually snaps.

"I really hate you," my wife would say to Vova, her eyes a-goggle. We beat her up once again. Bitch! We've only winged this bird! Till she was black and blue in the face!... No effect whatsoever! But it was sweet. We exchanged glances. We embraced, and it was sweet. We prodded each other in the stomach.

Suddenly my wife declared to Vova:

"Either him or me!"

"That's a fascist way of popping the question," I noted gloomily.

"What do you need him for?" my wife asked Vova. "OK, you've had your fun and games, now call it a day!... He won't give you a child in any event. What's the point of him? But I will bear you a son."

"You've had one child already!" I observed.

"You will have a son, Vova," my wife said with conviction. "You will be proud of him."

"I am your son, Vova," I said timidly.

My wife burst out laughing. A laugh of pure contempt. For a second or so I lost faith in myself, in Vova's and my mutual love... It was a second of unforgivable weakness. Vova saw all this and grew sad. My wife built on her success. She smelled of woman. Vova pulled pensively at his little red beard: five steps forward, five steps back. *Either/or*. He didn't take long over his decision.

He ran into the room. The shears snapped. I was sitting in

the armchair with a glass of tomato juice. I was drinking greedily. She boldly went toward Vova. Her body suddenly seemed to me so desirable, and I cried out in joy:

"Wait! I want her!"

Vova gave a smile in response to my cry. He wasn't a jealous guy and placed a high value on people's passions. But he made a terrible sign, which signified: AFTER. I was gripped by horror. No! But my wife boldly made for the shears. Vova made for my wife, red-haired, intelligent, dear, just like a tank.

"I love you," my wife said to Vova in complete ecstasy. "I love! I love you, Vova."

Vova grabbed my wife by the hair—she had fair, shoulder-length hair—twisted her hair around his hand and tipped her unto the soiled carpet. He pressed his knee into her chest. We were all as naked as newborn babes.

"I love . . ." wheezed my wife, in loving admiration of Vova.

Vova quickly started cutting off her head with the shears.

"Oh!" Vova cried at long last and lifted up his trophy by the hair.

I sat there, covered in blood, tomato juice and cum. The strongest sexual impression imaginable. I know who I am. I am Renoir.

And so, my dear reader, I became a widower for the second time. The wheels knock. I am walking along the narrow corridors of railway carriages, I fiddle with the loose handles of the heavy metal doors between carriages, beneath me I see the silver ribbons of the rails, the smell of the railways is in my nostrils. I am going to the restaurant car to eat a railway burger and to wash it down with beer. Soon will be the hustle and bustle of midday Kharkov; I am free, I am sad; I have just buried a wife who died from a childhood disease.

Vova took the body by the legs and tried to tear it to pieces. He was strong, my Vova, but he wasn't able to tear it apart. Then he mounted the body on himself. He bellowed. I closed my eyes. I am very, very tired. And AFTER I've finished, I say to him:

"Take her away."

Wearily—he was also tired!—he grabbed her by the foot and lugged her onto the landing on the stairs, toward the refuse chute. He drags her toward the refuse chute like a large imported doll. I see the sweep of his freckled back. Vova! . . . I never saw him again.

Blanks! Blanks! . . . I passed through the dull red light. The guard greeted me like I was one of the family. I bit and sang in a mocking falsetto:

> A birch was standing in a field,
> Was standing leafy in a field . . .

I bit like an adder. I lost a lot of teeth. Yes, I was that tall lad with the protruding ears and the completely human face. Kraig Benson picked me, the fake foreigner. Instead of diplomatic immunity he offered me the lash and order. I'm grateful to him! I'm now starting to wield a skillful pen again. I write about you, Vova. My Vova! My punishment! Give me back my punishment! And if he has died—no, you will never die, Vova—if he has died, tell me where his grave is. I shall bring him an armful of spring tulips. We are a monument, Vova, wrecked by warring whirlwinds. I hear the swan song of my revolution.

A WHITE NEUTERED TOMCAT WITH THE EYES OF A BEAUTIFUL WOMAN

ON ACCOUNT of my nervous exhaustion I couldn't distinguish the stripes and cockades of the judges, but it seems that this was all happening either during the Tsarist past, or perhaps even in some foreign country, not that any of this changed the sense of the sentence which has been passed on me.

At this point I leapt up and shouted, addressing myself to the military-judicial nebulousness, You have made a mistake, this isn't fair, you have placed me and yourselves in a crying shame of a situation. First, I yelled, I don't have anything in common with either the army or even more so a military tribunal. Second, I am opposed to the death penalty, so that you're not just adding insult to injury, you're mocking and taking diabolical liberties with me. Third, I love my wife, who will not be able to endure my death, she'll hang herself or take poison, or throw herself out of a window, or drown herself, and our son will be left a complete orphan, and he will never forgive you this. Fourth, all this has been described many times over, played out, and has become so much of a cliché that out of a prisoner of conscience, which I happen not to be, you're turning me into a prisoner of plagiarism, which I as a writer categorically have no desire to be. Fifth, you are taking too much upon yourselves in intruding upon the transcendental, in usurping the functions of Providence, and even if I never loved policemen, could never bring myself to love them even though I recognized their relative usefulness, I have to admit that when a tire was stolen from my car I did go to the police station, and there I was heard out in full, though the tire still hasn't been found, I have to confess.

I came to in a cell, from the smell of sal ammoniac. Squatting before me was Colonel Diamant, the head of the military faculty of Moscow University, from which I'd graduated seventeen years earlier. I recognized him immediately from his light-colored curls and his exemplarily Slavic facial features. In my time I'd suffered much at his hands.

"Well, my boy, you've really lost it," said Diamant disapprovingly but at the same time with some fatherly feeling, taking a sniff of the sal ammoniac for his own amusement before closing the flask. "Don't feel like dying, is that it?"

"I'm not guilty of anything, Comrade Colonel," I explained in a weak voice.

"Oh, yes, you are," said the colonel firmly.

He was a fat, youthful-looking man with light blue eyes and small narrow lips. I felt that his energy field was far stronger than mine. He had the energy of a fifty-five-year-old man who has tasted power, I was never able to cope with such types in open battle, I would take back stage, become a yes-man and fill up with hate.

"It's boom-bang-a-bang for you tomorrow," Diamant informed me confidingly.

"What do you mean, tomorrow already?" I couldn't help exclaiming.

"At o seven hundred hours precisely," elaborated the colonel, having looked at his watch. "You've got more than enough time. Are you going to write?"

"An appeal?" I livened up.

"What for?" he said in astonishment. "Something artistic. Some sort of address to the people."

I thought about it.

"No," I said. "I've got absolutely nothing to say. Will it be OK to write a note to my wife instead?"

"No point," said the colonel.

"You're mistaken," I said. "I loved my wife more than anything on earth." And I lowered my head, realizing that I was talking about myself in the past tense.

"Bullshit!" The colonel didn't believe me.

"Once, many years ago, before we were married even, parting from her for the summer, I spent three hours howling, leaning against the frame of the door. One can experience true love only once in a lifetime."

"Write about that, then," suggested the colonel.

"One may not write about that," I said sternly and sadly.

"But did you screw any black women?"

"I didn't have relations with any black women, and I didn't betray the Motherland," I sighed.

"Oh, yes, you did," said Diamant firmly. "Do you know what I like about you?" continued the colonel after a short silence. "That you don't wear a wedding ring. A real man doesn't wear a wedding ring."

We each took some time out to think our own thoughts.

"Do you want to know my secret?" I asked, bringing my face near to him.

"Well?" He went all tense, froze, his face a deep purple.

"I'm a romantic by nature . . . Come, listen to this silence. Like in the countryside . . . Only there are no dogs barking. I am a disguised romantic, Colonel."

"Go and fuck yourself!" said the colonel in fury and spat on the floor in anger.

"Aren't you ashamed to spit in the cell of a man on death row?" I said reproachfully.

"I'm sorry, it was an accident," said the colonel, shamefaced, and wiped the spit with his boot.

"I bet your wife's an old witch."

Diamant nodded his head in assent, despondent.

"But mine is a white angel with white wings."

"What is she, sportswoman or something?" asked Diamant.

"Well, not as such," I said and started to walk up and down the cell with my hands stuck in my pockets, like a pendulum, as I remembered my wife. "But maybe they won't shoot me. Perhaps they'll only give me a fright, like Dostoevsky, and exile me. And I'll live in a peasant hut and write novels. After all, what would have become of Dostoevsky if he hadn't undergone a mock execution?"

"Who the bloody hell knows!" said Diamant, puzzled.

"He would have become Chernyshevsky, got it? True, on the other hand Chernyshevsky served out so many years in Siberia and—nothing. He remained Chernyshevsky."

"And quite right to do so," Diamant said approvingly.

"I've got somewhat carried away," I said, pulling myself up short. "I suffered in life most of all because life did not correspond to my ideals. In school I had a teacher of history whose name was Tsilia Samoilovna Littlefinger. That was her surname—Littlefinger!" I showed Diamant my finger. We burst out laughing together.

"Oh, you're impossible!" Diamant waved me away, wiping tears of laughter from his eyes.

"Littlefinger! Littlefinger!" I shouted, guffawing.

"Enough! I can't stand it." Diamant was splitting his sides with laughter.

"Khlebnikov has a poem about laughers. And he was writing about us. 'O, burst out laughing, laughsters! O, bust with laughter, laughers!' Are you fond of Khlebnikov?"

"Who isn't?" said Diamant, surprised at the question.

"Don't suppose you've got any chow?"

"I've got some chocolate. Milk. Want some?"

"Yeah, gimme some. You don't mind that I'm so informal with you? After all, what does it matter to me that you're a colonel when tomorrow everything will end?"

"I've read that thought somewhere before," said Diamant, pensively. "By the way, speaking about thoughts." He reached into his briefcase and pulled out a large notebook. "See, I've got an album. I collect thoughts. Well, the thoughts of those whom we boom-bang-a-bang here. Write something. And I will preserve it and reread it from time to time."

"And what do the others write? May I see?"

"Wait. You write something first, otherwise it's no fun."

"Oh, go on, then," I agreed.

"Excellent!" The colonel was radiant and opened up his album on a clean page. "Here's a pen for you. And I'll have a sit-down in the meantime, have a smoke."

I rested one leg on the other and set to thinking. I thought for a long time about what to write.

"Only please make sure you write legibly," Diamant pleaded.

He smoked his cigarette, then a second, then a third. Finally I gathered my thoughts together, my hands grew damp and cold. Not recognizing my own handwriting, I produced a few words.

Diamant took the album from me, put on his golden glasses and read thoughtfully, aloud:

MAN IS BORN HAPPY AND FREE,
BUT IS EVERYWHERE ENCHAINED.

"Well, what do you think?" I asked.

Choked with emotion, he couldn't utter a single word for ages. He kept on shifting his gaze from me to the album and back again.

"Are these your own words?" Diamant asked at last after what seemed an eternity.

"My own," I answered modestly, but without concealing, however, a proud smile.

"It's just like a hymn!" rejoiced Diamant, his glasses shining. "Words of genius."

He even embraced me.

"Thank you, thank you, my dear friend!"

"No big deal . . ." I said, affecting modesty.

"I must tell you something," Diamant was speaking in an inspired whisper, bending close to my ear. "For such words . . . for such words . . . I'll think I'll go and report to my bosses. Such words might just earn you a pardon!"

"What?!" I leapt up on the spot.

"What's the time now? Four-thirty? OK, I'm off, perhaps I've still got time."

"Give me some chocolate!" I said.

"Here, take the whole bar." He hurriedly took the chocolate from his briefcase, grabbed the album and, winking at me, vanished.

I imagined him hastily pulling on his greatcoat and fur hat, running out through the gates and hailing a taxi, I see the car stopping, the late-night taxi driver switches on his meter, I see them traveling through the city, leaving the scars of tracks behind on the fresh snow, it's warm and cozy in the car, the driver doesn't have much to say for himself, the colonel keeps on looking at his watch, the car leaps out onto the embankment road and gathers speed, the yellow lampposts shine, I eat chocolate and see the snow falling on the black water of the Moscow River, the car brakes next to a multistory building which looks like a wedding cake, I am filled with love for this cake; I see the colonel knocking at the carved front door, and I see a sleepy elevator attendant, she's wearing a scarf and spends a long time fiddling with a bar with which the door has been secured, and a spacious hall in front of the elevators, and the grand cabin of the elevator with its spacious mirror, in which the colonel is reflected, shaking off the snow, and, finally, the precious door; a short ring, silence, a second ring, a third, and lo and behold, from the distant depths of the apartment paces are heard, not the mistress of the house, but a servant,—one can hear close to the familiar Moscow sound of the chain and the click of the lock, the door opens. "Hello, Dusya!" "Hello"—slightly surprised—"Semyon Yakovlevich!" "Where's Pavel Petrovich? Is he asleep?" "I don't think the master's gone to bed yet. Working. Come on, I'll hang up your overcoat." The corridor. A chink of light. His master's voice. Out from the study, arching a long back, steps a white neutered tomcat with the eyes of a beautiful woman.

"Well, then?" I cried out.

Colonel Diamant, a worried morning look on his face, stopped dead in the middle of the cell.

"Sorry, mate," he said, coldly but sick at heart, and, avoiding my eyes, as is the Russian way, started to undo his holster.

SHIT-SUCKER

OH, THE spring in the Moscow countryside is so beautiful it's scary! Everything flows, shivers, trembles. Fall is also unspeakably beautiful. The forest is literally enveloped in yellow fire. And the silence! The silence is deafening. All you can hear is the jolly hammering of the moonlighters' hammers, and their screeching saws spraying sweet-smelling shavings, and the quiet song of occasional migratory birds. Beyond the forest, close by, is the Moscow River. Here it is taut, capricious, virtually a mountain stream. On July middays it lures thin-necked blokes with white lines left from their vest straps, beckons nervous women with eyes so deep-set they seem to be in bunkers, entices badly brought up Young Pioneers and schoolchildren. The river, thanks to its wiles, manages to turn some of the aforementioned into victims of drowning, and drags their weak-willed bodies verily unto Zvenigorod itself, where they surface opposite the befouled monastery, like submarines, as a warning to sinners. Some time long ago the young Herzen lived in this area. Gossamer clung in a thin veil to the tender face of that illegitimate youth. Now there is an airfield nearby. One after another the silvery carcasses of red-starred fighter planes rise into the air. The chorus of drumming hammers halts for a moment. The moonlighters throw back their colorful sun-hatted heads. Ours! Those are our jets! The moonlighters breathe heavily. Yeah, they're just the sort that shot down the Korean airliner! Mushroom soup bubbles in a bucket. Their eyes become flecked with blood: Had it coming to them! American arse-lickers! Soon it will be lunch. The youngest of them has been sent off to the shop. He walks along the forest track, his frog-like mouth grinning from ear to ear. His are the large palms of a true worker. Suddenly his muscles tense, he goes deeper into the forest. He squats under a small pine tree, and starts rummaging among the rotting leaves. He uncovers a large, strong cep. He twists the mushroom in his hands, croaks approvingly and puts it carefully inside his padded waistcoat.

During lunch it starts to rain. The moonlighters sit in the dacha, they have a roof over their heads, they couldn't care less, let it rain! They are drinking, eating soup, having snacks with the booze. The best educated of them is Viktor. He spent a year studying at the aviation institute. After he was kicked out he had to serve in the German Democratic Republic, in 1968 helping liberate Prague from the hooligans. As a memento of his service in the tank corps he wears a tank commander's headgear. The most skilled worker of them all is, of course, Evgeny Ivanovich, he's the one in charge, even though on paper the brigade leader is Pavel. But Pavel's expertise lies elsewhere, in the evenings he slips off to the nearby Resort for Rest and Relaxation, but he's lazy, which is why he specializes in easy game, from forty-five to fifty years old and up. Sometimes they stroll up to the dacha building site— perfumed, made-up, thin-haired matrons, each evidently with a sweet tooth—to watch him hammering in the nails, to spend some time there, to offer invitations to come over and see them sometime; but Evgeny Ivanovich doesn't need these young birds anymore, he's had his fair share of that, and he gets off more on work nowadays. The dacha they have to build is a complicated one, in accordance with some sort of crazy vision, out of a fairy tale, the sort that are built in the Swiss mountains apparently, with steeply sloping roofs, with rafters right down to the ground on one side,—on the other side, the window looks up into the heavens. It's funny, Viktor says, he's seen similar in Germany, and the Kraut birds are so easy, no problems with them, he explained to Pavel, hey, hold on a minute, says Evgeny Ivanovich crossly, tell us about the houses. But his eyes have already become glassy, for some reason he doesn't hold his drink as well as he used to, he's not as young as he used to be, and the owner is an idiot, why build in such an incomprehensible style? Look here, he's told them to redo the staircase to the first floor, he doesn't like the way the staircase turns, don't you know! OK, you'd understand it if he was a Jew, but he seems to be a Russian, so why does the bastard have to act like Lord Muck? We should just torch the whole bloody thing! Evgeny Ivanovich grew angry and dozed off. The others finished off the second bottle of vodka and were happy that it was raining: no one felt like getting up or doing anything. Zhenya said that he wouldn't go for any more vodka in such rain, and the rain poured down even more heavily, it lashed down so strongly that it was as if the fighter planes really had blown up the skies; so then they started trying to persuade Boris to go, he's still young too, he has a motorcycle. Boris was the trendiest of the lot of them, he wore the snazziest clothes, and his job was decent enough in all senses of the word, if not very contemporary: he played the accordion in a Holiday Camp at the opposite end of the Moscow region, but he'd just got married a few days before, although for some reason you couldn't tell from his face that this was so. Viktor had absented himself awhile also, for two or three days, for family reasons, and you also wouldn't think that his father had just died: our lads know how to hide deep within their souls the most varied emotions! The owner of the still-unfinished dacha would visit them on Sundays to check up on them. They would prepare for these inspections, though not very thoroughly. On the first floor, in the room which was earmarked as the future owner's future study, Zhenya had been scraping off the floor the puke which had turned hard there three days ago. Evgeny Ivanovich, in specs, effing and blinding, had been reassembling the staircase, checking it against the draftsman's version. Boris had driven off into the rain to get a third bottle. They slept on the floor without getting undressed, in their padded waistcoats, Viktor slept in his headgear, they got up during the night to drink water and urinate through the window. Just before dawn Pavel returned, soaked through, terrified, and woke them all up. They rushed down the staircase, leapt out of the house, stopped and stared.

While they had been asleep, rivers of dirty water had completely flooded the basement of the house. They had a smoke. Everyone realized that the water could wash away the sandy foundations, and then the reinforced concrete piles would start to lean, and the Swiss crap would tumble down. Everyone also realized that it was their fault: they'd dug the pit, but they hadn't thought that rainwater might flood it. The new iron roof of the house sparkled threateningly and wailed gently in the wind.

Their boss was enjoying a Sunday lie-in in his nice warm bed on Gorky Street when he was disturbed by an early morning alarm call. He arrived an hour and a half later in his own cherry-colored Volga car. Pavel spun some heated and incoherent yarn about a dam which had burst its banks. The sickly face of their boss, exhausted by long days in the office, was yellow and unpleasant. "So what are you waiting for," frowned the owner, "get some buckets over here and start bailing it out." "Take three days to bail it out with buckets," announced Pavel. "We need a shit-sucker." "What the hell is that?" asked the boss, taking an instant dislike to this word from an alien and absurd life. They explained it to him. "OK, so where do we get this shit-sucker?" asked the owner. "We'll have to ask Uncle Kolya, the night watchman," they replied.

"Let's go, then," said the boss coldly. He took Pavel with him. When the brigade had finished putting the roof on the house, their boss, as is the custom, produced some bottles of vodka. The moonlighters had knocked together a table and some benches next to the house. They'd quizzed him about the Korean airliner. "Is it true that there was an atomic bomb on board?" asked Zhenya. "Of course there can't have been an atomic bomb on board! I've told you a hundred times!" shouted Viktor in a fit of temper. He knew everything about airplanes, but Zhenya still wasn't convinced. The boss liked these lads. They loved their country, though they were exasperated by the various shortcomings, and it's a shame they drink so much, of course. "You know," said Viktor quietly, "I feel I ought to warn you." He rotated his head and his tank headgear. "Pavel flogs your stuff on the side. That's why we keep running out of materials." It was already dark. They lit a campfire. Zhenya told them the story about how once he was once put on trial in Mytishchi. In the courtroom he started acting crazy: he stripped down to his underpants. The militiamen jumped on him. The trial was adjourned. Evgeny Ivanovich with undue familiarity asked the boss why on earth he'd wanted a dacha in a non-Russian style. The boss gave his answer, but by the next morning Evgeny Ivanovich had forgotten exactly what the answer was and just couldn't bring himself to remember. Then Viktor whispered to the boss that Pavel had made the whole damn dam up out of thin air. For all that, Pavel was the one the boss took with him.

Uncle Kolya had been drinking at breakfast and was on a high. He took noisy delight in his guests: he drummed his fists on the table and struck up a Russian song. Uncle Kolya was always informing people that in his youth he'd been an engineer, but that just before the war he'd been unjustly repressed. The boss suspected that it was Uncle Kolya who was stealing his building materials. Perhaps he and Pavel were in on it together, thought the owner. But where else would he find workers? Uncle Kolya had had his leg broken in the prison camp. He walked in a circle, like a pair of compasses. His nickname was Old Shufflefoot. In lines Old Shufflefoot claimed to be an invalid from the Great Patriotic War.

"Shit-sucker...shit sucker..." The cripple fell into deep thought. "Let's go!" he yelled out in triumph.

He explained: they'd have to go to the village, he knows the stove mender there, one could almost say he's a relative of his. Old Shufflefoot sat in the front, Pavel in the back, looking like a teacher's pet, a blue-eyed boy with light hair, just slightly and elegantly balding. If Gogol's Chichikov had had a fling with a domestic serf, then their love child would have been the spit and image of Pavel. Several kilometers into the autumn forest they caught a fleeting glimpse of a solid green fence.

"We have this special local sanatorium here," said Uncle Kolya importantly with a smack of the lips. "There are armed guards."

The boss, it appeared, didn't hear.

"All the rooms there have Arabian china cabinets with crystal glasses and refrigerators," said Uncle Kolya, addressing Pavel.

"And every morning they place a free bottle of vodka, a free bottle of cognac and also a free bottle of sherry in each refrigerator."

A forced smile crawled along the boss's tired face.

"They serve you caviar three times a day, whichever type you like, including the best pressed caviar."

"It's salty if you eat a lot of it," declared Pavel in a sweet voice.

"There they give you special caviar, not salty," said Uncle Kolya severely.

"Cool!" said Pavel, animatedly. The boss held his tongue.

"What's more"—Uncle Kolya licked his lips—"they have armed guards there with machine guns and they even have a can-non. Imagine what it's like when it fires!..."

"Leave it out!" said the boss calmly.

"I've seen it myself, with my very own eyes!" exclaimed Uncle Kolya. "It stands in the bushes, next to the entrance."

Suddenly a huge red combine harvester headed straight toward them from around the bend.

"Stop him!" yelled Uncle Kolya.

The boss flashed his headlights. The combine harvester came to a halt. Uncle Kolya dragged his leg out of the Volga, and started circling toward the combine.

"Listen, mate," said Uncle Kolya, making his way toward the young combine operator. "Tell me this, please: can we get hold of a shit-sucker around here? Perhaps the fire brigade will let us have one?"

"They won't let you have one," said the combine operator.

"I know they won't let us have one," agreed Uncle Kolya. "So where, then, can we get one, Mikhail?"

"Donno," said Mikhail. "Ask Vovka."

"Which Vovka is that?"

"Our top worker."

Having been demobilized four years ago, Vladimir Sorokin,

member of the Young Communists' League, had returned to his native village, not too proud to get his hands dirty in shitty work on the farm. Now the whole region was trying to emulate this cattle breeder.

"But where do we find him, this Vovka?"

"Where else would he be?" said Mikhail in astonishment. "He's always with his piglets."

"Well, goodbye, Mikhail," said Uncle Kolya severely and shook Mikhail's hand.

"We haven't seen you around here for a long time, Uncle Vasya," said the combine operator.

"Lots of work," explained Uncle Kolya. "Only I'm not, you know, Uncle Vasya. I'm Uncle Kolya."

"Ah, yes, of course!" The lad gave a broad smile, revealing a fine set of teeth. "And in fact I'm not Mikhail at all. In fact I'm Bodunov, Aleksandr."

"Bodunov?" Uncle Kolya looked closely at him. "Well, I never! But it's true. Yes, you *are* Bodunov."

After talking for another minute or so about various important matters, they went their separate ways.

"To the farm! To their top worker!" commanded Uncle Kolya. "He has a new shit-sucker, I know it! It shines like a new kopeck!"

The somewhat reassured but still gloomy boss stepped on the gas.

"Uncle Kolya," asked Pavel cordially, "tell us a bit more about the sanatorium."

"About the sanatorium?" Uncle Kolya thought it over. "Well, OK, then," he agreed at long last. "In general, this is how the place operates: each patient, on average, has two consultants assigned to him, a Sister, and several nurses. Only American drugs are used."

"I bet the nurses are real crackers too?" interrupted Pavel.

"Only crack staff, no two ways about it," Uncle Kolya assured him.

"I wonder where they live?" asked Pavel as casually as he could manage.

"That's enough of that, lad!" Uncle Kolya called him to order. "They live in a special restricted zone. Behind barbed wire."

"Like nuns," said Pavel, thinking aloud.

"The nurses—that's nothing!" Uncle Kolya said dismissively. "The main thing is that they have a special section there."

"And what's there?" said Pavel timidly.

"I'll tell you what's there," said the invalid cautiously. "The dead are there, in special underground buildings, preserved in crystal, bulletproof coffins."

The boss looked at Uncle Kolya with alarm.

"It's true." Uncle Kolya met his glare without flinching. "You think that when our leaders die, they bury them in the ground? No way. Those are plaster casts being buried. The real ones are deep frozen and hidden here. They're all gathered here: all the marshals with Zhukov at their head, and the culture vulture Zhdanov, and old man Kalinin, and Malenkov, and Molotov, and Mikhail Andreevich Suslov, chief ideologist. And in the doorway to the Main Cabinet lies a huge frozen idol, the fiery comrade-in-arms Klim Voroshilov, ready for anything . . . When they are needed again, they'll be defrosted, and once again they shall be our leaders," Old Shufflefoot concluded his speech with a solemn look on his face.

"Now I get it! . . ." Pavel even covered his mouth with his palm. "Just in case there's a war!"

"Well, just to be on the safe side in any event," added Uncle Kolya instructively. "That's the reason for having both the machine guns and the cannon."

"Listen here," said the boss suddenly, irritated beyond all measure, "I'd be grateful if you could refrain from mouthing all this—all this pernicious nonsense while you're in my car!"

"But what do you mean, nonsense?" said Uncle Kolya, offended. "They lie there in their uniforms, with their medals. They've even got Beria, Stalin's Chief of Secret Police. When he was being tried he said to them, 'Don't shoot me. I'm a talented organizer. I may still come in handy.' Khrushchev thought about it and complied with the request of his sworn enemy."

"Hold on!" said Pavel, his heart beating quickly. "So how then will they be able to wage war, if, as they say, technology is advancing all the time?"

"Well, perhaps somehow they teach them about it there?"

"How can you teach dead men?!" the boss said, enraged beyond all measure.

"How should I know?" Uncle Kolya shrugged his shoulders and lit up a stinking *papirosa*. "Think about it, what do I have to gain from lying?" he said angrily. "After all, when they defrost Stalin I'll be the first one he puts behind bars."

"Why?" wondered Pavel, slow on the uptake.

"Because he'll put all those who'd been in prison during his time back inside again."

"But what if they go off in there?" worried the moonlighter.

"They shouldn't," said Uncle Kolya, shaking his head. "A military doctor, rank of colonel, stands next to every coffin. Though sometimes they give them a rapid defrost and flip them over, to avoid bed sores."

These bed sores finally drove the boss to breaking point and beyond.

"That does it!" he roared at Uncle Kolya. "Just leave it, OK! There's nothing there! There are no machine guns, no coffins! I spent last summer in that sanatorium—last summer, get it! Is that clear enough for you?!"

Uncle Kolya looked thoughtfully at the road ahead and smoked his *papirosa*. The forest was literally enveloped in yellow fire.

"So is it true what they say," said the invalid, screwing up his eyes, "that in every room there's an Arabian china cabinet with crystal glasses?"

How We Murdered the Frenchman

IN FACT, we didn't really kill him. We merely wanted to cut him open to see what he had inside him. Shiryaev took pity on the lost soul which death hadn't stopped for and decided to keep him as a roommate. He doesn't ask for food, and two's jollier company at the end of the day. Only make sure you behave yourself, don't be a ruddy hooligan, you foreign prick!

The Frenchman turned out to be complaisant, but sometimes at night he would suddenly start to vibrate a lot, so much that even the chandelier would start moving and the glasses and plates on the table would tinkle. Shiryaev was a light sleeper and the sound would wake him up immediately. I'll chuck you out of the window in a minute, Shiryaev would threaten in a hoarse voice. Nevertheless, the Frenchman wouldn't stop vibrating straightaway. Now all because of you I won't fall asleep again until morning, Shiryaev would reproach the Frenchman. He would lie and listen to the Frenchman bouncing around the room, hitting himself painfully against the walls. Scallywag, mumbled Shiryaev.

In the morning the wild sounds of music came through the wall.

The newlyweds were getting ready for work. They would slam the doors, make a racket in the kitchen. Then suddenly there would be a tormenting silence. Shiryaev had no one left: his wife, his relatives, his acquaintances had all died. Shiryaev used to get up early, leave his apartment block, ride the trolley bus to his daughter's to take his grandson to the kindergarten. One morning he arrived to find no daughter and no grandson. Strangers were living in her apartment.

The newlyweds would return late at night, often somewhat drunk, judging by the smell, and would greedily fish pieces of greasy meat out of the saucepan. Relations with the neighbors weren't good from the very start. Shiryaev guessed their plan and moved his small refrigerator into his room.

"In case they poison the food," Shiryaev explained to the Frenchman.

He would deliberately go out into the corridor and pace around there, just to show that he was still alive.

Shiryaev wore warm underwear all the year-round, because he was a tired old man and knew from experience that winter is stronger than summer. Shiryaev would make his way slowly to a laundry to hand in his dirty washing. The young girls who worked there hated him. He would show the line his veteran's identity card wrapped in cellophane and would squeeze his way forward to the counter. His ID card lay in the breast pocket of an army shirt. Shiryaev wore military clothes, but without epaulets.

"You ought to be embarrassed to bring in such stuff," the girls would say, who'd seen all sorts of laundry in their time.

Shiryaev's hands would start to quake at this, but he would control himself and stand in gloomy silence.

The girls would set about marking the clothes, and the stink would make them feel sick.

"Take your laundry back home," the girls would say rudely to Shiryaev.

"You show me your instructions first," he would answer. "I know my rights."

The Frenchman giggled as he listened to Shiryaev's story. The girls didn't have any instructions concerning stench. The Frenchman had come for an internship at the university and, once he'd found his feet, he had started hanging around with all sorts of people. He was warmly accepted everywhere, because he was French, and, despite everything, he got to like the Russians more and more. At home in France he'd been lonely, his mother lived in Toulouse, and he saw her once a year, his teeth were always aching there, whereas in Russia suddenly they'd stopped aching, and then he took to visiting the Moscow theaters and even started to smoke a little. But he didn't know how to smoke, always managing to choke and have coughing fits, and this made a considerable impression on the women of Moscow, who started to teach him how to smoke. He traveled to Zagorsk and was amazed, his eyes filled with understanding, he liked the way the candles crackled in Russian churches, even though he was an atheist and didn't believe in God. Then, one Sunday, he was taken to Pasternak's grave in Peredelkino and had explained to him the role poetry plays in Russian life. Next to the grave stood jam jars full of flowers, people kept on coming to worship the poet, someone started to recite by heart some immortal verses, others were silent, the Frenchman was stunned, he got hold of *Doctor Zhivago* in French from somewhere, he walked around with a raised collar, he threw his long thin scarf over his shoulder, he squinted myopically—all this also impressed the Moscow women. Shiryaev would listen to the Frenchman in silence, stooped in his chair, holding his palms together between his knees. "Once my grandson," said Shiryaev, "pushed, like, one boy in his kindergarten group. The boy was a real swine, put on airs, he'd bring his foreign-made toys to show off, so, my boy grabbed him and pushed him a little . . . Oh no, they've switched the music on again!" Shiryaev got upset. "They kick me out of the laundry, there's no peace at home whatsoever, they switch it on on purpose, they know I can't stand it." No one asked the Frenchman about Paris. Well, only sometimes. They would ask, "But have you seen such and such a film?" "Yes, yes, I've heard about it." The Frenchman would nod his head, deep in concentration. In fact in Paris he'd rarely gone to the cinema, practically hadn't gone at all.

This time the manager of the laundry arrived on the scene, she'd heard Shiryaev yelling and, without even touching the client's laundry, said firmly: "Take it home!" Shiryaev realized that if he lost this battle, if he lost, then he was well and truly done for. And the crowd of those handing in their laundry was also ill-disposed toward him. Enemies everywhere. The newlyweds' wild screams of laughter could be heard through the wall. "You see," said Shiryaev, "I made inquiries. She left for Mongolia. What for? Why Mongolia? She didn't say anything, just went away. And took my grandson. I arrive: strangers. I ask, 'Where's Lyuda?' They shut the door in my face. I rush hither and thither making inquiries. No one knows anything. Then I find out: she's gone to Mongolia. I say, 'What do you mean, gone to Mongolia?' Without even sending a letter to me, nothing. Gone to Mongolia. What is one to make of that?" "Oh, yes, Mongolia," nodded the Frenchman understandingly, "the Trans-Siberian railway." "My grandson's a good lad," said Shiryaev. He chewed his lips. "I just don't get it. Some Mongolia or other. Why did she take him away?" "They'll come back," the Frenchman said, trying to set his mind at rest. "They'll return, what else can they do? They'll return." Shiryaev shook his head. "They'll return and ask where I am. And I'll be feeding the worms—that's where I'll be. The neighbors will have poisoned me." "My mother in Toulouse," said the Frenchman, agreeing, "also suffered in the same way from loneliness, but she never complained..." "Do you think I'm complaining, then?" Shiryaev turned on him. "I wanted to go and work for a bit in the Voluntary Society for Collaboration with the Armed Forces, and at first they said, 'OK,' and then, 'No, you can't, you smell.' I didn't used to smell, everyone was OK with my smell before, but now, like, I *smell*. There must be a new breed of nose in town: they sniff out bad smells everywhere." "You don't have to tell me!" agreed the Frenchman. "I ask the woman in charge, 'What sort of manager are you, if you're afraid even to touch the laundry? I've got more awards and medals than you've got gold teeth! If you don't take my laundry, I'll write to the Central Committee!' That's it, my dear friend, Soviet power is at an end! I show her my identity card, but she just waves it aside. 'I don't need any ID card of yours,' she says, 'if your laundry's in such a state.' 'What sort of a situation is this,' I say, 'how can this be, what, are we supposed to bring clean washing to the laundry or something? I'm sorry, but that's a real act of sabotage.' They cut you open, they want to poison me and they're getting away with it scot-free, yes?" "Yes," agreed the Frenchman, "now no one at all will write a letter to my mother." "You should have spent a bit less time loafing around all those Zagorsks and places," Shiryaev flew at him. "You should have sat in your university, done some work." "Well, of course I didn't think for one minute that things would turn out like this," said the Frenchman in astonishment. "After all, I didn't do anything out of the ordinary. I went to the theater, I traveled to Pasternak's grave. Then I started getting invitations to go to artists' studios. They're all very nice. Surrealists, avant-gardists, conceptualists." Shiryaev belched. "Sorry," he said, "continue." "No, it's OK," said the Frenchman. "I went to the john today," said Shiryaev, bothered by the bitter belching, "you know, I got up and turned around to have a look, like, do you also turn around when you get up after a shit? Our ideological instructor always used to say, 'There isn't,' he said, 'a single person in the whole world, be he proletarian, capitalist, Chinaman or nigger, who,' he said, 'doesn't turn around to have a look; such,' he would say, 'is man's nature, which we are attempting to change.'" "There is an ancient fable about this very matter," modestly interjected the cultured Frenchman. "Remember you're a fable yourself," Shiryaev reminded him. "And what do I see, do you think? Everything is red. Everything's just swimming in blood. Well, I think, my guts have burst, I'll die now. But first, I think, I'd better check. Trust, but verify. Don't rest on yesterday's laurels. Two steps forward, one step back. Or the other way around, I've forgotten. In short"—Shiryaev livened up—"I take a cloth, dunk it and swirl it around." Shiryaev belched again. "I have a feeling that tomorrow my legs will be paralyzed," said Shiryaev. "What will you and I do then?" "But what about the cloth?" asked the Frenchman, apparently wanting to distract Shiryaev from his black thoughts. "Yes, so then, you know, I move the cloth around. That is, you know, I move it through the water and then lift it up carefully. And what do you think? I see that it's not blood at all, but you know, that thing, red, got a 'B' in it, damn and blast it! No, not cranberry, it's gone." "Beetroot!" guessed the Frenchman, delighted. "That's it!" shouted Shiryaev. "But how did you know?" He screwed up his eyes suspiciously. "You ate beetroot for breakfast yesterday." "Well, gosh, you don't miss a thing," said a disappointed Shiryaev bitterly. "So OK, I ate beetroot. So aren't I allowed to eat beetroot?" The newlyweds switched off the music. "They're fed up with it, the bastards," said Shiryaev. "Now the bed will start squeaking." Shiryaev paused for thought. "I have a grandson," he said. "And so, just imagine, once in the kindergarten he accidentally pushed one boy, and that kid just went and hit his teeth against the edge of the sandbox. I arrive in the evening to collect my grandson, as usual, and there's a state of emergency there. The helpers are running around, the teachers are screaming. 'Your grandson,' they say, 'has knocked a boy's front teeth out.'" Shiryaev got up, scratched his back and hobbled to the ventilation pane in the window. "Is there a draft?" He stretched up to the ventilation pane and spent a long time fiddling with it, but just couldn't shut it.

"It doesn't shut," said a distraught Shiryaev and gave up in despair. "They've fucking ruined everything!" He pressed his brow to the glass and looked at the two streetlights glowing dimly in the yard. "So they went on and on about electrification, electrification, electrification, but what came of it? The lights are on, but there's no order. I say to the manager, 'I won't let you get away with it. Your laundry service tears our sheets, and you're making a big fuss over nothing.' So then she turns to the people, shaking my long johns before their noses. 'Comrades,' she says, 'look at the disgusting object he's brought for us today!' I say to her, 'Stop indulging in demagogy. I'm going to call the police now!' And, like, they're all against me. The women with their painted faces, and the blokes in hats. 'Go on,' they say, 'take up your laundry and go!' 'No,' I say, 'you're messing with the wrong guy. I'm a Siberian wolf, me, an old hand.' Oh, no, the bed's started creaking." Shiryaev nodded toward the wall. "Indulging in perversities with each other. Now it's the in thing: they lie in opposite directions and lick each other like dogs. That's why so many cripples are being born." "It's in fact more likely due to vodka," suggested the Frenchman. "What, don't like Russian vodka, then?" said Shiryaev angrily. "How was I to know," sighed the Frenchman, "that with Russians you have to keep your ears pricked! I was going around like a crazy guy, from guest to guest, and not suspecting anything. All my stereotypes were being destroyed. I had expected a herd of sheep, that you'd all be simple as worms, and then suddenly all this!—they're cultured people, they know poems by heart." "Silence!" whispered Shiryaev. They both listened. "She's a real goer!" said Shiryaev disapprovingly. "All of Moscow will hear her screams.

Animals," he added. "So tomorrow, when my legs are paralyzed, I won't be able to crawl to the telephone. I'll die of hunger. Do you think they'll call an ambulance? They need my room. When I die, they'll live here, my room is bigger than theirs." "This is how they put it to me," said the Frenchman, highly agitated. "'Everything in your country is, of course, better, but to make up for it we are better people than anyone else.'" "Who said?" asked Shiryaev. "Soon I'll see my mother," said the Frenchman, even more worked up, "then I'll calm down and fly away, following in Napoleon's footsteps along the road to Minsk." "I'm not trying to get rid of you," explained Shiryaev. "Live here. To hell with France." "I have to go," babbled the Frenchman passionately. "So there you have it," said Shiryaev, upset, "one's gone to Mongolia, the other to Toulouse. But what does that Toulouse of yours have to offer? Do you have winters?" "We have winters," said the Frenchman, remembering. "Soft and gentle, like fruit jellies." "And she's taken away my little grandson," sobbed Shiryaev. "And do you know what he is like? When he grows up he'll sort everything out in his own way. He takes after me. He'll establish order, have no fear, this isn't Toulouse." "They say, 'Do you know any French songs?' 'Yes, I know some.' 'Well, come on, then, lad, sing us one.' Well, OK. I thought and I sang 'La Marseillaise.' They say. 'That's not it. Do you know something soulful? Why is it,' they say, 'that you're drinking and yet the person inside you doesn't come out? Why,' they say, 'doesn't a person come bursting through to the surface?'" "Who said that?" Shiryaev pricked up his ears. "You know, that same lot," said the Frenchman. "You'd better stop acting like one possessed," said Shiryaev. "You'll break all the plates!" Shiryaev heavily plonked himself down on his bed. The newlyweds ran in turn to the bathroom and again started to make the bed groan. "When I was doing time in the prison camp," said Shiryaev as he undressed, "a Frenchman was killed there, I've forgotten his surname, or perhaps a Swede, I don't remember, it was a long time ago." "You haven't mentioned this before," said the Frenchman. "What is there to tell?" said Shiryaev. "In those days many decent people were put in the camps. On the border with that very same Mongolia. And what made her go there? Perhaps she fell in love with someone?" "I understood that things were bad," complained the Frenchman, "and I sang what I knew, from childhood. '*Marjolaine, tu es si jolie...*'" "You're a real fool!" said Shiryaev, falling asleep. "I shall miss you."

The Maiden and Death

IT WAS the most fashionable murder of the season. Everyone went around under its influence for a long time, until the impression wore off. I remember it with affection. And all because of the blonde. I don't clean my boots often, but this time I made an exception. My wife asked gloomily, as if for a joke, "Going to a rendezvous, are we?" With a laugh I answered, "Well, we'll see about that, we'll see about that."

"But you hardly knew her."

"So?"

She looked at me distrustfully, disapprovingly.

"Buy some mayonnaise on the way back."

I was happy to oblige.

"With pleasure!"

Excited, full of anticipation, I flew out of the house.

Fall!

The leaves of the chestnut trees and maples rustled beneath the wheels of my white automobile. We'll see about that, we'll see about that. Don't even think about missing it, darling! I felt that I

was the creator of a great mystery play. The high September sky—
that's the cupola of my theater! I rubbed and rubbed my hands in
pleasure. Dreams were coming true.

The original idea flashed through my mind a year ago, in just
such a sunny fall, in the inner courtyard of the Sklifosovsky Accident and Emergency Hospital, by the doors of their grubby morgue.
I was waiting for them to bring out the body of one old woman. Suddenly the doors opened, and they brought them out: men, women
and children—fucking loads of them! Wreathes, a flurry of activity,
hearses. Almost everything here is unexpected: poisonings, people
run over, fluke accidents, a bloodbath, apotheosis, wails, a hymn to
accidents, sorrow, brief glances, and not forgetting the ugly mugs of
the drivers. And an unusually large number of young people, quite
different from the cemeteries. I was so dazzled by all this that I forgot about the old woman as I stood there, rocked by the powerful
whirlwind of human emotions.

And I started to pay calls on this yard, in the morning, before
the hour when all the bodies would be released, I found myself
drawn there more and more—I stood with my head uncovered,
the September, October, November wind ruffled the remains of
my once full and fluffy head of hair; snow started to fall, I raised
my collar, flowers grew fewer in number, the meteorological
backdrops changed, people fell from icy steps, brides in black
kissed male corpses long and hard on their lips, sometimes a forbidden stench arose, there was much lively, genuine formalism
too—stealthily, not letting anyone in on my secret, I always rushed
here as if to rehearsals, with increasing frequency, fearing expo-
sure, and I was gorging myself.

A stranger to everyone here, I soon felt completely at home
and familiarized myself with everything to such an extent that I
could read on the faces of the deceased all the details of their het-

erogeneous torments—and this reading turned into a passion. I understood that I was entering a forbidden zone, the zone of some inhuman whirlwinds of instability, that I was being transformed, that this was life-threatening, but I didn't have the willpower to resist my passion.

The consequences weren't long in coming. The world split in two, and the leaves fell. Words broke into separate little letters, the letters turned into senseless signs set out in military columns, they were marching somewhere, marching somewhere, along a desolate boulevard, and then disappeared around the corner. My wife shouted at me, bitterly aggrieved: Why have we stopped going to the movies? What answer could I give? I bought tickets. The movie was heavy-going, over-fussy, about the war. In the middle of the movie, to my surprise, I burst out laughing. Someone behind me struck me in the back with his fist. We quickly left the stuffy auditorium. We stopped in front of the poster in dismay.

"What's the matter with you?"

I shrugged my shoulders.

"I've been working too hard."

The theater was an even bigger disaster. During a performance of some trashy, infantile production of Dostoevsky I simply threw up everywhere. It was a very small theater, a studio theater, the actors were inexperienced. We were sitting in the second row. It was a literal showstopper. The stupid head of the director poked out from the wings. My puke was beetroot-colored, with white macaroni. I mumbled something, stooped and apologized.

My wife decided, of course, that I was having an affair. I wasn't sleeping with her. And like they all say in such circumstances:

"Is there someone else?"

I made a strange reply, answering her question with a question:

"Do you think that love conquers death?"

Without saying a word, she burst into tears. She'd decided, apparently, that I was making fun of her. And it's true: what I said was stupid. Enough! I didn't go for a whole week. I held out, held out, and then started up again, like a good little boy. It was the only place I wanted to go. What did those beautiful words of Stalin have to do with all this? I belonged to the generation which even now cannot be indifferent to the Georgian. But the more often I visited the yard, the more I understood that we were all wrong. And it isn't about Stalin, but about one's direction in life. What did I get out of that yard? Only an idiot could think that I carried away graveyard thoughts, some un-Soviet melancholy. It was not depression that had possessed me, but passion. I was grasping the all-embracing, organizational gift of death; I had learned, with my collar raised, to value the genre's high purity. I had learned to appreciate there, in the courtyard, that inimitable example of Stalin's sense of humor. But to hell with the details, although they led me to the idea. The idea started to stir inside me, but even its outlines were vague as yet.

All I understood was that there were three stages. The first is crap, the imaginary health of the spirit (in other words, intoxication, women and other types of upsurge); the second, then, is a most marvelous illness, and I am dangerously ill; but as for the third . . . to reach the third stage . . . and it wasn't Hegel directing me here, but that same old courtyard: how to turn blind chance into a triumph of will and handiwork? How?

But she thought, wearing herself out, that I was not screwing her because I was being unfaithful to her, but I wasn't being unfaithful to her, I was being faithful to the changes within me, perhaps I was even being transfigured. But she, stupid woman, was at the breaking point.

Clarity arrived later, in the spring, when one whirlwind became entwined with another—and then the stormy season really started.

In the spring Snakeeater had decided to get married. That's his nickname, Snakeeater—he's basically my only friend. And he's got such a nickname not because he's a slippery little shit, but simply because, when we were still students, a hundred years ago, for some reason he was always looking for words with lots of *e*'s and *a*'s close together. The one he said he liked best was Snake-eater. So from that time on he was Snakeeater. It's even quite a charming name—Snakeeater; I was teased in school, for example, they called me a monkey (like they called Pushkin) and teased me, and I used to get very upset—it was on account of the shape of my skull—and I suffered terribly, but with time this somehow resolved itself. Anyhow, I always enjoyed success with women. Always!

And so, Snakeeater invited us to his wedding on the nineteenth of April.

After the ceremony a modest celebration, in a small, narrow room at his place, but the food was nice and there was lots of wine. Among the guests—that very same brunette with a fat bottom and a delicate neck, whom today we are seeing off on her final journey. We were seated next to each other. She fizzed and frothed all the time, she kept slipping nasty comments into her conversation—black emanations were coming from her. I didn't realize what the reason for this was to begin with. She'd been quite different on our only previous meeting—I remembered that she'd drunk a lot without getting very drunk, I remembered that she'd been a real giggler, tousled, red-lipped, with her glass of white wine, on Snakeeater's lap—on that one and only evening, so much the student then, with her girlfriend sitting next to her on this very same sofa,—and suddenly memories came to the surface, like entrails spilled from a ripped-open stomach. The forgotten blond friend, erased from my life, suddenly made her presence strongly felt. How could I have forgotten her? How could I have taken pity on her that evening? Everything came back to me immediately, and I felt like seeing her, felt like plucking and picking her out of the pit of my lapsed memory.

Back then Snakeeater and the brunette had locked themselves in the bathroom and had bathed there for a long time, until morning. The blonde and I had remained on the couch. We heard their shrieks of delight. We talked about literature. We didn't notice that we'd started kissing. She leaned back and said: You've got really nice *eau de cologne*. English, I answered. And suddenly she informed me, laughing, that she's afraid. Whereas I was all in a lather. And her hair was so, so fair! I even rubbed my hands in delight. It's a habit of mine. Big deal, everyone's afraid! I got mad and lost all potency. I skillfully hid my weakness from her, as if I had in fact taken pity on her. And so I remained in her eyes the most noble of men, although the only uncertain thing was: was she grateful or not? You never can tell with women.

"So," I say, "where's blondie, then?"

"Which blondie?"

"Well, that one," I say, "your friend. You remember, she was here with you, that evening?"

Silence.

I say:

"Give me her telephone number."

Silence.

"Listen," I say, "I really need it: give me her number. I need to get in touch with her. Come on!"

She looks at me with distaste.

"For God's sake," she says, "just fuck off."

"Watch out," I say with a heavy look, "you'll regret it!"

"I'm really scared now."

"OK, your funeral."

She didn't give me the number.

By the end of the wedding celebration she was drunk as a skunk. Snakeeater led her off into the bathroom. I don't know what they got up to there—for old times' sake. Snakeeater's wife was on edge. I was silent and sullen.

We left in the early hours. My wife and I, this brunette and also one young theater-type with an ignoble face. My wife said, even as we were bidding farewell to her:

"You should walk her home. She can hardly stand."

"Nothing will happen to her," said the theater-type with conviction.

The brunette started walking in the direction of the avenue. I never saw her again. The theater-type had put the evil eye on her.

So many congratulations, Snakeeater, dear friend. She dreamed of marrying you, but you were enticed by a wife cut from coarse but heavy cloth.

Snakeeater didn't answer. He was simply overwhelmed with sorrow. Looking at him made me feel terrible and terribly happy.

The funeral took place in Veshnyaki. The memorial service was young in spirit, contemporary. The coffin with her body was placed in the middle. The other coffins, with the bodies of old women, were crammed in the corners. A young priest, the picture of health, talked after the liturgy about the link of science with religion. He talked about how it was helpful to believe in God, particularly in such moments as these. I could not help but agree with him. The only thing that irritated me was that he wasn't paying any attention at all to the old women, hardly waved the censer in their direction, no equality, not at all Christian. All sorts of people present there, leaving thoughts for their dead relatives to one side, were discussing the murder. They were all whispering: the husband did it, hacked her to death. This greatly excited everyone. I climbed out of the white car. I just knew it! So many maidenly faces! The sweetest of sweet girls, with independent views and free movements, and small but very attractive breasts. In winter they wear sweaters and nothing else underneath, and all sorts of jeans under which you'll find nothing but the briefest of briefs, which they change every day; and they wash their hair almost every day, and they smell sweetly of *eau de toilette,* they hate tights and in the coldest of weather get by in thin woolen socks; they have *no problem* with obscene language or Nabokov, a flexible timetable is what they value most in a job, they don't like dancing very much, but instead they're really rather keen on food, and they also love to say, pointing at a chap: "I've screwed him." And so this, then, is the young generation, an independent bunch, but here they all stand huddled in a group, summoned by me, charmingly tearful, with flowers, in black, one even has a veil for the occasion, they crowd around—the sweet! the sweet!—pale as pale can be, without makeup, terrified, tear-stained—and each one, each one has under her blouse warm breasts with hazel nipples, and lower, lower,—tender, moist, hairy little mice! One grayish, one ginger and somewhere around there should be mine too, the blond one.

People were gossiping about the details. I pricked up my ears. She'd been ambushed and killed near her dacha, in the evening, on her way to the shop. She'd been dragged into the bushes and savagely butchered with a knife—several blows to the neck, the back, the stomach. The country cottages are deserted in September, the children are all back in school. Her husband—and by that time she'd already got married to spite Snakeeater—waited and waited, she wasn't returning, so he went out and saw a shoe on the path. He saw something white in the bushes, rushed toward it: it was her. Covered in blood, he dragged her home. There was still some life gurgling inside her—she had nine lives like a cat. It gurgled a bit more, and stopped. Her carotid artery had been severed. He then grabbed an axe and—covered in blood—rushed off to the station. That's where he was picked up by the police, with an axe. And they put him in jail. And accused him of the murder. And who is her husband? Well, like, he's some sort of, well, not an architect exactly, but something else, he's a wacko and a psychopath, a childhood friend. That's cleared that up, then.

In the church I hid behind a column, poked my head out—I couldn't see well, but I noticed that they'd stuck a piece of paper on her forehead, as is the custom. I was, however, terrified of approaching her. I thought that she would wink at me, like the Countess in *The Queen of Spades*. Overcoming my fear, I went up to her. Her face was severely disfigured—even I was taken aback. You could see that her eye had been punctured, her temple was smashed, her face was dark blue with cuts and bruises. She'd put up a fight, the bitch! I quickly went outside, had a cigarette.

"Why do you look so shifty, as if you've been caught with your hand in the cookie jar?" said Snakeeater, coming up to me.

And I didn't even know that I looked like that. I would have to be more careful. And suddenly I wanted my blonde so badly. I'd even tried sleeping with my wife as if she were the blonde, but it wasn't right, wasn't right, it wasn't the same thing at all. I wanted the blonde—it was the same thing as sleeping with one's own memory. That's neat! I muttered something indecipherable to Snakeeater, "What made you say that about the cookies?" That is, I felt the need to demonstrate my innocence.

That's when he said that we were all being filmed by a hidden camera, that the investigation hadn't revealed anything, that her husband was a bastard of course, but not the one responsible, that he'd gone to the police morgue on the outskirts in the Moscow suburbs, had seen her undressed—it was monstrous! Then we helped carry the coffin to the hearse and he pointed out her mother to me, Kseniya Petrovna, an old woman, completely distraught.

"So why are they cremating her?" I asked.

"Kseniya Petrovna will take her ashes to Gomel and bury them there. You see, she's from Gomel."

And I hadn't even known. But where's her father? Her father didn't come. He's an alcoholic. Searches have been carried out already. Even the theater-type had his place searched. It turned out that he was a monarchist. What sort of secret could the young girl have had? And then in the heat of the moment it all came out: she'd been involved with some sort of sect, and there'd even been illegal money exchanges, and she was a druggie, and a whore, and a dissident.

"Oh, Lord," I said. Someone had made threatening phone calls to her. No one knows who. Recently she'd been living in fear of her life. I was shocked. I hadn't made any threatening phone calls to her. We followed the catafalque to the crematorium. Kseniya Petrovna's hope will come to nothing: she won't bury her daughter in Gomel. The husband will be released due to lack of evidence, he'll steal the ashes and will wear them in an amulet around his neck. So who was it, then, making threats to her on the telephone? The investigation is trying to establish that at this very moment. The idiots! Let them establish it.

"I don't understand," said Snakeeater, "why they tortured her so."

"Well, you know"—I gave a short laugh—"there are maniacs about."

"No," he said. "This wasn't a sex maniac. A pervert would have raped her."

"There are lots of different sickos," I parried gently.

"The evidence suggests that he hit her with something heavy in the pit of her stomach. His boot, probably. The poor thing shat herself."

"The favorite trick of South American police forces in the war against free thinkers. A young girl is transformed instantaneously from a proud beauty into a terrified pisshead."

I lowered my eyes. She thought, shitting herself, that I'd come for her friend's phone number. I just grinned. The white car cooled down in the roadside woods.

"Perhaps that's the reason why she wasn't raped, cuz she'd shat herself?" was the groundless hypothesis I put forward after a pause for thought.

Snakeeater said nothing. Then suddenly he announces that last night he'd summoned her spirit. That is, presumably, spiritualism. And she came to him, her ghost came into his kitchen. He said that he'd lost two kilos in weight overnight, that spirits feed off the energy of the living. This blew me away. I had suspected that he had mystical inclinations, but I hadn't known that he was a medium.

"Why did you raise her?" I said in alarm.

"To find out who murdered her."

I was terribly frightened, but I tried not to give anything away. There was a long silence.

"So what of it?" I asked at last. "Did you find out?" And I looked at him out of the corner of my eye.

"It was her, all right," Snakeeater said in a wooden voice. "I recognized her intonations immediately. She was moaning and groaning. She was still very embarrassed and confused. I didn't expect anything like this. She wailed: 'Oh, silly cow, I allowed myself to be slaughtered!' I waited for a long time for her to stop groaning. Then I asked her directly: 'Who murdered you?' She said: 'A bloke.' I asked: 'Did you know him?' She said: 'Yes.' "

The car swerved sharply to one side: my head was spinning dangerously out of control. Snakeeater continued:

"Then I asked: 'But do I know him?' She answered: 'Yes.' Then

I asked: 'Who is he?' To this she replied: 'Not saying . . .' You see, she explained that this was very dangerous for me, that, if she reveals the secret, then I could be killed too. Then she said that she'd always loved me."

When we were already drawing close to the crematorium, outside the city, I said:

"Do you remember, that night . . . she had a girlfriend?"

Snakeeater couldn't remember. He remembered that there'd been someone there, some girlfriend or other, but he couldn't remember who.

"Why?" he asked.

"Oh, nothing," I said. "I wouldn't mind seeing her again."

"I feel sorry for her," concluded Snakeeater.

"I should say so!" I agreed.

I thought that, when I die and my spirit gets called up for a chat, I won't go. And then I thought: it's like at a disco. Some get invited to dance, and they refuse, whereas others sit and mope. And spirits, most likely, pine when they are wallflowers. So perhaps I'll go after all.

It was solemn in the crematorium, and not as cramped as in the church. I took up my observation point next to the mistress of the ceremony, who was wearing a dark blue suit. I could see the whole crowd of pretty young girls. After all, she'd been very sociable, liked company. I saw Kseniya Petrovna with her bowed head right at the coffin's side. And her—with her sticker—from afar. Everyone was sobbing and no one said a word. I saw the musicians walking on tiptoe to the balustrade. They too felt there was something special here. Then they began to play, with real feeling. The performance was going beautifully. There were many blondes—I realized to my horror that I couldn't remember her face. I wanted her, but couldn't remember the face. I wanted the victim of my nobility. The funeral director in a voice cracking with emotion invited us to say our last farewells. The thought came into my mind that if one gathered all these mini, mousy holes, these mousy, different-colored pussies into one and molded them up into a ball you could end up with a fat rat or a fat cat! You are little mice, I'm a cat! I'm a cat, you are mice ... Mini-mice with mousy holes ... Everyone started saying their goodbyes. Some kissed her on the forehead, others simply stood for a bit and then walked on. I approached too, stood for a while, looked. Well, farewell! Au revoir! The final sobs of the young girls rang out, these were echoed by the young men there, the plainclothes police, musicians, and even the funeral director with her leonine face. The whole world wept as it came together at my show. The fear soon evaporated. The funeral director hammered a symbolic nail and announced the death of a citizen of the USSR. With a rumble the coffin shot away into the crematorium's inferno. The small curtains drew shut. Brothers and sisters! No, not blind chance, but the human mind brought us all here today, to this vale of incomparable sadness. Is this not proof of the limitless possibilities of our reason, which has become lord of the most implacable and destructive force of all?

I bowed to them all, right down to the ground. Flowers and applause flew at me. I pick them up mechanically, wave and with the flowers stuck under my arm, I applaud frenziedly in reply. But people are already complaining in the doorway: your time is up, a new round has begun. Till next time, my friends!

With an armful of roses I walk out into the great outdoors, which is cluttered with the catafalques of September.

A blond shadow timidly detaches herself from the bus.

"Hello," she says, with a slight lisp, in sweet agitation. "It's me. Congratulations on your premiere."

"How beautiful you are now!" I can't help saying. She laughs, pleased.

"So you see"—I narrow my eyes—"I did everything correctly." And I give her the flowers, and I lead her by the hand to the white car. "Ah, well, to resurrection!"

We kiss in full view of everyone. Couldn't care less. Let's leave the city! We shall walk through the fall forest, we shall emerge on the bank of the Moscow River, we'll throw off our clothes and, naked, stuff the rest, we shall splash in the chilly water, we shall swim out far, we'll make a bonfire, we shall drink vodka . . . "And at long last I shall become yours." "Yes," I say. "But why did you mutilate her so?" "I don't know," I say, "I felt like it." She nods her head understandingly. "But what about the yard?" she says, smelling my cheek. "English?" "Yeah, that's right . . . And as far as the yard goes—it's over. Fuck the yard. Those times are past." "But will you kill again?" "How do I know?" I laugh. "Only time will tell."

We speed along the ring road. The forests are alive with noises. And everything is good. Stalin is right. Gorky is right. All of us are right. Man—that has a proud ring. Love conquers death.

Anna's Body, or the End of the Russian Avant-garde

Anna! Anna! Anna!—her heart leaps up.

Anna Ioanna! Anna Ioanna!—crashing in her ears.

An-na-Ioan-n-na . . . —announces her stomach, like a distant steam engine, and instead of steam sends a shot of mucus up her nose.

Anna was awakened by the shot. Like a large fish, like a whale beached on the shore of a crazed ocean, Anna lay in the middle of her bed in the middle of the night. Pensively she sucked her fat, cracked lips and reached for a cigarette. Something fell with a plop to the floor from the bedside dressing table. Probably a book. Probably Borges. Anna continued to rummage in the darkness. An ashtray fell but didn't break. But its entire contents were probably strewn all over the floor now. Anna breathed noisily and rummaged.

Anna! Anna! Anna!—her heart was jumping.

Anna raised herself on her elbow and set about feeling for something else, and she found it. A yellowish night-light came on.

Amid the creams, medicines, saucers, evening papers with unfinished crosswords she found a rumpled packet of cigarettes. With heavily trembling, damp hands Anna lit a cigarette and sat up in her bed.

Anna's body had got out of hand for some reason recently. Anna's body would by turns get fat, get thin, get fat, get thin, get fat, get thin, get thin, get fat. In addition, something was dripping from her ears. Drip-drip. Her earlobes were damp. The dripping of melted snow in the spring thaw, and buds. And the grocery store. Anna took great pleasure in the fact that she was able to communicate with waiters. "So what, then, just for the fun of it, is your name?" And they always answered honestly: Volodya, or Tolya, or Slava. Drip-drip, dripping from her ears, and her ears were itching. In despair Anna stuck her fingers in her ears. Sometimes she was seized by a strong desire to rip them off. This particular night Anna's body was already fat and greasy enough, it still hadn't reached its apogees, but it was already nicely glossy, like salmon, and Anna, looking down, could contemplate the ovals of her spreading cheeks, the burning buttocks of her face, inflamed by an allergy, in between which a cigarette smoked. In the corner of the room the Christmas tree with its rufous needleless branches still held, here, there and everywhere, on the very ends of its bare, ruined branches, Christmas toys and decorations. Smashed multicolored baubles glittered on the floor. February was coming to an end. In October they'd celebrated her fortieth birthday. Drip-drip, dripping from her ears. Lenochka, a student, pale-faced, had flirted with older men.

Anna's right eye had ceased to obey her. Close the left eye, and instead of the world you see French landscapes, a mauve Rouen, a frog's pond, pointillism. Close the right eye—Russian realism. The right eye had at most fifteen percent vision. The left eye saw everything, our entire reality.

Sometimes Anna felt that she was Anna Karenina, sometimes

Anna Akhmatova, sometimes simply Chekhov's burdensome Anna-round-the-neck. Her acquaintanceships changed in accordance with this, so she would either be falling in love, emigrating to Paris, or burning the snow with a tear, until she fell in love for the last time. Some Jews or other would visit her, would bring sometimes hundreds and sometimes thousands of faded rubles, her husband, who was abroad, would compose anti-patriotic brochures, would keep appealing to her to join him there, but what was the point? Sometimes the local cop would drop by, cast a sidelong look at the empty bottles. He'd stand there for a while and then leave.

Anna reached for a bottle of cognac, poured herself some, spilling a few drops, and looked at the fir tree. "I'll get rid of it by March, before Women's Day," thought Anna and drank her cognac.

That made her warmer. Anna took a deep puff on her cigarette and plonked herself back on her pillow. Then she drank another glass, her face grew redder and more life returned to her legs. Anna's right leg bent at the knee and slipped far out to the right, so that all her five toes with their long toenails, which hadn't been cut for ages, poked out from beneath the sheet. Anna's left leg, also bent at the knee, slipped away to the left and came up against something living.

She shook throughout her whole body, did Anna, took fright, froze in horror.

A man was lying to her left. He lay with his back to Anna, facing the window. Anna recognized him from the back of his head and almost shouted out. It was the man she loved, her most dearly beloved, the most loved of all, who had left her two months ago, after they had returned from a winter vacation in a resort in the Caucasus. He took her home from the airport, and, tanned and gray-eyed, he said that he'd phone the next morning and would drop by, kissed her forehead with the easy casualness that he alone possessed, and didn't phone, and didn't drop by, never, never, never ever.

He skied on the downhill slopes—she slept.

He, full of *joie de vivre*, puny, splashed in the swimming pool— she slept.

He came from the sauna, rubicund, slightly embarrassed— she slept. He said to her as he woke her fat body from sleep, "Moscow girls wear nothing in the sauna; but the Leningrad girls—to a woman—wear bathing costumes."

She answered, still half asleep, "This is all so boring!"

In the evenings he would get drunk with the Leningrad girls, the black marketeers and the Circassian men, and then she too would also get up and get drunk with them.

Every day when the non-Russian sun was at its greatest height, she would wake up with the intention of getting a medical certificate from the local woman doctor which would allow her to swim in the swimming pool. At long last, on the eve of their departure, Anna stood before the fastidious, ugly little face. Anna stood, like a clash of two worlds, like a fight to the death between Picasso and Botticelli, generously unleashed her Slavic breasts on the doctor and, stunned by this beauty, the infidel grudgingly wrote out the necessary piece of paper.

How did you get in here, my little boy, without keys and clothes? How did you penetrate my warm, dark burrow?

Her beloved man—the most intelligent and most beautiful in the world and very, very talented, and sometimes just from looking at him she would be seized by erotic convulsions, which had never happened to her previously—was sleeping, curled up in a ball like a dormouse, in his dear khaki-colored shirt and with no underpants on. Anna reached out to him with a trembling hand, but suddenly withdrew it. She sat upright, took her brush off the table and started to brush her light hair quickly. Then she looked in the mirror, and, no longing rushing now, started to do her eyes, applying green eye shadow.

And now, and now—but first she'd have another drink, agitated as she was. Anna had a drink and smiled. She knew what she would do. She wasn't going to wake him. Let him sleep, let him sleep until morning! He's probably tired, let him sleep, and I shall caress you nice and slowly all night long. Sleep, I shall come to you in your dream, and I shall eat you up, my little boy! Sleep, and I shall, . . . yum-yum!

Anna burst out laughing, holding her hand over her mouth. Anna wrapped herself up in euphemisms, as in secondhand furs.

Anna! Anna! Anna! trumpeted her heart.

"I knew that you would come!" whispered Anna. "I knew! I knew! I knew!"

"How wrong you are, my joy!" laughed Anna. "So, why on earth do you waste your talents on rough trade? Hey, why do you need tarts when *I'm* here? There you go, writing and writing and writing, but never what's needed! You can't show such filth to a child or to decent people. You write such disgusting things"—she wagged her finger at him threateningly—"so write about us instead, about how you came back to me, about our love, about the snow, which is falling in silent snowflakes on the tired town, about the branch of lilac in the garden, write about that which is in each of us, in even the most completely lost soul . . . Write about how I longed for you, how I suffered without your embraces and your eyes, and how my breast is burning from the loss. Sleep, and I shall turn my little boy into you know who—well, I won't say!" Anna laughed again. "You'd be better off writing about how under the cover of your cold iron, scarlet blood babbles—go, take pity on the cripples and resurrect the dead—go and resurrect the dead, go—and resurrect!"

"And so you're sleeping," prattled Anna, stroking the sleepy male belly, "and you don't have the faintest idea that you are sailing above the world, that you are growing here with me like the Eiffel Tower or like the leaning Tower of Pisa, or some other textbook monument... And God... after all He's in each one of us, in every apartment building and in every apartment, and in this Christmas tree, and in this cognac, and even my Mummy, who spent her whole life teaching materialism, and even in materialism!"

Anna tightened the small loose knots of the bandages on her wrists with her teeth.

"Little white cuffs," she sobbed. "Yes, I'm a fool. I was a fool... forgive me! But now you are mine once more, you came, you are all mine!"

Anna! Anna! Anna!—said the loving heart as it was tearing into pieces.

Anna put out her light, and then put out the light, then made herself more comfortable, ran her dry tongue over her lips and, as in an old fairy tale, gobbled up the man she loved. So that's how, on this night, the history of the Russian avant-garde came to an end.

THE PARAKEET

WITH REFERENCE to your inquiry, most esteemed Spiridon Ermolaevich, to wit, requesting information about the fate determined for your son, Ermolai Spiridonovich Spirkin, who compelled a dead bird to fly in defiance of natural law, my reply will not be forthcoming immediately. But why? Why, my dear sir, because I must confess: I am confused. My breast was bursting with emotions as I read your petition, written in the blood of fatherly feeling. You have deeply vexed me, Spiridon Ermolaevich, deeply agitated me! You have cast such a cloud of melancholy over me that no words can describe it, only the howl of a beast. However, I bear no grudge toward you. My bosom echoed in response to your fatherly urge to protect that son of yours, Ermolai Spiridonovich, from the full force of the law, as you hint in obscure terms that your son, Ermolai Spiridonovich, so you assert, had from his early years a deep love for those of God's creatures capable of flight. I am willing to grant that your hint is correct. Nay, I shall even go further. Every child has a weakness for birdies, whether this is expressed in catching them in the coppices, the forests, and also in the open fields with springes, or in buying them for copper coins at the bird market, in order to set the birdie in a cage, especially if it is a songbird. The law sees nothing wrong in such activities and indeed displays indulgence toward children in their innocent childhood amusements. This is of course the case, but, joking aside, world culture, my right honorable Spiridon Ermolaevich, as I most humbly understand it, thinks predominantly in symbols, the interpretation of which is the task of learned men. From ancient times, for example, it has been fashionable to read the auguries in the guts of birds that had been flying by. On the other hand, if any live bird were to fly into your room, albeit the humblest goldfinch, would you welcome such an event, Spiridon Ermolaevich? No, you would not welcome such an event! And why? I shall tell you why: because you will see in this a terrifying symbol. I could give you many more similar illustrations of man's ignorance, except that I'm hastening to reach my conclusion, which bears a certain relation to your son, Ermolai Spiridonovich: viz., a bird is a creature that disturbs the soul, a bird is an enigmatic creature, not subject to our whims, and it therefore follows that it is not to be trifled with. And meanwhile what is your kid up to? He is kidding around! Ermolai Spiridonovich deigns to kid around with a dead parakeet—a particularly suspect type of bird to boot! A parakeet is already a symbol in its own right, and the Devil himself would be stumped to come up with an adequate interpretation of its meaning, insomuch as all world culture from its very inception has done nothing but gossip about the parakeet as its favorite idol. What's more, it's a foreign bird. Yet you, Spiridon Ermolaevich, with a lightness of touch which would be far better employed elsewhere, dash off in your petition that your little boy's prank bore an entirely innocent nature. Really, it's no big deal! My son, you say, Ermolai Spiridonovich, took a parakeet whose name was Semyon and who had gone to his last resting place, nimbly climbed up onto the roof of your very own home, which is to be found on Swan Street, and began throwing it upward into the air, like Ivan the Fool from the fairy tales, in the hope that in its native element the dead creature would get its second wind, flutter and chirp, that is, in a certain manner of speaking even come back to life. If one judges by your overhasty words, Ermolai Spiridonovich's deed owed everything to a lack of understanding and nothing to any criminal intent, owed everything to an overactive imagination, a nervous disposition and shaking spasms throughout his body, and nothing whatsoever to a coherent plan of intrigue. At the same time you are, it goes without saying, outraged and disgusted by his actions and offer to give your own sonny, Ermolai Spiridonovich, a damn good lashing, with no leniency whatsoever. No two ways about it: fatherly feelings! I repeat again: we have no quarrel with you, Spiridon Ermolaevich. You are a respected man and remain so for the time being. But be so good as to try to understand us as well, who have served the fatherland for many years also, put yourself in my boots, for example. For what if such experiments become more common, what will happen then? And what if that foreign crap had flown? According to the statement made by your mad son, Ermolai Spiridonovich, it did in fact flap its nasty wings a few times, that is, made some sort of attempt at resurrection! So what if suddenly, against our expectations, it had gone and completely resurrected itself? What words could we have found to explain such an awkward and unusual situation to our well-intentioned and trusting fellow countrymen? I shudder to think how it all might have ended.

HOW WOULD WE HAVE LOOKED THEN?

Ah, yes! No question about it! Your son turned out, Spiridon Ermolaevich, to be delicately built, one could even say frail. We marveled. Who does he take after? "Well sir, well then, young man," I inquired of Ermolai Spiridonovich, having examined him carefully, "answer me this question: why did you dig up the bird from its place of burial or, to put it another way, from the midden? Why the hell, I'd like to know, did you exhume it?" He answered evasively, but promptly and with unquestionable politeness, sawing the air with his little white hand during his answers, using his hand, that is, to make it all easier to understand. On observing such manners, I was immediately put on my guard. I see that not only his build but his manners are unusual too, almost perfect manners. There isn't a bit of Yid in him by any chance, Spiridon Ermolaevich? He kept on trying to win us over, helping himself, if you please, with his little hand—a real sight for sore eyes, one might say! But the trick didn't work—we're not in the circus now! And I'm sitting there thinking to myself: this baby's tarred with a different brush! What sort of story was emerging from his words? What picture was taking form? "Tell me about it," I say, "from the very beginning, and stop waving your pasty white hand in front of my nose, I can't stand it!" He was profuse in his apologies, as though I were in need of his apologies, as if he were doing me some huge favor by apologizing! But I say nothing about this. However, in the meantime, I ask him: "So you, Ermolai Spiridonovich, wanted to resurrect this bird. But this bird, according to reliable information received from competent sources, had already been pretty much devoured by earthworms, didn't you notice? White worms, looked just like your fingers? It was all covered in worms, and ants were participating in the feast in equal measure. So how could such a bird hope to be resurrected? Didn't you feel just a teeny-weeny bit squeamish about taking it into those nicely kept hands of yours!?" He answers, head bowed: "But what about the Phoenix?" I see, my dear sir, Spiridon Ermolaevich, your little son is very bright, Ermolai Spiridonovich, bright be-

yond his years. Well, I never, the Phoenix! "Where," we ask, "did
you obtain such information about some sort of Phoenix, what
sort of bird," I say, "is that?" "Well," he says, "it was a red-feathered eagle which flew from Arabia to ancient Egypt; there, when it
had reached the ripe old age of five hundred years, it would burn
itself alive, and then it would be reborn from its ashes young and
healthy, so that worms needn't necessarily be an obstacle here."
He's a smooth operator, I can see that. "I see. So what," I ask, "do
you see as the point of this fable about the red-feathered eagle?
How," I ask a supplementary question, "did you manage to come
to the pass of believing wop fables?" Once again his answer is eva-
sive: "A fable," he says, "is supposed to be amazing." "Don't you
wriggle," I say, "don't conceal anything from us, otherwise you'll
end up starring in your own fable! Give us, hooligan, the truth."
"But I am," he shouted angrily, "telling you the gospel truth!" and
once more he flapped his hand. "OK, have it your way: speak, and
we'll just sit here and listen to what you have to say. But don't get
angry and don't shout. Who," I say, "do you think you are shouting
at? At whom, so to say, are you raising your voice?! I'm old enough
to be your father, Ermolai, and yet you've taken it into your head to
yell at me!" He is silent. He turns red. "Am I old enough," I ask
him, "to be your father, or am I not?" "Of course you are. And I address you as I would my very own father." Well, I never, I think to
myself, he's calling me father now, he's thrusting forward and saying yes yes yes like a randy tart. There's more to this than meets
the eye. So I investigate further. "So this parakeet of yours, this
turquoise-hued Semyon—he too, no doubt, was also some sort of
symbol, yes?" Everything in world culture, Spiridon Ermolaevich,
is a symbol, nothing but symbols, wherever you care to look,
parakeets in particular. But he, your son, Ermolai Spiridonovich,
in answering explains it all as a consequence of the weeping of
children. He tells us a story we know well: how this parakeet

called Semyon kicked the bucket in the family of the Physician to
the Boyars Agafon Elistratovich, your neighbor on Swan Street,
who had purchased the foreign bird to amuse his two young
babes—five-year-old Tatyana Agafonovna, and the three-year-old,
snot-nosed toddler Ezra Agafonovich. He bought it, as is proper,
at the bird market, from the Dutch merchant Van Zaam, or as we
call him, Timofei Ignatievich. This merchant, Timofei Ignatievich,
is in no way remarkable, he is mild-mannered, apart from the scar
on his Dutch nose, which he received after arriving in our neck of
the woods and realm as a result of a minor domestic dispute with
his wife. I am letting you in on these details so that you may know,
Spiridon Ermolaevich, that I earn my daily bread: you can't re-
create the full picture without the details, especially when there's
some monkey business afoot. Accordingly, your neighbor, Agafon
Elistratovich, bought this foreign parakeet of small build, probably because he was too stingy to buy a bigger bird, and christened
it Semyon. They confined the bird, as is right and proper, in a
cage. They fed it, according to Tatyana Agafonovna's statement,
on millet. But this parakeet, sadly notorious for its, thank God,
unsuccessful resurrection, utterly refused to eat millet or indeed
any other bird food, exhibited foreign ways and, the efforts of the
children notwithstanding, started to turn up its toes as a result of
declaring a voluntary hunger strike. On the third day Semyon
popped its clogs to the mixed chorus of tears from Tatyana Agafonovna and Ezra Agafonovich, the three-year-old, snot-nosed
brat, who, the bastard, still hasn't started talking yet, or pretends
not to be able to. The death agony lasted for three and a half hours,
sometime after lunch, and ended with the bird's dying a natural
death.

These are the terms in which your son, Ermolai Spiridonovich,
describes the story, after which he himself becomes its main hero.
But not straightaway. As is right and proper, after the bird died the

ceremony of burying it in the midden was held, so as to prevent the spread of disease. A small crowd of some twenty-six ugly mugs gathered at the burial, drawn there by the howls of the physician's youthful brats. As Ermolai Spiridonovich (who participated in the funeral procession as an observer) has told us himself, the night before the procession he had heard all sorts of voices in his head, despite the fact that Physician to the Boyars Agafon Elistratovich had promised his children to buy them something even more amusing to replace the dead parakeet, something like a billy goat. Next morning Ermolai Spiridonovich left the house with the firm intention of freeing the bird from its chilly grave *at exactly the time* when it started drizzling, making the streets dirtier, and Mademoiselle Shelgunova *distinctly* saw from the window of her parents' home, in a break between her lessons on the harp, how your son, Ermolai Spiridonovich, dug the parakeet out of the midden with his nails, looking for all the world like a mangy cat, which, you know, feels like treating itself to some tasty carrion.

The following disgraceful chapter is already somewhat familiar to you, dear Spiridon Ermolaevich, judging by your precipitate inquiry, one that is completely incredible coming from a man of your stature and experience. But really, tell us, how *did* you manage to rear such a mad brain, and what's more, one who would go on to become in consequence a real troublemaker? How? You pass over this in silence as you supplicate on your son's behalf, but one would like to know all the same, so as to discourage the others. I for my part twigged straightaway, the moment he came before me, that he wasn't *one of us,* his show of allegiance notwithstanding, and so I say to him as soon as he finishes: "And now, sonny, tell us what *really* happened." "That really is what happened," he argues with me, "it is," he says, "the whole truth and nothing but the truth!" "I bet you," I say, "that it isn't!" My Jolly

Rogers are standing in the doorway, in their red caps, having a good laugh. "Hey," I say, "hold it there, my Jolly Rogers, it's too early for you to be grinning yet, perhaps this young man will think again, and win from me one hundred rubles, and an honorable booting out into the street, and freedom into the bargain." "No-no"—my good fellows shake their heads—"he won't win, he's as dishonest as the day is long, wherever did they dig up such a liar!" "Sssh!" I say. "It's not yet your turn to be laying down the law!" and I turn to address your dear son, the sweet young adolescent, moving close to him: "Too hot to handle, eh, Ermolayushka?" Ermolai says, recoiling from me: "I have nothing more to say to you. I've told you everything. But I didn't do anything bad, believe me . . ." "So it turns out to be the case, apparently, that it was simply out of some childish pranks that you decided to dig up the bird, is that it, Ermolayushka? You dug up the bird, and leapt nimbly up onto the roof. You whisper sweet nothings in its ear, 'Now fly, my Semyon, fly, my pretty! fly, my little dove!' And at this point the worm-eaten turquoise Semyon parakeet flapped its turquoise little wings, flapped them a couple of times in the futile hope of returning to its former life. Aha!" I said here, finally losing my temper. "Aha, there's your SYMBOL, Ermolayushka!" "There's no symbol here!" cried out your son, the sly rogue, Ermolai Spiridonovich. "There isn't!" "Well, you go and tell that to the marines . . ." "Why is it," asks Ermolai Spiridonovich, "that you keep on seeing symbols everywhere you look?" I didn't reply immediately, but looked more intently at your young man, Spiridon Ermolaevich, and then I answer after wiping my bald patch with a handkerchief, and say, "Well the reason why I keep seeing them, my splendid Ermolai Spiridonovich, is that world culture, forgive me, Lord, from its very inception, as we are assured by the most learned of men, is stuffed with symbols, and there's no way we can leap out of this cage, try as we might!" And I struck him, your hazel-eyed son, I punched him right in the teeth, wholeheartedly, because I suddenly felt sad, as a prophylactic measure, and that fist of mine, well, you know yourself, Spirry. And his little teeth went flying in all directions like pearls falling off a broken thread—they scattered and rolled along the floor. We were silent . . . When dear old Ermolai Spiridonovich regained his thoughts, he looked at me with his toothless grin in amazement. "What," he says, "have I done to deserve such treatment?" "Don't cry," I reassure him, "they *were* only milk teeth, weren't they?" My Jolly Rogers are standing in the doorway in their red caps, splitting their sides with laughter. But Ermolai Spiridonovich himself isn't jolly at all, he counts his losses, he doesn't even smile at my joke. "It's the done thing," I admonish him, "to smile when your elders joke with you, especially when they're old enough to be your father. Why, you yourself," I exclaim, "taught us to laugh at jokes, what with that trick of yours with the parakeet!"

We tortured and tormented your son, Ermolai Spiridonovich, we interrogated him zealously, using all the tools at our disposal, we can do no other, we haven't been taught differently. We were shocked by the frailty of his build! Fragile goods! For the most part we used methods of torture which gladden the heart. We submerged him headfirst, for example, in a pool of manure and we suggested that he might like to swim around a bit; we impaled him, blindfolded him, we were joking, naturally, and instead of a stake we used the male member of our giant Fedka, who goes by the nickname of The Honorable Fedka. Do you remember him, Spiridon Ermolaevich? He remembers you most well, he says that when you were nippers you played together once at bat and ball, along with Sashka Shcherbakov, who drowned in a hole in the ice last winter. We also introduced ants into his prick; we pumped air up his asshole, inflated him like a frog, with the help of an Elizabethan pump; we tore his nostrils and fingernails with pliers; we called some bawds and asked that he, Ermolai Spiridonovich, lick their poxy wounds, just in case this might heal them. He licked. Well, what else would you like to know? In the end we tore off the balls—had no use for them. Threw them to the dogs. So at least they didn't go totally to waste. And what would he need them for? Do you and I, dear Spiridon Ermolaevich, want to have progeny from such a one? I think not. And then he completely overreacted to this loss too, he got really angry and started swearing as soon as he regained consciousness. He was saying that we were inhuman monsters and savages, which is hurtful even. Of course, there's nothing wrong with cursing on the rack, everyone does that, but there's no need to hurt people's feelings, is there? We are not free agents, we are obeying orders, we fulfill important commissions out of a sense of professional duty, and for that he calls us, so to say, savages. No, my dear friend, it's you who are the savage in the fullest sense of things, you're the one who went against the world order, not us, and on the rack people say what's really on their mind! Just as drunks tell the truth, so on the rack the truth is in whines! And consequently, my supposition in relation to the fact that he is not one of us, my dear sir, was being reinforced with every passing hour. I, thank God, know this business, I earn my daily bread, and that's why, therefore, I have a good sense of how *our* people scream on the rack and how those who are *not one of us* scream. One of our people would never call me a savage, because that's not what he thinks, but your bastard came out with it. And he behaved, I regret to inform you, without much spunk. No sooner had he gone through the pool of manure and puked his guts out than he started begging for mercy and, like a little child, was promising that he wouldn't do it anymore, and that he in-tended, he said, not to give himself airs in the future, to behave quietly, that he would be an enthusiastic servant of the state. That is all very well—but who needs his repentance? But we asked him nevertheless: "Dispel," we say, "our doubts with regard to the resurrection of the parakeet nicknamed Semyon. Perhaps you and your neighbor, Agafon Elistratovich, had had some disagreements?" He squealed that there hadn't really been any disagreements as such, but the physician, he said, was a real old soak, and that when he treated people his hands were trembling. But we've heard so many good things about Agafon Elistratovich, and so we responded to this denunciation concerning his chronic drunkenness with the utmost indignation. More to the point, how is one to explain that not even three full days had passed from the purchase of that parakeet when the said parakeet started to peg out, suffering terrible convulsions, as if someone had poisoned it, and that even before that it had seemed to be pining away, it didn't chirp and had turned down all food? Wait a minute, I think, let me consider this carefully. I wiped my raspberry-colored bald patch with a handkerchief and, following up on this, I ask Ermolai Spiridonovich, your son, having first clutched his scrotum in a vise (his testicles were at this moment still attached to him), as a precautionary measure: in case he tried to deceive me. "Wait, wait," I ask, "weren't you the one, scumbag, who poisoned the foreign bird in an attempt to vex your neighbor, the Physician to the Boyars Agafon Elistratovich, and also those broken-hearted children of his, Tatyana Agafonovna and Ezra Agafonovich?" "No," replies your son Ermolai Spiridonovich, his eyes popping out of his head from pain, "no! No-o-o!!" But his little eyes had gone white—we're biting our lip, that means that we're in pain—"No-o-o . . . I mean ye-e-s!" We squeezed harder, struggling to work out: is that your final answer? "Yes! Yes! It was me!" Ermolai Spiridonovich shouts at me, as though he thinks I'm deaf. "I did it! I did it," he says, "in order to vex him!!!" "Well, that's great. To vex him—but why?" "Oh," he shouts, "that hurts! stop it!" He's twitching all over, poor chap. "Stop it! I can't think like that!" "You don't need to think," we say, "just give us the answers . . ." Still, we eased up a bit, because we feared that otherwise he might do serious injury to his tongue, and how would he speak to us then? "The reason I wanted to annoy him," he explains, "is that I don't like him." "Why?"—we pressed him a little more firmly on this. "Well, naturally because," he yelled out, "he was a faithful servant to the fatherland!" "Now we're getting somewhere!" I say. "Now why didn't you say all that earlier? Fine, have a rest, my dear chap . . ." And as soon as he'd had a bit of a rest I say: "But perhaps you wanted to poison Agafon Elistratovich as well as the parakeet?" He is silent, thinking. And I was literally just about to start putting the squeeze on him when he comes out swiftly with his answer: "Yes!" So there you are, you can see yourself it's an open and shut case we're dealing with here, my respected Spiridon Ermolaevich! We decided, however, not to make a rush to judgment: we are suspicious people, pardon my French. So on the following morn we took him to have some fun on the rack, that's of use to him, for he's a bit of a stooped one, your son, Spiridon Ermolaevich, it wouldn't harm to stretch him out longer for good measure. This is a real killer, this activity, I inform you, it's particularly funny if it's a wench, but I must say that your son is a delicate fruit, so he's as good as a woman, if not better . . . While I do not presume to exhaust you further with details, allow me instead to make one digression of a strictly philosophical nature. You and I, Spiridon, would be pretty poor philosophers, nay, we would be deceivers, if we failed to note man's great passion for torture and all its works. Why does our state protect its loyal subjects from arbitrary rule, arbitrary violence and petty tyranny? Why, the reason why it protects them against all this is that otherwise there wouldn't be anybody left alive in this country, because they would already have tortured and exterminated one another beforehand . . . To give an example: my dick doesn't get very excited by women, it doesn't really see any difference in the minimal variations between them, having tried more than its fair share; but no sooner do I really get down to business with a man, with the authority of the state fully behind me, there's nothing I can do about it, it reaches for the sky, and in fact sometimes I get so worked up that I cream my hose, and my woman thinks I've been playing away from home, but she's wrong: I've been at work... This passion is a deep mystery, and for the most part philosophers pass over it in silence, hiding their head in their shoulders, like ostriches; this mystery is a more serious business than turning your finger in some mossy hole, here your guts get turned inside out, Spiridon, but nobody knows why. Yet at the same time I also love humble martyrs who merely fart and whinny on the rack, I respect them, and I would never ever swap one such martyr for a hundred Englishmen, for enduring torture and suffering are things pleasing to God, but what's an Englishman—a piece of shit, that's all he is! Or let us take, for example, the prophet Elisha, who was once teased by children who called him a bald old coot. Come hither, chrome head!... The offense was not great: every decent man ought to have a bald patch. And Elisha did not speak a single word in anger to the children, and he set two she-bears on them, and the bears tore the forty-two children to bits... Exactly, brother Spiridon, here's food for thought! Yet you keep on writing your inquiries, you do not fail to pester us with messages, wasting paper. That a man will sell everything and everyone is something I am utterly convinced of, but the approach mustn't be rushed, you mustn't scare him off, just give him time! But we are not given enough time, we are hurried, rushed, pressured to get results. That's why mistakes occur occasionally in our line of work, and from these mistakes, Spiridon, civil disobedience grows...

So now, please judge for yourself, Spiridon Ermolaevich, what would have happened if that worm-eaten parakeet had taken wing? HOW WOULD WE HAVE LOOKED THEN?! As it was, according to the words of the troublemaker, it flapped its little wings a couple of times, although later on the rack he renounced these incautious words of his. But then again he, the parasite, was telling porkies like there was no tomorrow by that point! In one version, can you believe it, he himself poisoned the parakeet; another time he says that he and Agafon Elistratovich were in it together to try out the poison; another time he even went so far as—I'm telling you this in confidence—to denounce you by claiming that you, that is his very own father, Spiridon Ermolaevich, were the one who persuaded him to exhume the rotten creature. It was on hearing this (or could it have been earlier?) that we tore off his nuts, so that he would no longer take his father's name in vain, especially without good cause, we tore them off and threw them to the hounds, a tasty morsel for them . . . And he agrees to anything, he's ready to sign anything, to affirm whatever we say, no matter what, he replies to every question in the affirmative. What is the use of that, I ask you? We realize that he's trying to confuse the investigation, to send us off on false leads and to conceal the shameful truth. But, after taking a few wrong turnings, at the very least we all concurred in our opinion that the reason why your son Ermolai Spiridonovich wanted to resurrect the parakeet was to show that this foreign bird was superior to our sparrows, and to lessen thereby our national pride and show us up before the whole world in a ridiculous and unbecoming light. When both we and Ermolai Spiridonovich had agreed on this joint conclusion, we embraced in celebration: All's well that ends well! Bring us, my lads, viands and victuals, let's party! And our good fellows bring us sea salmon, piglets and lambs, various soufflés, and wine that has the ribald name of Milk of the Mother of God. We started eating and started chewing the fat. . .

However, I have a vague suspicion that you, Spiridon, inflamed by fatherly feeling, which naturally we don't hold against you in any way, are interested further in finding out what happened next to your son, the unforgettable Ermolayushka, whom I remember with such fondness. Well, what could have become of him? Nothing became of him. Everything, thank God, worked out well. Early one morning, yes, about five o'clock, just as the sun was rising and turning the onion domes of our holy churches to bright gold, he and I slowly ascended the bell tower, hand in hand. We marveled at the view. Capital City stretched before us in a sweet morning sleep and mist, the cocks were crowing and the orchards were rustling. The grain storehouse, the public squares, the hooting of steam trains, the university—everything was in its appointed place. The river ran through the city like a silver snake, and on the higher bank, on the other side, stood a forest—a sight for sore eyes, no mistake about it! And the aroma rising up from the grasses, Spiridon! The smell of clover, Spiridon, it's such a strong smell! "Beautiful!" I said as I looked around. "Beautiful!" said Ermolai Spiridonovich. I looked at him from the side. Only one word for him: handsome! Even his morning-after-the-night-before pallor was starting to acquire a subtle blueness which only enhanced his appearance. Led astray through no fault of his own by lusty demons, his hour of liberation had now arrived, and, foreseeing the new life to come, he already looked just heavenly. "Well, Godspeed!" I said and led him by the hand to the bell tower's parapet. "Fly, Ermolayushka! Fly, my pretty! Fly, my little dove!" Stretching his arms out in the form of the cross, he stepped out and swallow-dived into the emptiness. For a second I was tormented by doubt: what if he soars like a turquoise parakeet, to the demons' great delight? Holding on to the handrails, I leaned over and looked down somewhat anxiously. Thank God! Smashed to bits! I see he's splattered splendidly, he landed with a real plop, nay, even to the extent that there are tiny pieces of brain scattered all over the pavement like a ripe sun melon. My good fellows in their red caps rushed to put Ermolai Spiridonovich in a body bag. I crossed myself.

Cheer up, Spiridon Ermolaevich! Don't let it get to you! It's not as if he's worth it! Don't feel sorry for the bastard! He also pointed the finger at you, but I've filed that particular piece in my own special place, well away from prying eyes, I didn't allow it to circulate. As soon as your fatherly feelings cool down a bit, do call on me— we'll go to the bathhouse, have a steam, drink some beer. My missus brews some strong beer, it's got a real kick! Just drop in, no need to make an appointment. And you'll still have time to sire some little children, you're a man in good working order for now, I dare say, even if you are getting on a bit. And if you don't father any kids—it's not the end of the world, you'll get by! We won't grow short of heirs! But your son, Ermolai Spiridonovich, he, of course, went directly to paradise: a martyr's place is always in paradise, even if he's a martyr for an unjust cause. And he's looking down on us from there tenderly, he's amusing himself with his turquoise parakeet, he strokes its feathers, and gives thanks. When you think of this, when you imagine such a scene, you even envy him, honest to God, Spiridon...oh, well, fair enough, balls to him, let him be happy...

PERSIAN LILAC

BELLA ISAAKOVNA KOKH skipped merrily through the dacha settlement in her transparent mackintosh, her face as red as meat.

Jewish women differ sharply from Russian women. Not many people know this. But even among Jewish women Bella Isaakovna is undoubtedly one of a kind. This is our secret, Bella Isaakovna's secret and my secret. We swore to preserve it, but there are some things that are greater than us. I mean metaphysics. Perhaps this is precisely the reason why the Jews became the chosen people. Thanks to Jewish women like Bella Isaakovna. She is a young woman, she's given birth once. She is twenty-six years old. She has curly hair.

Chewing a piece of grass, I stood in her path.

Intellectuals of both nationalities would desire to smooth over the differences or even deny that they exist. But they are wasting their time. I shall speak in hints, so as not to make anyone mad or offend anyone.

There are various proofs of the existence of God. The majority of them have been refuted.

Bella Isaakovna and I weren't acquaintances and we didn't say hello to each other, but we each knew a few things about the other.

What I'd heard about Bella Isaakovna was that she was a sloven and that her house was a mess, that she was a bad cook and that she had a hysterical nature and that Bella Isaakovna's husband, a physicist and also a Jew, gave her the occasional beating. I'd also heard that Bella Isaakovna had strained relations with her mother. They say that as a nineteen-year-old girl Bella Isaakovna suffered an illness for which her mother, seven years on, still can't fully forgive her. Apart from all this, I knew that when I was standing there chewing on my grass, Bella Isaakovna was coming back from the bathhouse. She was no beauty, but her skin was so soft, which she rubbed with wild strawberries—you wouldn't find a Russian woman with such skin.

However, I'm talking about something other than skin-deep differences. A different difference is under discussion here. Only the elite know about it. I'll explain myself in a minute.

Bella Isaakovna had also heard all sorts of things about me and was convinced that I was half- or at least quarter-Jewish.

"Why do you think so?" I asked.

"You know fine well why," replied Bella Isaakovna. "But why, isn't it so? Am I not right?"

"My great-grandfather was Romanian," I confessed. She was disappointed. She was panic-stricken that her husband would at any minute burst in on us and kill us both. She was simply a bag of nerves. I too wasn't too keen on this prospect of mutual immolation. She muttered:

"His work is top-secret. He doesn't have the right to leave work in the middle of the day."

But this still wouldn't calm her down. She didn't know what to do with herself. She threw herself on me and asked me to kiss her on her lower lip. I kissed her, listening carefully to the rustles. She was simply all aquiver. I had never suspected that one could be so excited by a kiss on the lower lip. She was asking me to say something tender to her. I was lost. I didn't know her well enough. We'd only just got acquainted. I said:

"I like you."

She grunted in disappointment. I tried mentioning her skin. This cheered her up unexpectedly.

"So you are a Romanian, then?" she asked, and, not listening to my protestations, shouted out:

"He's here! We've had it!"

I rushed to my clothes. There was no one there.

"Come on, say something tender to me," Bella Isaakovna asked. "Hey, come here, baby."

This put me off, but I went. Now I'll pick my words with care and say everything I need to. So here it is: Jewish women, in distinction to Russian women in any event, possess one extraordinary feature. They have talking vaginas. That is, the vagina doesn't talk by itself, of its own accord, but it can be made to speak, like a cat can be made to speak, by putting your fingers inside its mouth. So there it is. It can even sing, something uncomplicated, of course, naturally, some musical phrase or other from Moscow Nights. But this is amazing nevertheless. Russian girls are far more pragmatic and silent. They don't utter a sound. They communicate only through the mouth. Whereas here you have this extraordinary feature. But very few people know about it, because the senses simply aren't developed enough. The relationships are too crude. A lack of curiosity. I don't know. I'm not a scholar, I haven't searched for the causes. I'm simply making a statement. But Bella Isaakovna was a complete exception. In everyday life she was mercantile and even rather thick. She knew all the models and modifications of cars made in the USSR and liked to rank the various dacha settlements: for example, she ranked Nikolina Gora far higher than Krasnaya Pakhra. She could read English and in bed asked for spades to be called spades. So that's what we did. She'd never been in a train in her life, but her vagina was a miracle. It didn't just speak. It answered questions. I didn't understand at first when she said:

"If you like, ask something. She'll answer."

I didn't understand and asked her what she meant.

"Ask and we shall answer. Welcome to Question Time."

For starters I posed a very easy question.

"What is it now: winter or summer?"

She answered faultlessly. It was a wormy, rotten summer.

I asked:

"What is your name?"

This smacked somewhat of spiritualism. She answered with a complete lack of shame. Bella Isaakovna's laughter could be heard in the distance.

And then I gathered up my courage and asked the question I'd been wanting to ask for a long time. For many years. I asked:

"Is there a God?"

She answered:

"Yes."

"Is that the truth?" I asked, my voice trembling, my cheek pressing into her.

"The truth," echoed the impassive answer.

I am not saying that Kant was put to shame. I don't care about that. This was the voice of nature and of eternal femininity. A completely autonomous voice. I didn't hide my tears. Leaning on her elbow, a surprised Bella Isaakovna was looking me up and down.

"You really pick your questions!" grunted Bella Isaakovna. "You really pick your questions!"

She looked disappointed. Chewing on a piece of grass, I stood in her path. The Persian lilac was coming to an end all around.

BERDYAEV

IN THE ravine the dogs barked, sensing freedom. Their pack spun around in circles. The dog owners, bunched in a group, played with the leads, smoked, clapped their mittens to keep warm. Wary because the dogs were going mad now that they'd been let off the leash, I took a path to the left, bypassing the ravine, and got lost in the darkness. As I tramped through the snowy nooks and crannies of the copse coated with hoarfrost, I was gripped by doubts, I had visions, dark crepuscular pictures, I had stood for two weeks in the middle of my apartment in an open dressing gown, stretching my arms into the air, to my rotund wife Dorothea's howls and under the gloomy gaze of my blond children, looking like a Turk disarmed into a state of mad terror and nakedness, telling myself off for my cowardly weakness before the seasonal genius of Kruglitsky, whose voice held such friendly overtones that I couldn't resist and immediately agreed, despite the fact that with the imminent passing of my two-year-old illness, on the eve (as it had seemed to me) of my recovery, I should have been more careful: I had hidden away, like a mouse, slunk away into private life, become a total lone wolf.

Kruglitsky passed the receiver to a hostess whom I didn't know, the organizer of this sumptuous climax to Mardi Gras week, and she set about describing, in so many words and so unartistically, how to get to the house, which was the distance of a mere morning constitutional from my house, that I suspected that topographically she was a cretin and, alas, I was not mistaken. I didn't like her from the very beginning, this Natalya, and I didn't alter my opinion of her later, when I met her and saw her inviting, turned-inside-out lips, reminiscent of a regimental trumpet, her skinny behind, into which her velvet bit, her manner of dancing solo facing her reflection in a dark window, or when I heard how with strict regularity and feminine chic the most vulgar words flew from those lips, obscenities which she had become proficient in pronouncing in so enchanting a manner that they seemed like plucked wild fowl. Deprived of down and feathers, they produced above all a gastronomic impression, at any rate, they didn't reek of an animal farm, yet in their nakedness there lurked some particular indecency, one that brought to mind the appearance of a roasted chicken. Add to this that instead of trembling before her family ties I merely felt a vague irritation, for in the activities of her long since largely forgotten but, as soon became apparent, still very much alive father I had constantly seen not concern for the welfare of the fatherland, but the arrogance of a favorite who had gone too far. I remember how in my childhood I observed him once in my parents' house, at the birthday table, at my mother's right hand: she was the birthday girl, and was wearing a low-cut dress in honor of the occasion. I remember the greediness with which he ate the tasty morsels of turkey using his hands, and how every minute he kept reaching for his wine glass, leaving on it the grapes of his fingerprints and the imprints of his lips, lips he'd passed on to Natalya; I remember how, pulling open his mouth with his pinky, he sensuously picked away with his toothpick at remote molars, just as if he were establishing order in distant provinces, and how later, having stuffed himself, he fell asleep over dessert. My mother interceded for him before the speechless guests by explaining away his snores as a consequence of the high political importance of the activity he'd just been engaged in, and I also remember how, a mere six months later, when he was already yesterday's man, my dear mother got very angry when she told the story of his gluttony and snoring.

The recollection was on the tip of my tongue as Natalya assured Kruglitsky and me that her father UNDERSTANDS EVERYTHING and that the disfavor that had fallen upon him signaled the beginning of our common troubles, to which Kruglitsky nodded his head, a serious expression on his face. But I stayed silent, and what is more, I too nodded out of loyalty, as if I sympathized with the overthrown grandee, who had earned the reputation of being a *reformer* on the strength of the wildness of his endeavors. Well, to hell with her, that Natalya, I didn't begrudge nodding, when it comes down to it I'm just as much up shit creek without a paddle as she is, and moreover I certainly don't exclude the possibility that she had nothing directly to do with the EVENTS THAT FOLLOWED, although of course as the hostess . . . I don't know—who can tell?!

My paranoia had long since known limits, approximate limits at least. I would mock those wretched fools who saw in every under-the-weather vulgarian who happened to come up to them on the streets to ask them for a light both a threat and a warning. I used to laugh. I reckoned that the sphere of your threats was confined to matters of the utmost urgency; I used to treat stories about your messengers, greetings, poisoned cigarettes and deadly umbrellas, your all-seeing eye and other fairy tales with distrust, if not to say with hostility, for, Your Highness, my memory was not your ally in the same way as it was not the reformer's ally either. It is not for me to create a myth about you, if only for reasons of family history. I should point out that my dear mother, whose womanly instinct in this particular case triumphed with true zeal over the Table of Ranks, frequently spoke of you, the groom who was not to be, with disdain, about your prissy philandering, your bombastic love letters, full of spelling errors and inappropriate Gallicisms, about your amorous souvenirs, in which (until recent times, at least) were preserved her hairpins and carefully smoothed-out wrappers from the sweets she'd eaten, picked up surreptitiously by you at balls. You were, naturally, a prestigious and desirable pair, but Granny decided that you yourself were too young and that you were lacking in "finesse."

Later, when you got together with my father and used to stroke the back of my head, visiting our house as a friend, I heard plenty of times (and this also *didn't help* the myth) how dissatisfied you were with your angels, how, affecting a look of mock squeamishness, you swore as you described those oafs and loafers, and how my father laughed tensely as he listened to your confidential chatter.

But since the time when, blazing with anger, you shuffled off your earthly coil, much has changed. Two years of tiresome dialogues left their mark. For two years I conducted with you, Count, a never-ending conversation; for two years, I had only to cover my eyes, lie on the couch, move away to the window, for a Jupiter on duty to descend on me in a dry shower of words, and I, caught in freeze-frame with a spoon of cabbage soup in midair 'twixt bowl and lip, with my hair covered in shampoo or on a cross-country skiing stroll, again and again took a seat opposite you, and we fell into conversation, which the more it went on, the more it turned into a competition to see who was the champion at abstracting himself from his own essence. Virtuosi, we kept on establishing records, we abstracted ourselves to such an extent that we turned into the allegorical china statuettes of the animals from Grandfather Krylov's *Fables*, whose proneness to gluttony was, as you must surely know, a topic of conversation during that sumptuous Mardi Gras feast at which, having wandered through the copse, I was a late arrival. And so when I entered the house, Kruglitsky was already concerned about what might have happened to me, though still eating blini with salmon and swilling down vodka. The feast was in full swing. Kruglitsky and I took noisy delight in our meeting and kissed each other three times like old comrades. The small number of guests treated these kisses with enough respect, and for a certain time they looked after me as if I'd had a preservation order slapped on me. Natalya, the lively hostess with the mostest, wasted no time in piling a mountain of blini onto my plate, Kruglitsky spiritedly splashed a generous measure of vodka into my glass, punishment for my late arrival, and, having clinked glasses on the occasion of this little meeting, we both threw back our heads in a single movement, and Natalya cried out as she was leaving the room, "Fucking ballsy!"

Our conversations took many different forms: sometimes you would be polite and shower me with all sorts of attention, even going as far as, on one occasion, providing a lit match when I took out a cigarette, and I was profuse in my thanks, but sometimes things would suddenly "smell of Siberia," if one thinks of Rozanov, whom Julia, and this does not surprise me, COULD NOT STAND (oh, you, my little ducky!); the wind of change was blowing, and your face, now darker, was acquiring a miserly, ascetic look; I was nervous, I got all tangled up in lies, I fussed and fidgeted—but the tempest moved away in some magical way, and again afresh, almost in a friendly manner, we set about discussing the global problems of building a better way of life. Then, screwing up my eyes in sweet hope and lauding your mercy and leniency, with the infirm voice of a friend of order and loyal citizen, I exhorted you that cosmetic changes were needed not for the purpose of disturbing the status quo, to which, believe me, I wholeheartedly belong, but in the name of, believe me, patriotic considerations, and it seemed to me that in your youngish-looking face I could see for a moment something resembling hesitation or even sympathy. Inspired by this sign, I gave free rein to my eloquence, got carried away and even became a little impudent. But you looked at me with a faded gaze, you put me in my place and gave me a real dressing down, as if I were a boy, for being so indiscriminate in my choice of acquaintances, for all those dubious Poles, Yids and Magyars who had taken to visiting me during the last month.

I expended so much spiritual strength on this dialogue that at times I would start to grumble at myself, at you, at EVERY-THING. Lord, I would grumble, I am wasting the best years of my life ON WHAT?—and I felt like rushing headlong out of the house where Dorothea was absolutely at the end of her tether from my chronic silence, and on every suitable occasion and even without any occasion would emit her favorite hiss, "Bloody hell!" I fled from my blond twins, fled across town to my parents' apartment, into an atmosphere of deepening fear and fading away, in order to burst into my aging, ailing mother's bedroom and to shout from the threshold, "Mama! why did you have to have me, Mama, Mama..." Well, and so forth... all this tear-stained *plagiarism,* for which you, it goes without saying, did not fail to reproach me with malice aforethought, having hinted at a certain lack of modesty, in our subsequent conversation, and I agreed: the comparison is inappropriate, but what is one to do, given that Providence sets us all in motion, *from small to great* ("speak for yourself!"), OK, that is, it sets me in motion, finds it fun to play with me, making me go around in circles like a toy train, around and around and around and around!

But how can one shout or say anything at the door of one's parents' bedroom, in an atmosphere of deepening fear and fading away, that is, when Mama, having noticed me through glasses fitted out for reading French novels, hurriedly putting aside her book and sensing my agitation, will hurriedly ask, "Has something happened AGAIN?" *"Mais rein,"* I shall answer, as casually as possible, *"mais rein du tout!*...It will soon be Mardi Gras. Mama!..." And Mama will say, "Why did you get involved with all that riffraff and low-life? Why do you need all those Kruglitskys?" And you, Count, will echo her from the wings, "Indeed, why do you?" Well, naturally you agree with her. You have a grudge against Kruglitsky. Everyone still remembers those verses of genius of his which circulated in numerous manuscript copies:

YOUR HIGHNESS! HOW HIGH ARE YOU FLYING?
HOW SLYLY ARE YOU DYING, YOUR SLYNESS?

A semi-official parodist, a certain scumbag like Nestor Kukolnik, tried to lessen the impression of the apocalyptic decline, to turn everything into a little joke. He composed a playful little number:

YOUR HIGHNESS! HOW DRYLY ARE YOU CRYING?

But the attempt to cheat society failed. The manuscripts continued to circulate. Soon everyone was repeating:

YOUR HIGHNESS! HOW HIGH ARE YOU FLYING?

Kruglitsky experienced problems with the authorities. They called him in. "We won't allow you to go around claiming to be an unacknowledged genius!" "Then acknowledge me!" Kruglitsky replied wittily. I awaited him on the front steps. He composed all of this later, but it's still witty.

"But Filonov was on the front steps then," said Kruglitsky,

pointing at me. The young ladies were envious of me. The white, wet face of Kruglitsky floated in front of me, his mindless gaze, and I said, "Let's drink!" And we had a drink, and started to ask Kruglistky to recite something.

"Oh, please, Kruglitsky!" begged the young ladies.

He did not put on airs, he said that he would read *one* thing, because he doesn't want to read more than that, and that this poem is all about Mardi Gras. The young ladies cried out, "Of course! of course!" and Julia, anticipating, declaimed:

WE STOCKED UP ON PANS AND PATIENCE...

"OK, you recite it yourself, then," said Kruglitsky. Everyone protested, and Julia, now holding her tongue, most of all. She was wearing a beautiful moiré dress, wide and long enough to enable one to part one's knees without worrying when sitting, as is the done thing among Parisian women nowadays, who love to relax. But unlike Parisian women, Julia was not taking it easy, quite the reverse: she was fidgeting all the time, she didn't know what to do with her arms and legs, which meant that her dress rustled in a special way and crimson patches glowed on her cheeks.

The hollow-cheeked, apostolic visage of Kruglitsky lit up with emotion—he started reading. I don't remember it by heart, I've also forgotten the number of the apartment, but I'll convey the gist of it to you, without spilling a drop and with running commentaries, carried along as I am by its magical putridity.

We stocked up on pans (though a double pun on pain and *le pain* is undoubtedly present) and with patience (here the martyrdom theme is directly alluded to). We even managed to get hold of amber salmon (a reference to inconsistencies in the food supply system). As winter is coming to an end, when, so to say, the shoulders have grown weary from the weight of the fur coats that had preserved during cold times our meager warmth (in the discussion of the poem the owner of the house, a man with a trendy little beard whose name was Lyosha and who in all other respects remained for me a complete enigma, expressed his amazement at why, he wanted to know, the warmth was *meager*? The young ladies set about trying to show him *why*, but he, despondent, kept repeating that warmth is *not* meager, that indeed this was practically an insult *to our movement,* and that this, comrades, was right out of order. Kruglitsky, in lieu of any commentary, ate a pancake with relish and demanded that his host put on the favorite record of his youth, *Snow Is Falling,* at which point the discussion came to an end), and so, when the shoulders have grown weary from the weight of the fur coats that had preserved during cold times our meager warmth, that had protected us from the intrigues of influenza, when the neck for the last time burns in woolen embraces, when sweater elbows are wearing thin, and handkerchiefs lie in sticky snotty lumps in all the pockets (this anti-aesthetic element is one of the main features of Kruglitsky's poetry and is sometimes expressed much more forcefully, sometimes too explicitly, but here I like it), and so, when . . . when . . . then, my friends, how marvelous are pancakes! Their lace (or lacy texture—I don't remember exactly) is worthy of libations!

After this the meaning of the poem takes on more and more of an allusive character and comes down to the fact that, no matter how long it may all drag on, no matter how slim our chances of winning are, no matter how flat and unprofitable we find this hippodrome and this low sky, pulled down over our eyes like a fur hat, or these inconsolable races, where, no matter which horse you bet on (I'm slipping into the poem's meter here, I feel) it trips, and even a pig in a poke would run his race more swiftly—all that is true, but irrespective of whether it is true or not, the calendars don't lie, March is at the door and it promises a thaw and changes.

The poem contains the poet's conviction that the changes will affect everything other than the feelings of the poet's beloved for him, and it concludes with a very refined lyric ending: they stand together and watch the streams flowing and the buds busting out all over.

"Fucking ballsy!" whispered the hostess Natalya, stunned.

"Even a pig in a poke runs his race more swiftly!!" I quoted. "An amazing line!"

"As if there were only one amazing line there!" Julia snapped at me.

As a rule, I am prepared to sacrifice the truth in order to observe social proprieties, but understanding as I did that in this particular society social propriety is to be observed in its breach, I left the manners of the chattering classes to one side and casually unmasked myself in the following judgment: I said that the allusive part of the work had been less to my *liking*, because the time scale dragged on for too long, that is, it all went on for so long that when the *thaw* would begin at last and the streams would start to flow and the buds would burst, the ones gazing on this marvelous wonder of nature would be not the young poet and his passionate girlfriend, but an old man and old woman who had long since lost possession of all their faculties, with walking sticks, losing their hair and with liver spots on their face and hands, or even two skeletons, two bags of bones, so that, I concluded, the cleverness of the meteorological allusions comes to nothing, as it has been crushed by too long a waiting time.

Kruglitsky made an indistinct exclamation. All three young ladies looked at me and frowned with knitted brows. Then the host with the beard whose name was Lyosha uttered words to the effect that warmth is *not* meager and how is one to understand the image of *the fur coats*, to which Kruglitsky replied that he felt like listening to the gramophone record of *Snow Is Falling*. He invited his companion, a silent young lady with *an absolutely enormous*

forehead—I had never seen such a forehead on a woman before—
to dance, while the hostess followed them with her eyes and said:

"Fucking ballsy!"

And Julia said:

"I love it when Kruglitsky is sentimental. It suits him."

But I didn't say anything. I took a bite of a dry pancake and kept
silent. I wondered whether I should go home, but at this point
Kruglitsky finished dancing, sat down next to me, and he and I
started up our own separatist conversation about our former comrades and girlfriends, and we were overjoyed that our opinions co-
incided so often, and if one of us succeeded in saying something
particularly sharp we guffawed so loudly that it was unseemly.
When I noted that Fyodor's eyes, as a consequence of his fondness for hard drinking, had started "to see trebles," Kruglitsky
laughed so deafeningly that the young hostess, dancing a solo in
front of her reflection in a dark window, decided that this laugh
was on her account, and ceased her dancing. Julia, resting her
crimson cheek on her fist, was smoking and making out that
nothing here concerned her, but at this point she couldn't contain
herself either and asked who we were laughing at.

"We're laughing at Fyodor," the tipsy Kruglitsky replied eagerly.

"What's so funny about him?" asked Julia sharply.

"He finds," said Kruglitsky, nodding at me, "that Fyodor's eyes
'see trebles.'"

"What does that mean, 'sees trebles'?" asked Julia, deliberately
addressing her remarks not to me but to Kruglitsky.

"Let him explain it himself," said Kruglitsky, who himself had
only a vague idea, in my opinion, as to what it meant.

"It means," I said, addressing the young lady, "it means, young
lady, well, how can I best explain it to you? Are you familiar with
the workings of the internal combustion engine?"

"I don't understand," said Julia in agitation, "what Fyodor has to do with the internal combustion engine! You talk about him as if he weren't a living person!"

"Don't get your knickers in a twist!" I exclaimed. "I can assure you I think at least as much of Fyodor as you do."

At this Kruglitsky leaned over to me and, scarcely able to stop himself from bursting out laughing, started to whisper hotly and incoherently in my ear that this was probably *not the case*, inasmuch as Julia had been Fyodor's lover for a whole year, and Julia, of course, understood what he was whispering to me, and her face turned completely crimson. So as to change the subject, I asked Kruglitsky what had become of Michel, whose friendship he had much valued. "What, you don't know?!" "No!" I said, anxious. Kruglitsky told me the sad news. "Fucking hell!" I burst out. "When?!" "What is it with you?" Kruglitsky's eyes goggled. "What planet have you been living on? That news is a hundred years old!" "It was Marya Nikolaevna taking revenge!" yelled out Julia. "It was her!" "No, surely not," doubted Kruglitsky. "How do you know?" "I just do!" stormed Julia. "She wanted to give herself to him, but he took fright and told her where to go." "Hold it, you two. Which Marya Nikolaevna?" I asked. "Well, that one!" said Kruglitsky and pointed at the ceiling. "Ah, that one." I understood who it was. "But I," said Kruglitsky, his eyes shining, "if I'd been in Michel's place I would have banged her once, and go fuck the consequences!" "But can a coward be a good poet?" responded Julia rhetorically. "Yes!" I asserted, rather too familiarly. "You consider that Michel was a good poet?" "How should I put it?" I cast a sidelong look at Kruglitsky, but he, the swine, was maintaining his neutrality. "In my opinion he was a relatively good poet." "Relative to what?" asked Julia. "Relative to Byron?" Kruglitsky guffawed. "He still nicked his best line from Bestuzhev!" snorted Julia. "He never got rid of that Scottish sediment," said Kruglitsky angrily, "that Scottish smell of cheap whiskey on his breath." He grew gloomy and added, "It's a shame."

Sparks were flying from Julia on all sides, as from a tram. The conversation, as is always the case, turned to the Marquis de Custine. I allowed myself several critical remarks. Julia ridiculed me as an arch-Slavophile. Julia laid into Rozanov for not understanding anything about Christ. She and I grappled with each other, but not because Rozanov understood nothing about Christ, but apropos equality. Julia was yelling that all people are equal, and that therefore a constitution and a republic were needed. I said that a constitution, most probably, was an imperative, but that the people, I regret to say, weren't really mature enough for a republic. "What? You don't believe in the people?" Julia was indignant. "The people are not an icon," I retorted, "there's no point in praying to them." "Well, you're wrong there," reasoned Kruglitsky. "I idolize the people!" "Bravo! Bravo!" yelled Julia. The hostess also participated in the argument, got very worked up and kept on repeating all the time: "The poor people! Poor! Poor!" "Put *Snow Is Falling* on again," said Kruglitsky to Lyosha and once again went to dance with Big Brow. "When will they finally get around to reforming the orthography?" said an indignant Julia, turning to our hostess. "I'm just so fed up with all those obsolete letters, those Yats and Yers." "And Izhitsa's even worse!" chipped in Natalya. "Well, I like Izhitsa," Kruglitsky hiccupped as he danced. "It's a cool letter, isn't it?" he asked me. "I personally like all the letters," I said jokingly. "Creep!" Julia shouted at me. "But you," I threw at her in return, "have filled your head with the penny pamphlets of European *Communism* and think you've found the truth!" "Yes!" said Julia to me arrogantly. "Just imagine—I'm a Communist!" "Real Communists," I exploded, "don't sip champagne or gobble chocolates!" "Fat lot you know!" yelled Julia. "The Erfurt Program doesn't forbid it!" She made a big show of finishing off her champagne and said with contempt, "Stoolie!" "No personal insults, please!" said the alarmed master of the house whose name was Lyosha. "I do ask you, comrades . . . no personal remarks!" "He's no comrade of mine!" exclaimed Julia. "Stop that!" said Kruglitsky, sticking up for me. "He's also had run-ins with the authorities." "Shut up!" I yelled. "He was almost exiled in Vologda!!" added Kruglitsky. "Ah, but he wasn't!" laughed Julia with completely crimson cheeks and added, "do you remember, Kruglitsky, our trip to Vologda?" "Fyodor took some photographs, of us having a picnic," said Kruglitsky. "You can see your knickers in one of the photos." He chuckled and poured himself some rum. The remains of his cigarette fell on the encrusted table and burned through the encrustation. Natalya went pale, but didn't say a word. "So what!" said Julia. "I've got nothing to be ashamed of. I have nice legs." "But the knickers were even nicer!" Kruglitsky kept it up. "American," giggled Julia. "Have you heard?" asked Kruglitsky. "Berdyaev was exiled to Vologda *also*." "Sack of shit!" snapped the young lady with the VERY LARGE FOREHEAD. "He was against equality too," exulted Julia. "Perhaps he was *too*," I said, "but I don't like Berdyaev!" "You don't like him?" Julia responded animatedly and looked at me with unexpected friendliness, as if she had forgiven me everything all at once. "Yeah, he's not a bad lad, really," Kruglitsky assured her, his tongue faltering. "So will you be fasting for Lent?" Julia asked me brightly. I lost my nerve and didn't know what to say, so that's how I answered. "I don't know." She guffawed and snorted. "Invite her to dance instead, she's in the mood for dancing," said Kruglitsky, matchmaking. "Rubbish!" yelled Julia. "Just try it! I'll say no! How is it then that you don't know?" she said, returning to the fast. "I'm indifferent to rites," I announced. "However, at Easter I eat *kulich* with pleasure, and at Christmas, goose. But when religion clashes with the demands of my stomach . . ."

"What unbearable vulgarity! Stop it immediately!" Everyone looked at me in shock and horror.

I realized that I'd put my foot in it big-time, hadn't *fallen in line* with the prevailing religious spirit, so I decided to get my coat. Kruglitsky had also made up his mind to leave. "But you're staying the night with us here!" exclaimed the reformer's daughter indignantly. "No, no! I'm going!" He made jerky attempts to stand up. "Where are you going?" Big Brow asked affectionately. "I'm going away," announced Kruglitsky. All fell silent, crushed by the news. "Don't rush!" I advised cautiously. "I want some fresh air!" growled Kruglitsky. "I've eaten too many blini!" He started to struggle into his huge sheepskin coat. "You look like Pugachev in that!" I observed. "My dear!" said Kruglitsky, touched. "You really are the only one who understands me." He embraced me and asked, "Well, how are things with you now?" "Despite my infamy, they've no longer got it in for me," I whisper in his ear.

For revolutionaries we all were very well dressed.

Outside the fresh air made Kruglitsky go completely crazy: he started to gasp for breath, coughed and belched frequently. Without hesitation Big Brow grabbed him by the hand and dragged him back indoors. "He'll probably die soon," said Julia, with tears in her eyes, "he lives on the edge." "In my opinion"—I nodded sympathetically—"he simply wanted to puke." "He'll die soon," insisted Julia, not listening to what I was saying. "We will all die soon," I said. "No!" said Julia maliciously. "You, for example, will hang on for a long time, you'll be loafing around polluting the atmosphere for some time to come yet, like a smoldering firebrand!"

Despite the insults and the ideological disagreements, we entered the copse together. The crust of snow that had melted slightly during the day crunched underfoot. Julia went first, along the narrow pathway which had been established over the course of a long winter. The air was special. Although it was both cold and biting, the moistness caressing the face (it seemed that when we got to the end of the copse we would emerge not in the city but at the seaside, by the gray Baltic waves) softened it, it held the promise of spring. "Why have you taken a dislike to me, Julia?" Not answering, she continued to walk, but after a few paces she halted so suddenly that I almost fell over her. "So you think that everyone ought to like you?" And, without waiting for an answer, she carried on walking. "You, miss, are the one who thinks that everyone likes you," I mumbled, hurrying after her. "Nice legs indeed! Just a pair of legs. We've seen better. Or perhaps you think that your bangs suit you! Your bangs are crap. Your bangs make you look stupid, sort of canine! As for the fact that you were the lover of dissolute, drunken Fyodor, well, that doesn't do you any credit either. You probably were the one who went and *offered* yourself to him, yes? A real plain Jane, and no mistake!"

An empty street. Windy here, as always. "I really don't like these new apartment blocks," she winced. "So where do you live, then?" "In Kuntsevo." "Well, I'd hardly call Kuntsevo old!" "Of course it's old!" "I don't know about that"—I shrugged my shoulders—"but I don't like that Kuntsevo of yours. And no passing motorist will take you there." "We'll see about that!" she said, throwing down a challenge. We started trying to hail a private taxi and *to check things out.* Cars stopped occasionally, but no one wanted to go as far as Kuntsevo. Despite the wind, I was kept warm by a strange *schadenfreude.* "Well, why are you standing here?" she said after slamming the door of yet another car. "Go! Go! Goodbye!" "No worries," I replied grimly, wrapping myself up in my scarf. "My, what a beautiful scarf you've got there!" said Julia. I made a movement which she rushed to interpret the wrong way: "What do you think you're playing at! That really does it! No way! No way! I know your sort. Out of boredom you decided to amuse yourself with the revolution, to play at noble feelings—but you burned your poor little fingers and started whining." "God forbid! I'm no revolutionary! I find the sight of a revolting peasant repulsive, and as far as materialism is concerned, it smells of garlic sausage to me." "You're a clear-cut case," said Julia, screwing up her eyes. "After the revolution we'll hang you over there, from that streetlight. Your legs will twitch to a different tune." She raised her head and gave the streetlight the once-over. "Do me a favor!" But she didn't hear me, she ran up to a car, smiled sweetly, twittered away, haggled—and slammed the door in disappointment. "They have no desire to go there, you see . . ." she said, curling her lip. "Why are you so bloodthirsty?" "I'm not bloodthirsty. But I'd take great pleasure in hanging you. And I'd hang you in such a way to ensure that you would really suffer before you died!" I couldn't contain myself and burst out laughing. "Tell you what," I suggested, still laughing, "before you hang me, why don't you let me be the one to take you to that Kuntsevo of yours?!"

I shall not describe how she mocked my suggestion, or how with even greater passion she kept waving her arm, throwing herself at every car. I wonder, Count, how things would have turned out if someone *had* agreed to take her to Kuntsevo. Surely that could have happened? Or can it really be that this element too had been agreed and rehearsed in advance? And what kind of operation has such universal dimensions! "I hope you're not planning to flirt with me?" she asked dryly. "You can rest easy on that account," I replied, just as dryly.

My house is five minutes' walk away. We walked quickly and in silence, like strangers, until she observed suddenly: "I know why you don't like Berdyaev. In the same way as a copy doesn't like its original." "I'm prepared to refute your opinion," I said, "but then you will think that it is my wounded pride speaking. Still, think what you like! Berdyaev gives top priority to the concept of freedom. It is more important to him than the concept of God! Freedom, you will agree, Julia, is the privilege of a strong personality. Whereas I would assign top priority to weakness—I preach A PHILOSOPHY OF WEAKNESS, although I don't have the slightest ambition to popularize it." "Thank God for that!" said Julia. "Otherwise we'd have had on our hands one of the vilest varieties of reactionary philosophy."

We approached the house. My shocking-red car, splattered with the mud of the last thaw, stood freezing in the wind. I oohed and aahed, rummaging through my pockets. I explained that my car keys were in the apartment. "I'll wait here," replied Julia. "For pity's sake! You're already chilled to the bone as it is." "It's not my custom to disturb at two in the morning the peaceful slumber of a family of complete strangers," Julia said haughtily. The delicate moment of truth had arrived. My wife Dorothea and both our blond girls were spending the night at her mother's. To say that *they* were home or that they were away were both equally impossible. On the way there, from the streetlight to Berdyaev, I had been preoccupied with this problem, but Julia's remark distracted me. "On second thoughts"—she stumbled over her words, but continued without shyness—"can I use your john?" "No need to ask!" I yelled, exulting inside and extolling the nihilism that had given her the unique chance to declare her need so daringly. "Naturally, by all means!"

A glass elevator took us smoothly up to my floor.

Switching on the light in the corridor, I placed my finger to my lips and, hinting at the presence of my family, said, "Shhhh!" Julia threw her fur coat into my hands and gave me a look of some bewilderment, as if she knew that there was no one there but us.

On tiptoe, trying not to catch the parquet floor with her heels, she set off for the bathroom which, in the revolutionary manner, she had called the john. You know, Count, at that minute she didn't look bad, yes, honest to God, not bad-looking at all, although you shouldn't think I was that enchanted. To be honest, even as she was creeping along the corridor I still didn't even know what to do with her next. You probably will ask what whim forced me to force her into this charade, this promenade on tiptoe. I shall explain. I was concerned about her well-being, I didn't want her to be a bundle of nerves from the moment she stepped over the threshold and, even as she was relieving herself, to be feverishly planning her escape. God forbid that she might have got it into her head to barricade herself in! I am in a certain sense a humanist, Count, yes, in a certain sense!

As soon as the door clicked shut, I ceased to be, and in my place in the hallway stood a large trembling EAR, just like the leaf of a banana tree, not missing a single sound coming from there. I heard the rustling of her dress as it was thrown up by an instinctive, captivating movement, like the blinking of eyelids; I heard a heel squeaking on the tiled floor as it tried to balance the body that had toppled forward, and I felt—even to the point of goose bumps—the coldness of the lavatory seat to which the dough of her flesh stuck slightly, and I *saw* how, resting her cheekbones on the palms of her hands, she pressed her fingers to her temple (a cheap little sapphire glinted for a second), and how her gaze did not start, in accord with some unwritten but fixed law, to wander in senseless concentration over the cherry-colored speckles on the tiles, seeking and tracing nonexistent patterns, but instead ascended through her bangs toward the light bulb on the wall—the light bulb which had been splattered with whitewash the last time we'd done home repairs, that we never got around to cleaning,

that will stay this way, will burn itself out and still be unwiped—
and then a taut, impatient stream hit the despised china and kept
on hitting, hitting the same spot until it

    start

      ed

        fad

          ing

            a

                way. It faded, revived, and then completely faded
away, like a dying swan; the last drops dripped with a dying fall
into the water, and this final drying up was accompanied by a
timid and wondrous sound which made my head positively spin
with delight!

But enough! Enough! How can one explain to you, Count,
guardian of the law and supporter of the state idea, the romantic
nuances of the naturalistic school? Oh, in the best-case scenario
you will make, squeamishly, a wry face! And only, perhaps, some
shrewd German, in some future, happier gyre, running his soapy
eyes over the papers of the Chancellery entrusted to your hands,
will stumble upon my secret raptures and will be just as secret a
sharer of these delights of mine, and, shaking his head sorrow-
fully over your notes in the margins—"Maniac! Psychopath!
Perversion!"—will be amazed at the spiritual coarseness of the an-
cien régime.

In short, I experienced real pleasure as I observed her tiptoe-
ing in the same old style, stealing along the corridor toward me, as
behind her the waters seethe and the plumbing moans, and this is
immensely dispiriting for her, turning her into the violator of the
peace of the night (as if she didn't know that we were alone); in
short, I waited for her terribly excited, in a fit of vertiginousness,
with blood throbbing and rushing loudly through my temples,
while she was creeping along the corridor toward me, and I was

still holding her fur coat in my hands, and with a sweet grimace she said: "I'm ready." Ah, that tinkle! It saved me from all sorts of beating about the bush, cups of tea, pontificating on the fate of poetry. It made me resolute. "Ready for what?" I asked derisively.

The moiré dress was creased. She tried to stand upright, but I stepped on her fingers with the full weight of my heavy boot. I stood over her, in my coat and fur hat, and my scarf was hanging down to my knees. "How dare you!" she hissed. "You stinking slut! You horny tart!" I said. "I hate you! I'll report this to the police!" "You need to be slapped up like a bitch!" "But surely you're against violence," prattled Julia. On her face the traces of my five fingers were appearing like a rash. Red sausagelike marks. I bent toward Julia and bit into her scarlet mouth. *How's that?* And what do you think, General? Did she bite? Clench her teeth? Have convulsions? With awesome passion she threw her arms around my neck.

Victory was mine to celebrate. The conquest that would follow, it seemed, would be uninteresting.

She got her breath back, took off her boots, etc., etc. I brought Julia some water, and we got talking. Everything about her was just as one would expect: thirty-something, an unloved, and, naturally, untalented husband who did not share her views, who loved neither music nor revolution nor poetry—"Just imagine, he doesn't even know who Kruglitsky is!"—she was at the very beginning of those death throes which still had about twenty years to rage, burning on her cheeks in fever, in trembling, in hysterics, exhausting the poor woman with a longing for a handful of sleeping pills, squeezing out of her, drop by drop, all the energies and pathetic feminine weaknesses, until she would finally wither, grow dark, give up the ghost as a woman—and a little dark withered old lady would enter God's church with a light step, in order to atone for the sins of an inflatable doll with her prayers, and with a frenzied question, "How is it possible to live like that? How?

How?". "Yes! Yes!" I said. "I don't know…" "This bourgeois word! this overindulgence! this stupidity! this cowardice!" "Yes! Yes!" I said. "How can one live?" "This savagery! this drunkenness! this filth! this coarseness!" "Yes! Yes!" I said. "An awful mess…" "And my little girl? What future awaits her?" "I have not one but two!" (She reached for her handbag to get a photograph; I boasted about my twins as well.) "Ah, what awaits THEM too? Why did I give birth to her? the country bumpkin! pen-pusher! office rat! get divorced? ha-ha!" Bitter laughter. "And what is one supposed to live on? walk the streets? prostitution? the power of money, the pauperization of the proletariat." I clicked my tongue in utter devastation. With pain in her face she scrutinized me. "You have TALENTED EYES!" I was embarrassed and pulled the ugliest face I could manage, pointing my eyes up toward the bridge of my nose. She didn't even smile. "I know, dear, I know. You also find it hard." "Oomp-pa-pa Oom-pa-pa!" I shouted, slapping my thighs, and made a suggestion, "Jules, darling, we'd be far better off having a screw!" Julia thought that things must be *really* hard for me, given that I was hiding behind such vulgar, blasphemous words, and whispered tenderly: "Not like that." I asked her for forgiveness. "You're not to blame," she said, shaking her head. "No? So who's to blame?" *"The system."* "Ah, of course!" I remembered. "You're a revolutionary after all!" "But you're also a revolutionary." "I'm no revolutionary!" I said morosely. "You're a revolutionary! Revolutionary! You're more of a revolutionary than the rest of them put together! You challenged your class!" She stroked my cheek. "I can just imagine how *they* hate you!" I shook my naked shoulders and uttered reluctantly, *"The feeling is mutual."*

How joyfully she clasped her hands! How genuine was her exultation! She tore the sheet off and set about covering me with kisses. "Mutual!" Julia kept yelling as she kissed me. "Mutual! Mutual! Mutual!"

Julia's shouts were getting louder and louder. I asked, "You wouldn't happen to write poetry, would you?" She yelled out: "Yes! yes!" I was delighted that my insight had been spot-on and joined her in yelling. You were shouting, and I was shouting. We shouted loud and long. I just couldn't stop shouting, although Julia was trying very hard. She was really, really trying, but the harder she tried, the more obvious became her lack of experience. I yelled as I thought with amazement about Fyodor. I had thought that he was a man of the world, but no, not on your life! I thought, "So much for Fyodor! And yet he'd been showing off and bragging, the alkie!" But at this point she cried out so loud that I forgot all about Fyodor and indeed couldn't think about anything else other than how on earth I might put an end to this awful yelling. We even grew hoarse: it was no longer a yell, but a hoarse yelping, but we nonetheless continued to yell with all our might, arguing with each other and trying to make points. I was yelling about how I was tired of yelling, but that I just couldn't stop, like a clockwork train on a child's toy railway; and she was yelling about how it was time for me to stop yelling, time to send everything to hell, to curse all this vanity and to set off for an encounter with the planets in my horoscope; and I was yelling sympathetically to her in reply, and in this way we finally ended up yelling that we would be faithful to each other till death us do part, and beyond the grave, during the time of disgraceful decay, and beyond that, right up to the Last Judgment, and after it too, *if we are granted this,* we shall also be inseparable. This wild feeling of eternity made me go into a fugue, and I yelled out my final scream, collapsing and fusing into an indivisible androgyne, and so, when I had crashed down and fused with Julia into an indivisible, philosophically unknowable but mystically accessible androgyne, I felt the unshavenness of a familiar cheek, as if I had become Julia and she had become me, Filonov, the namesake of the wonderful painter Filonov, a devoted cavalier in the eternal dance of love, she had become me, and I had become Julia: the beloved young girl of my sentimental bookkeeping, the vessel of passion and humbleness. I felt the un-shavenness of a familiar, forever beloved cheek, and I roused my-self. Oh, I knew for certain that Julia didn't belong to the foxy breed of bearded women displayed for money in fairground boots! Her skin was always smooth, just as I like it, and had a ripe-apricot-like quality. She had an apricotlike back and apricotlike shoulders, and delightful, as one finds only in the movies, apricot little cheeks, in reference to which I was saying:

"My darling, let me eat you!" and Julia answered, "Eat me! Eat me, Filonov!" and I had no choice but to eat her and take my fill, slowly. Ah, my God! No one on earth has ever loved anyone as pas-sionately as I loved Julia! I loved everything about her, absolutely everything: her intelligence, her apricotlike little cheeks, her soul, everything! I loved it when, having put her feet up on the couch, she would read to me her clumsy, but on the whole sweet, yes, very sweet poems. I loved her agitation when she received letters of rejection from various publishers: "Ma'am," Korolenko wrote to her, "in your compositions one finds at times lines both suc-cessful and completely civic in spirit, for example the line: 'And even a pig in a poke runs his race more swiftly!' but, ma'am, for the moment, as far as your literary craftsmanship is concerned, you still have far to go to be in the same league as Countess Ros-topchina." "He's right," Julia said in a crestfallen voice. "I'm no Countess Rostopchina." I comforted her as best I could, I cursed the liberal editors and the direction of the literary journals, I kissed her on her slender, undefended neck and said that in com-parison with her Rostopchina was ashes and dust, dear, nay, *trash*, and that for me her verses were the best in the world! With happy tears of gratitude she embraced me, and my heart stopped beating when I felt the most delicate aroma of her hair. I loved how she dressed, I loved the way she walked and talked, I loved her soft and gentle voice, I loved, I loved, I loved—she didn't even have any of that female hair on her upper lip, those unremovable female mustaches with which ladies struggle in vain with the help of hydrogen peroxide—everything about her was beautiful, she walked in beauty, but at this point, when for the millionth time we'd fused into an indivisible androgyne, I felt not only the unshavenness of a cheek, but worse! worse! I raised slightly my heavy, unwilling eyelids: ah-ha—a mustache! I closed my eyes and then raised my eyelids once more: a mustache! a mustache! The spell was not fading away. I briskly propped myself up on my elbows.

You will not believe me, Count, but I was genuinely taken aback: on the pillow, instead of my dear Julia, I discovered you, Count, in a state of utter *négligé*. Your military jacket with its high collar all torn, a creased and twisted lawn shirt, a grayish clump of hairs on your chest, long johns hanging off one boot like a disgraced military banner, and I, *Filonov*, drowning in some damn awful crème brûlée and having got myself into God knows what shit!

"Let me go, Filonov," you said in a weak voice. "Count, for pity's sake," I mumbled, hanging over you. "Kindly get up!" you shrieked. I leapt off the bed awkwardly. "Well, what can I say!" you said, wheezing as you got up in your turn. "Yes indeed, you gave me a really good seeing to, Filonov! Straight from the heart!" You picked up a gilt button that had come off, and squeezed it in your fist like a child. "Splendid job, there's no denying it, hmm, hmm! Where's your bathroom?" Unable to utter a word, I gestured toward the door. You dragged your pants over the parquet floor. The noise of rushing water came from the bathroom, but through that noise the spasms of weeping could be heard. I draped myself in my dressing gown and, dumb with amazement, discovered that several dried-up worms of vermicelli were stuck to the bottom of it. I started to peel them off in a businesslike manner. I was in a state of complete mental paralysis.

The water could still be heard. The thought suddenly crossed my mind that you had hanged yourself with a towel. I quietly scratched at the door. "Count!" I called. "Count!" "Get away from the door," was the cold reply.

I gave a start as you came out of the bathroom. As far as your uniform was concerned you looked, as before, somewhat creased and a few buttons short, but, nevertheless, you were saving face. You were managing to save a harsh face, one full of presence, I would even say, a fierce face, with pink swollen eyelids. In indignation you marched past me. In the hallway you turned to say: *"Well, Filonov! You've had it!"* and, hands trembling, you worked out the lock and departed, full of dignity. In the distance the iron door of the elevator rumbled.

Commander Sir! Have mercy.

So why are you taking so long? I am completely worn out. I stood for two weeks with my arms held high in the air. But in the end my arms went numb, and I understood: I had caught a glimpse of the imperial secret. Involuntarily, shattered by my passion for Julia, you had given it away.

Count, everything's clear, you and I are both victims! Victims of one and the same disgraceful scandal, a crying shame! Relax, Count, I shall keep the secret. I won't say a word to anyone... shhhhh! Even though Dorothea is crying, I keep silent. I have locked myself in and am not opening up. I don't even eat anything. Count, tell me, what about you? Do you dine? Only not a word about food! Count, I can honestly assure you, I'm not *in that department*!!! I always felt sick at the sight of public bathhouses and officers' clubs with their games of billiards. I don't know where Julia ends and you begin, where the *demarcation* lies, I am not trying to put you together, I make the sign of the cross in the in the air before me! Keep away from me! Keep away! Keep away!

If only I'd made the sign of the cross over you then!

Morning. I searched for Julia on the cornice.

Beware! I shall give you a bad name. You'll be forced to retire! This enlightened society of ours will split its sides laughing. Ha!-ha! Pants hanging from his boots. Filonov made sure the Count got his red box! Ha ha!

Where's Julia? Where are her apricot cheeks? Where is my only true love?

The Progressives won't understand, won't believe.

I'm locked up in the loony bin, behind seven seals. Hasn't happened yet, but it will.

You alone, Count, know the truth. You alone carry in your courageous heart the bitterness of our quid pro quo. So let us then forgive each other, and be reconciled.

Entre nous, stranger things have happened, haven't they? To tell the truth, I don't even need Julia. What is she to me? An inflatable doll. A nothing—or even less.

Dorothea! Girls! I love *you!*

I am not to blame that Julia tinkled so invitingly into the accursed faience. I accidentally overhead the divine sounds of the tambourine. Take Kruglitsky, he writes all sorts of poems, demanding changes, the rivers and buds, you be a bit harsher with him! But what is your bone with me?

Noli me tangere, Count! I exorcise you. *Noli me tangere!*

If anything happens, I shall yell! (Yell, then! Yell!) They'll hear me. Berdyaev, the one sent to Vologda, although I don't like him. Do you hear me, Berdyaev?

BERDYAEV: "I hear you! I hear you!"

So there, then! Did you hear the echo? Berdyaev is against equality and materialism. He was the one who taught me that materialism smells of cheap garlic sausage. We shall trap him and hang him from the nearest lamppost, Count! To hell with everyone and everything, except order. Don't knock at the door. That's Berdyaev trying to break it down. His tongue is well hung, he's dangerous, Count. Everything else is Kruglitsky's fault. He's the one who planted Julia on me. He whispered to me, "Take her." I took her. I led her through the dark copse at night. Kruglitsky is Lord of the Fleas. He betrayed me too.

I address you, Your Highness, with the following questions:

1. When did you become Julia?
2. What time was it?
3. When did Julia become you?
4. Who was Fyodor's lover: she or you?!

As a woman she doesn't suit me: she's a screamer. Secondly, I don't like her secret anatomy. But then again, what music! Just fancy, but shhhh! I gave my word. I am at your disposal, Count. Oh, Mama, what *were* you thinking of?

Attention, Filonov!

Long live Julia!

I salute you, Your Highness!

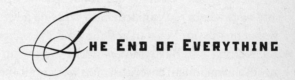HE END OF EVERYTHING

SKAFTYMOV WAS an early bird. Mornings saw him bursting with positive emotions. Even the monstrosities in the morning papers were no obstacle.

"Verunya!" Skaftymov shouted from the kitchen.

There was no answer.

"Verushenka!" Skaftymov called out again. "I'm pouring the coffee!" Skaftymov listened carefully. Blinova was keeping silent in the bathroom. Both husband and wife were writers and had started to be published even before their marriage and had even managed to achieve, well, not fame exactly, although why not put it like that, yes, fame, and so, having married, they kept their own surnames. It is true that the lovesick Skaftymov suggested that she should take the name of Blinov, but Blinova didn't agree, since she thought that this was not a very manly act. Skaftymov was slightly less complicated than Blinova, less conceptualist, perhaps.

He placed the cheese fritters on the plates, and knocked three times on the bathroom door.

"Vera Vasilevna, your breakfast is served!"

"I'm coming," replied Blinova, very quietly.

"The sun has got his hat on," said Skaftymov, his jowls quivering with joy, "hip hip hip hooray. The sun has got his hat on and he's coming out to play. Verun, hey, Verun, it's sixty-five degrees in the shade. Winter's gone, it's summer. Incredible."

Blinova came out of the bathroom. She was a large, tall woman and wore a light pink ankle-length dressing gown. She didn't look well. She was kind of wan and drawn.

"Verun," said Skaftymov, worried, "you seem to be a bit pale, my dear. You mustn't overdo it. You work until after midnight, and then you can't get to sleep for a long time."

"Do I stop you sleeping?" Blinova looked at him quickly.

"Heavens, no." Skaftymov waved his hands at her.

Over the breakfast he said, "When do you think the word 'jalopy' entered the Russian language?"

"What?" Blinova turned her absent gaze on her husband. "What 'jalopy'?"

"Just imagine, in nineteen hundred and forty-nine. At the very height of the notorious campaign against cosmopolitanism. Incredible."

Blinova shrugged her shoulders.

"And 'grapefruit'?" said Skaftymov.

"What do you mean, 'grapefruit'?"

"When did 'grapefruit' enter the language?"

"Well, in fact, Yura."

"What?" asked Skaftymov.

Blinova was silent

"No, it doesn't matter."

"Verunya," said Skaftymov. "You're just not yourself. I understand you perfectly. Before 1939, also, note, an interesting date, Russian didn't have a word for 'grapefruit.' "

"You know what you can do with that grapefruit of yours!" said Blinova viciously.

"Why?" said Skaftymov, confused.

"All these borrowings of yours," continued Blinova viciously, "have filled Russian heads with rubbish, just as nuts fill the stomach with rubbish."

"Verunya," said Skaftymov, amazed. "You've become conservative. You're being carried along on the wave of conservatism that's sweeping in from America."

Blinova loved America. She loved the starred and striped flag of that country, the proud name of President and all the rest, but she was silent now. She merely smiled a weak smile, screwed up her eyes and stayed silent.

At work Skaftymov gazed tensely out of the window. Suddenly he understood everything. She's pregnant. Of course, she is no longer thirty, and she's afraid, thought Skaftymov, she's afraid of giving birth, although I always wanted a second child, and now she doesn't know what to do, on the one hand, she also wants one, and on the other she's afraid, giving birth to Liza was too difficult for her, poor thing, she'd found out in the bathroom, she'd entered the bathroom with her head held high, as always, but came out shell-shocked, except that ... except that ... according to the dates ... that is ... the point is that this month ... we didn't actually ... she was working at night on her article, and then somehow ... well, in general ...

Skaftymov straightened up. She had some fatal disease. She'd discovered a tumor in the bathroom ... a lump on the breast. But that can be removed surgically. She will live. I don't care ... with a breast or without. I'd even love her if she had no arms ... I wonder how Venus of Milo's arms were positioned, Skaftymov suddenly thought. But what if the tumor is in another place? She has too many moles.

Skaftymov was inconsolable. He kept on phoning Blinova at work, but they told him that she'd gone to the library, and then that she'd asked for time off, that she wouldn't be in at all today. She has too many moles, grieved Skaftymov. How is it that this month we didn't even once... Vera... Skaftymov's ears burned with shame. There'll never be anyone like you again.

Blinova greeted him with a magnifying glass in her hand.

"Come here, you," said Blinova. "Come over here, Yura. I'd like to show you something."

Cancer. Everything died inside him. A magnifying glass! She wants to put on a brave front.

And yet it had been only yesterday that after supper she'd taken that very same magnifying glass in order to read aloud, before going to work on her article, a few pages of the monstrously tiny print of a beloved text. A photocopy of the book *The Spiritual Sermons and Meditations of Meister Eckehart* in a Russian translation from Middle High German. This was the very same Meister Eckehart from whom God never hid anything. Whosoever does a good deed not exclusively for the sake of God, but for other motives as well, apart from God, himself demeans the dignity of God. And when a man, in doing a good deed, also has in mind some other purpose, apart from God, then a part of his soul, no, that's not right, forgive me, it's difficult to make it out... a part of this deed he assigns to this other purpose, and in so doing thereby removes from God His part, and all such deeds bear no fruit and are needless.

"Incredible," said Skaftymov in amazement.

"You know, Yura," said Blinova, her eyes glinting beautifully. "Do you know what? I prefer to be in Hell with God rather than in the Kingdom of Heaven without Him."

"And what about me?" said Skaftymov in a childish huff. "What will happen to me?"

"Before I go to sleep I pray for you," said Blinova.

Skaftymov didn't know whether one was supposed to be grateful for that or not, looked into the book and said, "Do you know, Verusha, that only once before have we read a book with print as small as this?"

"I don't remember," said Blinova, deep in thought.

"How can you not remember?" smiled Skaftymov. "It even made my eyes sore. Khrushchev's memoirs!"

Blinova looked at him and burst out laughing.

"Heavens above! You're killing me. What a comparison."

And Skaftymov also burst into happy laughter. Blinova and Skaftymov had read a mass of various books and journals, but formerly they'd read more of all sorts of nonsense and less of the divine. In recent years they had grown spiritually to a significant degree.

"Take everything off!" ordered Blinova, fiddling with the magnifying glass.

"What?" exclaimed Skaftymov.

"It's very important," said Blinova. "You'll see for yourself in a second."

Perhaps I've got cancer too? flashed through Skaftymov's mind. His heart sank at this grim thought, and he obediently took off his clothes. Blinova switched on all the lamps in the bedroom. She went up to Skaftymov, squatted down and positioned the magnifying glass close to his groin. For three minutes she gazed uninterruptedly through the magnifying glass. Then she raised her eyes to him. Her pupils had narrowed in fear.

"Look for yourself," she said.

Skaftymov took the glass with a weak hand, sat down on the bed, bent over and froze.

An unexpected world opened up before his eyes. Between long black hairs he discovered a rich life. Small wingless creatures, somewhat resembling space apparatus as represented in science fiction novels, with little antennae protruding on all sides, were moving across a porous landscape. Some of them had burrowed half a body length into the bottom layer of skin and were filling up on dark liquid, others, sated, were resting in languor, a third category were intertwined for some purpose or other, either warfare or lovemaking, fourth, fifth, and sixth groups were incubating their eggs in holes, moving their feelers from time to time, and the remainder, the young, the dexterous, were climbing up the boughs, jumping from hair to hair, doing somersaults, playing tag. It was all one bubbling, bustling hive of activity. Skaftymov's procreative organ, which was abominably swollen in the magnifying glass, veins, vessels, protuberances and all, was also densely populated.

"Incredible!" said a stunned Skaftymov. "Simply incredible!"

"And there I was wondering why you were scratching yourself at night," said Blinova.

"Well, yes, you know, I did experience an itch, but I thought it was nerves. We're not living in the best of times."

"This morning," Blinova interrupted, "I discovered these creatures on me. Thank you."

"I thought it was due to nerves," babbled Skaftymov.

"After work I went to visit my friend. She opened my eyes."

Blinova's breath smelled of port.

"I didn't know," she said with a forced laugh, "that you have dealings with dissolute women."

The white Skaftymov, no trace of suntan, fell at her feet.

"Verusha, Verusha," he mumbled.

Blinova squeamishly shoved him aside with a pom-pommed, sea-green slipper.

"I didn't know that you fuck two-bit whores!"

Skaftymov stopped crawling over the parquet floor. Everything was swimming before his eyes: the dressing table, the slippers with the pom-poms, the mirror, the cross with Our Savior, the legs of the bed.

"But wait, but what..." Skaftymov just couldn't get his breath back.

"Don't you touch me, you dirty bastard!" yelped Blinova.

It seemed as if a whip were tearing off pieces of Skaftymov's flesh. Writhing in pain from the agony, Skaftymov lifted up two fingers.

"I swear," he said indistinctly, and his two fingers were trembling monstrously, "I swear by that which is most dear, I swear on Lizochka's health—"

"I don't believe you!" Blinova yelled right in his face.

Blinova bawled her eyes out in the bathroom until ten in the evening. At ten the phone rang. Blinova's worried mother was phoning from the dacha settlement "Crack of Dawn." Shouting because the line was poor, she said that their daughter, the twelve-year-old Lizochka, had suddenly for no reason gone down with a terrible attack of diarrhea. They were disconnected. Blinova pressed the receiver to her breast. Then she turned to Skaftymov:

"See. See what you've ... Monster."

She wanted to say or do something else, but suddenly a large grenade exploded inside Blinova's head. Her features became confused and shifted all over the place, her jaw dropped and she quietly crashed to the floor.

By the time Skaftymov had lugged Blinova to the bed, she, clearly, was no more.

The terrified parasites were running over Blinova's cooling body. Now they were doomed to an agonizing death from starvation. The sun had gone out. The blood had stopped and was now like aspic.

Skaftymov felt sorry for this nomadic tribe of bloodsuckers.

They are like gypsies, he thought, only a Hitler would dare offend these little ones.

Carefully he started to take the insects off the ends of Blinova's pubic hairs—they had ascended to the heights in an attempt to save themselves from the chill of the woman's stiffening body. He billeted some of them in his armpits, others he placed on his tongue and swallowed them very carefully. "It will be warm and cozy for them in there."

In the night he felt the parasites sucking zestily on the walls of his stomach and was delighted.

"They've settled in nicely!"

He wanted to preserve the insects in memory of Blinova.

But he did not significantly prolong the life of the wingless nomads. Toward morning he died from a terrible pain in the heart, but before he finally died he wheezed the borrowed loan word "jalopy" and simultaneously scratched himself furiously.

Their daughter Liza was sent to the Nakhimov Naval Institute. She will grow up and become a captain of a military vessel. She will avenge her parents.

Boldino Autumn

SISIN WAS staring out of the window in the half-empty train. The drear, dank autumnal Moscow countryside sailed by. It was a gray-ish day, but it wasn't raining. "If there is no God, then everything is permitted." Ivan Karamazov's thought suddenly flashed through Sisin's mind, and his affable face became pinched and mortified. "Everything is permitted! Everything!" thought Sisin furiously. "Who am I? Who? A man who has reached the age of thirty by pure luck. Every day I get up and walk through a minefield. A soldier from an unknown army, or to be more precise, without an army."

Two stinking, drunk, half-naked policemen were walking through the carriage.

"Pigs!" Sisin followed them with his eyes. "Titheads! Conts . . . stables. Well, what are you waiting for? Hey, come here! Come on, give me a good kicking! Come on, tear my clothes off, come on, fuck me up the ass!"

The policemen were gone. Sisin grinned limply and took his newspaper out of a wicker basket. He unfolded it, but as soon as he glanced at the headlines his hands started to shake and balls of fire flew before his eyes. He realized that he wouldn't be able to cope with reading today, and awkwardly stuffed the paper back into the basket. Five minutes later, when Sisin had come to his senses, a sepulchral mechanical voice hissed the name of Sisin's station.

He leapt onto the platform and took a deep breath of the clean pure forest air. "Heavens, how good, how marvelous!" He quickly made his way deep into the forest, which he'd known since childhood, devoting himself to the thing he liked most in life.

He knew every forest path and forest cutting here, every leaf and every blade of grass. Over there, a piece of half-rotten barbed wire, next to which two years ago Sisin had found six mushrooms, orange-cap boleti, all together, and had been photographed with them; over there, a nut tree with amazingly even branches, providing year in, year out the light springy staffs every mushroom collector needs. Sisin took out his knife and looked around. There is nothing finer than central Russia. These cherished mushroom glades! No peaks in the Caucasus, no Carpathians, no Guadeloupes can compare, no, Mother Russia, all is shit next to your inexplicable and immense sadness.

"Everything is shit." Sisin meditated as he squeezed the penknife in his hand. His brain started working overtime. Sisin snapped his knife shut, looked for a place to sit down and, not able to find a tree stump anywhere, sat down on his basket. Out of the wide old raincoat worn by keen mushroom collectors he pulled a thick notebook and a one-ruble Japanese ballpoint pen. The notebook was empty, pristine. Sisin hadn't put pen to paper since early spring. The white sheet seemed to have a hypnotic effect on Sisin, but Sisin overcame its evil spell and half an hour later he had already made his first entry in a beautiful swift hand:

The family is shit.

Approximately fifteen minutes after the first entry followed a second:

Women are shit.

Then he got down to serious thought, and thought until the wind started rustling in the yellow-red foliage of the aspens. Sisin raised his eyes, licked his lips and wrote down:

Parents are shit.

After about forty minutes he made, almost without a break, the following four entries:

The motherland is shit.

Lenin is shit.

Molly wally slapper is shit.

Life is shit.

Then, approximately an hour later:

Culture is shit.

Then, having waited another hour, he grasped his pen and started writing, but his hand was playing up, it wouldn't obey him. The entry ended up uneven, didn't come out easily:

Saint Augustine is shit.

After this he ate a piece of bread and sausage and drank coffee from his thermos. The sun broke from behind the storm clouds, and at the same time it started to drizzle. Sisin's face was dove-gray, clear and lucid. He poured the remains of the coffee into the grass and said happily:

Coffee is shit.

And once again he froze for about one and a half hours. It was obvious that he just couldn't bring himself to make the next entry, that he had already formulated the idea, but just couldn't bring himself to do it. Finally, in the encroaching twilight, he wrote carefully:

God is shit,

but immediately crossed out what he'd written in horror, thought again and changed his mind once more and firmly wrote below the words he'd erased:

God is the biggest shit of all!

and looked around in abandonment.

Twilight was falling.

LETTER TO MOTHER

DEAR MAMA,

Hurrah! Long live democracy! So we too, my dear, strange as it seems, have lived to see the day of radiant resurrection. Let us pray, then, quietly and joyfully, at our violated altars, for the health of the Liberator. May God be his help and guide! Amen! No retreat, no surrender!

My hands are literally itching with desire to write. That, indeed, is why I came here, to this unspeakably charming godforsaken hole, which vaguely reminded me of—oh, my childhood, travels with you in the yellow-blue express and Mademoiselle Grésillon, the walnut lover!—Switzerland, whose national flag, which fluttered at every railway halt, brings to life the smells of the pharmacy, of menthol and whooping cough. The hills, the ravines, the firs, the snow—not a sound! not a sound!—and in the woods a small miracle of nature: a spring that never freezes over, a silent orchestra of pulsating jets of water. It's no wonder the people named it "The Snowmaiden's Heart." In the mornings, having awakened from sleep, I gaze through the frosty lace and

see the luminary of freedom rising slowly over the northern lati-
tudes. Everything is fine, except that it's very cold—no point in
even thinking about skiing, I don't want to get frostbite. The
poverty of the half-abandoned villages—where for firewood the
women cut up the shells of their neighbors' cottages, which stand
with their windows like empty eye sockets—makes a very strong
impression on my sensitive nerves, but progress wins out, and
you wouldn't have recognized the men, Mummy dearest, they've
changed so much—they shave their beards and listen to Radio
Luxembourg.

The train journey passed, thanks to your prayers, without any
particular adventures, if one does not count, I suppose, that as we
were approaching Kineshma our train came under White artillery
fire, as a result of which the last three third-class carriages suffered severe collateral damage, having been blown to bits. And after that they still have the nerve, the vandals, to mouth off about
civilization!

No, honest to God, I can't help it, I shall write about it after all!
Here, in the native land of the national Russian Euripides, I shall
write in plain terms, without any fancy, highfalutin phrase-
mongering, the whole artistic truth about the vileness of our life.
My book, Mother, will be of use to the people.

At a point where a ferry crosses the Volga I got into conversation with the commander of a barrage detachment. He was about
thirty-five years old, he has become terribly thin, his face twitched
nervously, he gave me prickly looks, but his eyes, on the whole,
were kind, tender even. By his reckoning a third of the population
were for us, a third were against us and the remainder were a
swamp, pig-ignorant. The ferry drew up alongside. We embraced
and parted. The ferry made its way through a narrow, crooked
path of water which steamed through the middle of the ice. It was
a comfortable vessel, first brought into service last year. The

people here all stress the vowel "o," pronounce their "ch" as "ts" and steal left right and center. A young lady from Moscow, warming herself in the hold of the river giant, flashed her eyes at me. "Nice-looking," I thought reluctantly.

Zotov is also on our side, but he's suffering because of the disappearance of vodka. He says that unless there's a change of policy he'll go over to the other side. He told of how in a garrison town near Vladimir one major, his distant relative, saw with his own eyes, in a manufactured goods store, the following sign:

EAU-DE-COLOGNE COSTING LESS THAN THREE RUBLES IS ON SALE AFTER 2 PM.

I doubted the existence of such a major.

There are many rumors. In the canteen we exchange information greedily. The food is bearable, I hardly get the trots at all, and once, before the New Year, on the order of the deputy political officer, meat was on the menu. There's talk about an amnesty, a new calendar, that Russian will henceforth be written in Latin letters and that soon it will once again be permissible to wear round hats with ribbons. Mama, as soon as this is permitted, send me one without fail. Also send me some money, not less than eight thousand rubles, a box of Havana cigars (there's hardly anything to smoke here, the cigarettes—as in Orwell's novel, remember?— well, you can't hold them upright, the tobacco just runs out of them!) and a small amount of pressed caviar. I shall use the money to buy a new car painted in some trendy shade, since I have decided to stay in this local Palestine until the month of May, when I shall finish my book. I probably won't get to Paris this year, I want to take part in the renaissance myself. I am much preoccupied with the role of literature in a transitional period. It is important to get as mobilized as possible. Was Dostoevsky right when he responded to social upheaval with metaphysical doubts concerning human beauty? Are our pitiful wannabe members of the *Signposts* group right? On the other hand, art, having realized that it is a system of devices, has painted itself into a corner, which is where, like a naughty schoolboy, it will meet the arrival of the third millennium. And so, a bit less whining and resignation! Down with the Russian intelligentsia, Mummy! How are your alpine violets in the kitchen? In bloom? What of the breadfruit tree? The leaves haven't fallen off? You make sure you look after yourself. I have read an interesting book, one of the banned ones. I recommend it. Its plot might seem a bit silly to you, but the whole point is to be found in the lyrical digressions. A certain *kulak* travels from village to village and offers local landowners an illegal deal. From an economic point of view the deal is nonsense, however, once you've forced your way through all this rubbish you can't help feeling respect for an author who has revealed the mechanism for the establishment of capitalism in Russia. The book is sharp, useful, I would even say timely, though a bit of a mixed bag.

Zotov has just arrived this very minute, panting from happiness: "Herzen! Herzen!" he shouts, "is coming back. Starting tomorrow *The Bell* will be on sale!" Forget it, Zotov, cool down. I don't believe it, I don't believe it, I don't believe it!

Mummy, I was right: he's not returning.

But then again at least they now allow scores to be brought in from abroad. Anybody's notes, even Wagner's. Isn't it a miracle!

"Let's go to Pokrovskoe," said Zotov, "take a look at the church and buy some wine for good measure."

It was a long way. We were frozen to the bone. Out of nowhere we see, on a high bald hill, a high white bell tower. We even mouthed an astonished "Ah!" We enter the church: singing can be heard, candles burn, banners, gold, many well-dressed people. We squeeze our way forward. The frescoes, naturally, haven't survived. The wind. Broken bricks. Crows. A wedding. We move closer. The bridegroom is a short man wearing the full dress uniform of an officer in the air force.

"Let's leave," said Zotov, getting cold feet.

A scar above his eyebrow. A childlike smile. Bad omens. "'The world's great page begins anew,'" mumbled Zotov, as he scrutinized a portrait of a cosmonaut in the tiny cubbyhole belonging to a school's boiler man. On the way back, dispirited, we had happened to see the light in the window and decided to drop in. The function of the boiler man, I argue, is far more stable in the morphology of Russian mythology than the function of, let us say, group sex. In any event, either/or. Either a time out of joint, a period of utter stagnation *or,* at the end of the day, a bloodbath. "That's the last thing we want," responded Zotov. "Mustn't spoil the winter holidays, after all."

"Have you got any home brew, old man?" asked Zotov, unable to restrain himself any longer.

"It's shameful to drink in such an epoch!" the boiler man reproached him.

We exchanged glances. It seemed to us the old man's face held an intelligence which was not from these parts.

"Where are you from, old man?" I inquired, in my accustomed role of smart aleck.

"From the town of Aleksandrov," answered the old man unwillingly.

"Hey, my good chap." Zotov waved at him. "You're not by any chance..." My friend hesitated, searching in vain for the right words.

"Spot-on." The boiler man handed us a cup of very strong tea and gave a bitter smile in response to the unspoken question. "For possession of the Koran."

"What do you mean, the Koran?" I yelled. "You some sort of Muslim or what?"

"No more than you are!" he said angrily.

"No worries, old chap," Zotov calmed him down, gulping his tea. "We'll replace the requisitioning of farm produce with tax in kind, eliminate private property, give the government's official black cars to local doctors, and then we'll really begin to live!"

"But will the rural worker want the land now?" doubted the old man. "He's grown terribly unused to it. Oh, somehow I don't believe in these Commissar changes of yours," said the old man, shaking his head.

"Well, what do you expect from him? A real shit!" Zotov said with a contemptuous shrug of his shoulders on leaving the hospitable lair of the renegade.

But alongside this sort of thing these regions also provide one with cases of genuine heroism. I shall give you a simple example, Mama. The guide Valentin, a cultured young chap with puffy lips, anticipating Sasha Matrosov's Second World War exploit where he threw himself at the enemy gun emplacement, put his life on the line to protect the archive of the great dramatist from a furious crowd. A grateful People's Commissar, with a physical appearance that is just the ticket for a life-loving anti-Semite, immediately sent to the place where the incident occurred a congratulatory telegram, a punitive detachment and three carts for transporting the manuscripts to Moscow. The repentant savages, some of whom had been flogged in the stables, carried out of the manor house sacks full of papers and with a mean assiduity loaded them onto the carts under the watchful gaze of special advisers. At noon the horses were harnessed, and in the chiaroscuro of the July day the convoy set off on its journey to the distant southwest. It was last seen near Ivanovo. Valentin had grown old, become flabby, gone to seed. But even now, some sixty-odd years later, this cultural worker, honored by the state, paralyzed, hears at night the squeak of the wheels and the peaceful songs of the armed guards. He told Zotov and me that there is still hope and that by the year 2000 the convoy should reach Moscow.

"Surely that deserves a drink?" suggested Zotov encouragingly, but the paralyzed fanatic turned out to be insolvent in this matter. Tossed and torn by the contradictions of a transitional period, we rushed to Kineshma. In thirty degrees below, wrapped in scarfs, our eyelashes sticking together in the frost, we crossed the ice of the endlessly wide Volga, discovered a restaurant and, having shed our fur coats, ordered champagne. We were immediately refused champagne, but after lengthy negotiations a cheery waitress with a provincial face that had seen everything brought us some Moldavian cognac in teacups on saucers. We pretended to have suddenly developed a great passion for tea. The evening passed by unnoticed. Suddenly the sounds of a march burst into the restaurant from the street outside. With smiles of joy Zotov and I rushed out to look. Columns of workers marched in orderly fashion in the darkness. They were either burying Comrade Bauman or else celebrating Mayday.

"The Proletariat." Zotov was touched. "You know, Viktor, it's a grand thing!"

I decided that I would spend New Year's Eve at the sacred grave. The road to the cemetery lay through the forest. I must confess that I was a bit afraid of wolves, the more so since the local guide Valentin had just the other day encountered some on the trash heap in his yard. My fears, Mama, turned out not to be completely groundless. No sooner had I crossed a ravine overgrown with conifers via a small wooden bridge when two of these predators blocked my path, their eyes red and watering. "How unjust and ironic to perish at the jaws of wolves at the very moment when things have taken a turn for the better!" was the disturbing thought that flashed through my mind. However, the beasts were in no rush. They could hardly stand on their trembling legs; there was more entreaty than ill will in their eyes. With a certain relief I shared my supply of biscuits with them. They threw themselves greedily on the food, and then trailed after me for a long time, wagging their tails behind them.

A new trial awaited me at the dramatist's grave. Within the enclosure of the old country churchyard, which was illuminated from various angles by theater floodlights, a whimsical combination of tourism and mysticism was manifesting itself. A celebration of awe and horror filled my body. The heavens seemed swollen by an abundance of stars ... A male figure detached itself from the gravestone of the classic author and turned sharply toward me, shaggy fur hat in hand. A bald head and rather monstrous mug of some sort of mutant, an overgrown beard, folds of a black sheepskin coat fluttering in the breeze. "Erofeyev!" yelled out the mutant in an unpleasantly loud voice. "Is that you or not?" "Yes, well, it's me," I replied sullenly and without much enthusiasm. Without further words he rushed to embrace me. It was none other than the sculptor Zotov, my acquaintance from Moscow and the author of the well-known monument to Ivan Susanin which had been erected at the burial place of the martyr. It turned out that Zotov was in a state of deep depression. Thanks to détente and the Thaw he had in one fell swoop lost faith in everything. The last ethical props had rotted right through, and he stood there in the middle of the cemetery completely lost.

"Old mate!" proclaimed Zotov. "There's fine revolution here! The dead have spoken from underground, and a great purge of the graves of the *nomenklatura* is under way."

"No need to yell!" I said, checking on all sides from force of habit. "Do you really think that everything is permitted?"

"Unfortunately, most things are," sighed Zotov. "All my life I've been trampled underfoot, persecuted and suffered attempts on my life. In the end I got used to it and even became a bit proud of it. And now they've started praising me madly and showing me, like a performing chimp, on television."

"That won't last long," I said. "There's still time for them to spit into your ugly mug."

"Thanks for that, you're a true friend," answered Zotov, deeply moved. "You know what, mate?" The artist grew sad once again. "I've come to the conclusion that Susanin never existed."

"So who tricked the Poles, then?"

"Ah, well, but perhaps there weren't any Poles either," retorted Zotov, screwing up his eyes. "There was no one. No one!" he yelled suddenly and showed me, having unclenched his fist, an absolutely empty hand.

"So I suppose Suvorov didn't exist either, then?" I yelled in reply, feeling myself being borne along on a warm wave of patriotism. Do you know, dearest Mama, Zotov grew pensive. He took my arm in silence, and we hurried off to celebrate the New Year. On the way he told me how in Revolutionary Moscow the idea of erecting a common monument to all the victims of our nation's history is gathering momentum. Soon they'll announce that a competition is to be held to find the best design.

"At long last!" I said, exultant.

In the middle of the forest we kissed passionately. In the hall the television was blasting out rock music. I was overcome with emotion at all the innovations. I rushed to dance with all the girls in turn. It was like simultaneous chess. Large drops of sweat flowed down my grayish, charming face. The darkness was conducive to brief intimate encounters and unforeseen separations. Some young man resembling a cherub carefully protected me from any permanent relationships. I believe that all the girls were engaged in theater studies. I believe that I asked each one of them, with a sociological fervor which I don't fully understand myself, whether she used an IUD. At some time toward morning I got the impression that I was about to get the shit kicked out of me. But instead of this I was offered some incredibly strong home brew, and immediately several young men who resembled cherubs, crowding around me, started an animated conversation on various common issues, with extensive use of obscene language. I remember trying to ram something home to them hotly and at great length. When I came to the next day it was already after two in the afternoon, and I was in an unfamiliar single hotel room, on an ascetic bed, with a soundly sleeping woman in my embrace. After taking a good look at this unfamiliar face I could make out in it the strong-willed features of an Amazon, but it very soon became evident that the Amazon was quite probably old enough to be my mother. I stopped embracing her and examined her in greater detail. She lay there in a modest terry-toweling pajama of a heavy lilac color and smelled subtly of sweat, tobacco and perfume. I too was dressed any old how and was wearing green socks which came right up to my knees. I quickly felt myself: I couldn't make head or tail of anything. I made a delicate attempt to sneak away. The bed groaned furiously. The woman turned toward me slowly and stretched out her arm. I froze. The hand passed me by and grabbed a packet of Java cigarettes.

"Happy New Year!" she said in a low voice, after blowing out a whole cloud of smoke.

"Happy New Year," I replied cautiously.

"Don't be afraid." She gave a penetrating smile. "I won't torment you any more."

"Oh, it's nothing." I shrugged my shoulders and, despite my hangover, went pink from embarrassment.

"Well, of course it's nothing to you," she suddenly said despondently, which made her seem even older.

At that point I started smoking too.

"When I'm drunk—" I started to say in my defense.

"I must have had something to drink as well, I think," she interrupted me. "Otherwise I never would have told you the story of my life. Then again, it's your own fault. You were so skillful at asking the right questions."

"Really?" I couldn't help blurting out.

"Viktor!" It was her turn to blurt something out. "I even told you about Zhorzh. I've never in my life told anyone that ridiculous story, and never will. Oh, why, why did I confide in you? I'll never forgive myself. The fate of my children, nay, the fate of mankind itself depends on that secret."

"Calm down," I said weakly.

"Would you like an orange? I'll just peel one." With her long fingernails she started to tear away the peel. Then she tried one segment herself. "Why do they all taste of soap? Why"—suddenly there was steel in her voice—"does the Ministry of Foreign Trade deliberately import such crap?!"

"What did you say?" A terrible possibility had suddenly struck me. "You . . . you . . . who are you?! Surely, you're not . . . ?!"

"Quiet, fool!" she hissed at me. "I'm completely incognito here."

Zotov was sleeping in my hotel room in his clothes, on the rug, next to the empty bed.

"Zotov!" I quietly started to howl. "Zotov, be a dear, save me!"

Completely disfigured by his hangover, Zotov heard out my story gloomily.

"Well, you've been asking for it." In his anger his spit even landed on his own cheek. "It damn well serves you right, you idiot. Well, say you hope you can still be friends or something."

Being an honorable enough man, I was planning to follow his advice, but on the next day her husband turned up at her side, suddenly thrown up on the dust heap of history, a most repulsive creep, and she too is the foulest creature imaginable, and let them go to hell! To hell! And what about us? We shall build a new world on these foundations, and we who were naught, we shall be all!

THREE MEETINGS

SHE WAS born in a leap year, a year when the spirit of disturbance and change grabbed nature by the neck, when earthquakes drove the waters of the Mississippi upstream, and the river ran back to its sources as fast as a galloping horse, destroying forests in its path; when a comet with two tails burst through the sleepy night skies, and the squirrels, hundreds of thousands of simple red creatures, left their native habitat for the South, and they all drowned, every last one, lacking as they did the strength to swim across anything. Since that time nearly twenty years had passed, Stalin had been declared an enemy of the people and Stalin's Little Helper Kalinin had suffered a name change from Father of the Soviet House to All-Soviet bastard of the first order.

And then it was that he wrote her a letter, saying:

Dear Olympia,
forgive me for writing. The Russian word has grown weak and given up the ghost. It is so sick and tired that I'm embarrassed to resort to its services. It is like a stallion that has fallen to his

*knees. A whip! A whip is called for! The only whip we have is
laughter. Have a laugh, sons of bitches, at the torments of a
fallen word. I'll tell you more when we meet. I kiss your curls.
I switch to English,*

Your Mayakovsky.

PS *Do you understand, sweetie, why Mayakovsky? That's good.
Goodbye once more,*

completely yours, Mayakovsky.

No, I'm no Mayakovsky! Don't believe it. Don't believe, don't be
afraid, don't ask. Lord, what is happening? The Russian word,
Lord, is on its last breath!

Olympia F. grew up without a father, in an abnormal situation.
Before her daughter's eyes Olympia's mother ate tinned pineapple
compote with boyfriends, drank bittersweet Baltic liqueurs. The
young girl quickly acquired a taste for the bohemian way of life and
diverse perversions. Her school friends tell of how at the age of
seven she learned to examine her future breasts in the mirror.

Olympia shook her black mane and said languorously, "OK, so
sue me."

I felt like kicking some life into her. Perhaps that's the reason
why I took her with me, offered her to come. She didn't spend
much time thinking it over. She agreed right away.

"What's your opinion of socialism?"

She thought hard.

"I don't know what it is."

This was such a natural response, it possessed such chubby-
cheeked, provincial languor! I embraced her. She backed off
slightly and looked at me in amazement, inviting me to explain
myself. The tale that emerged was difficult to digest, not very tasty,
not properly reheated, my tale, told a hundred times before.

"I'm forty years old." Thus I began my story.

The room was silent.

"Forty years—that's the end of the line!" I added, after a short silence, painfully aware of my old, wrinkled, tortoiselike face, the face I deserved, the face for which from now on I bore the whole weight of responsibility, without the right of reply or replay. I plodded through my story as if up to my knees in water, hardly able to move my dry tongue:

"When I was a student."

I almost burst out crying from self-pity and couldn't continue for perhaps ten minutes. I took out my handkerchief, blew my nose, wiped my forehead covered in beads of cold sweat. She sat opposite me, motionless.

"When I was a student I had the good fortune to spend some time in Paris. Of course," I interrupted myself, "you can imagine how much Paris has changed since then."

No motion, no sign of life.

"Wake up, asshole!" I yelled at her. "Take up aerobics, or maybe the butterfly, damn you!"

"As you wish," said Olympia humbly. I saw her powerful body in my mind's eye, her shoulders emerging from the swimming pool waters and then submerging again, sending splashes all around. On her face—repulsive swimming goggles. The broad sweep of her giant arms. This vision made me go weak in the knees, unable to utter a word. This was our third meeting.

The first time I'd fed her with sturgeon à la Moscow. She ate with such appetite that I looked at her and thought, trying to suppress feelings of tenderness and revulsion, "She must be hungry." As a result I downed a load of sweet, cloying champagne, as I dealt with this Siberian Rastignac clad in slippery black snaky trousers.

"Among the young people in our town stupidity was positively encouraged," said Olympia, when she had polished off the sturgeon.

"That's amusing," was my response.

"Listen, can I ask you a question of the night? Do you believe in the powers of darkness?"

"What about you?"

Her eyes filled with moisture and grew red. "One artist from Anapa said that I ought to be taken to Red Square to the Lobnoe Mesto and have my head cut off there. What did he have in mind?"

I explained by means of a straightforward gesture. Her whole body started shaking, and it took me some time to realize that this was her way of laughing.

"I have a crack in the top of my skull," I said and came over all mysterious. "Energy comes out of it with a hiss. Take a listen!" She listened carefully.

"True, there *is* something hissing there," she said, but without much certainty in her voice.

"This sort of crack opens up when you reach forty," I explained. "Now it's too late to kiss it better, fill it in or put it back together again. This crack"—I livened up—"is proof of the fact that there is not just a body, but also something else as well. You understand, if victory is a defeat that didn't work out, then ..."

Now, I see, it is her turn to go weak at the knees.

The crack in the top of my skull is an anteroom to faith, it is, to put it more precisely, an anticipation of faith, because, since, inasmuch as, for, well, I don't know whether there are buffalo in Siberia, perhaps there aren't, but Olympia, undoubtedly, is precisely a buffalo, a Siberian buffalo—and if you shove your hand inside her tights you will find she has a cosmodrome there, it's the Boikonur launching site for rockets, with all its assets and equipment—and what sort of Olympia are you, then?

A forty-year-old man, with a metaphysical rent, finds the purse in his pocket weighs as heavy as a Lüger.

So there you are. The word is tired, and balls are sagging. The body *qua* body is becoming, if not more insignificant, then at least not completely corresponding to what it should be. It is hard to grasp the meaning of another's leg *qua* leg, women seem more liquid, in other words, the beginning of the inevitable separation is staring you in the face. You look at your hands—they'll soon rot. You feel sorry for them. You feel sorry for yourself.

The only thing you don't feel sorry for is this nasturtium reared on Siberian manure.

The game is simple. One—to the bar. That's number one.

Let's count to three.

You think tenderly, trying to repress nausea, "She must be hungry."

But she would strangle her own mother to avoid returning to Chita-Chelyabinsk, or—what are those other big cities of theirs called?—Cheboksary.

A beauty, tundra, Siberian fire, drinking yogurt, apples, a dietetic fainting fit.

The crack—it is the proof, it is the proof that the fourth dimension—the dimension of death—promises deliverance, inasmuch as, for, since.

I pay and I cry. I pay and I cry. I pay with my prematurely withered skin, the deep wrinkles near my mouth, my rotten teeth, with eyes that understand everything, with my sick arm, suspected of suffering from some trendy incurable disease.

Olympia looks up at me and licks her lips anxiously.

My car is becoming a four-dimensional point, and Olympia agrees with such elation that even I feel uneasy.

"Bear in mind that the crowd will tear us to pieces!"

"Let them."

And they did. But listen further. I pay with the swollen veins on my legs, the hairs sticking out of my ears and nose, my family, my worn underwear, that very same Paris.

"In Paris I went to the Museum of Contemporary Art. There was no Beaubourg there at the time. I've seen the Beaubourg only in photographs."

"Wake up, asshole!" she whispers almost affectionately.

We keep on falling into hibernation. At night she dreams of cops escorting her to the Kazan railway station in Moscow, each one taking turns to cop a hold of her bosom and pulling wedding rings out from there.

"OK, then," I continue my meager story, "in the museum, amid a multitude of different pictures, in an empty hall—culture's not appreciated much there—I see several Lenins hovering over a piano. Oh, well, there are also ants, expectation and all other sorts of metaphysics. It is Dali. A couple of Americans stop alongside me. Also students. Embracing, they look at Dali." I add, suspiciously, "Do you know Dali?"

She hesitates. In the autumn she had failed the entrance exams somewhere. She hesitates. Her face betrays a hard, cunning struggle to think how to dodge the question.

"Well, you're a one!" I say in horror. "You ignorant cow!"

"I love Vrubel," answers Olympia proudly. "He's a genius of the inexpressible."

The game is simple. Man is simple. Taxi. Slip a tenner. Now we're in fucking business!

The second time *they* kidnap me, take me up in an elevator to the top floor of the Belgrade Hotel and there they lock me in an empty, neat room; outside, the other side of the window, is the Moscow summer. Our general will meet with you in a minute. Half an hour passes. An hour. I touch the door. It's locked. Any minute they'll pipe in some gas, plant some incriminating dollars, throw me out of the window, directly into the summer.

"Daydreaming is a beautiful word," interjected Olympia.

A French kiss—a full mouth of plasticine. A mistake. The general didn't come after all. Her Moscow uncle kicked her out of the house.

"Moscow," said Olympia obscurely, "is the capital of anything you like, but never of the USSR. At what age did you start masturbating?"

"Forty."

I freeze, a stupid smile on my face. I don't want to repeat myself, but at forty years of age the body becomes more liquid, and everything—déjà vu, déjà vu...I freeze, a stupid smile on my face.

"My mother caught me when I was eleven. She said, 'Stop it, or else you'll grow a third leg.' I was scared, of course, at first, and then, OK, nothing grew there. I was in the Mausoleum yesterday."

"And how was it?"

"They should have buried him."

"That's what Krupskaya thought too."

"I should say so!" Pity for the widow of the leader of the workers of the world drove Olympia to tears. "Just imagine what it must have been like for her to visit him!"

"It's all Stalin's fault," I said, looking down. It turned out Olympia had a simple Siberian surname: Fyodorova.

"OK, then, tundra, how are you going to repay me for my kindness?" I asked Fyodorova, having drunk an unexpectedly large amount.

"I shall become your muse," she suggested modestly.

"You're already Olympia as it is," I said.

It's objectification time. They are bearing your own body to you, from head to toe, and they place you on the table, like on a counter. You can squeeze, you can pinch, you can touch, but you can't choose or swap. You are yourself: no more, no less. One and the same. And here it is: I pay with the crack at the top of my skull—the dearest thing of all—and have no regrets.

There's such a notion as the literary intelligentsia. It was invented by martyrs: Siberian political prisoners.

"No, you're not a woman," I say to Olympia. "No, you're a buffalo."

She looks at me, unmasked, scared, caught red-handed.

"Go away," I say to her.

"Go back to Mommy," I say to Olympia. "There's nothing here for you."

"Help me," asks Olympia and clings to me, stretching her Ingres neck.

And so it's her again. She stands gloomily next to the Metro station, in a fancy gray woolen overcoat, tailor-made and paid for by the man who keeps her, who does not please her in any way other than by the fact that he keeps her.

On this point the poet Joseph Brodsky and I part company. A forty-year-old man does not have gratitude gushing from his mouth. The magic of the figure "forty" is not in keeping, ontologically speaking, with gratitude. The fact that Brodsky didn't understand this both disturbs and gladdens me, because, insomuch as, and so he gets into his rusty old banger—which won't pass its next inspection in the spring, that's for sure, it'll be a case of having to gather some money together, get into debt, get one's act together, be lent some money—he starts his trusty engine, he's somewhat agitated, he pulls on his Czech driving gloves, this gesture is pregnant with unnecessary meanings and connotations of a time twenty years ago, the Triumphal Arch in Moscow flies past, in which there isn't a smidgen of triumph, the road leads to the center of life. I stop outside the shop opposite the block where Andropov and Brezhnev had lived as good neighbors. On this occasion she's in a white jacket, sporty, her eyes are burning, and she's without a fur hat, although it's snowing, and the setting sun is breaking through the snow, the sun of our defeat that didn't work out.

"I bought some grapes from some darkies at the market. Want some?"

We eat the grapes, spitting the seeds through the windows. Now it's declaration time.

"I shall love you like my own mommy," declares Olympia.

"That's wonderful," I say, spitting out of the window.

"What about you?"

"And I'll love you like my mommy too. Do you want a smoke?"

"Yes."

We light up and watch the Sunday snow falling merrily.

"So, shall we go?" I say, stubbing out the cigarette butt in the ashtray.

We're on the road. We drive through the tunnel, onto the bridge. We haven't got far to go. I brake by the Arbat Restaurant and turn sharply onto the pavement. This is my bowling alley: from this point to the large screen at the other end, the screen on which our Soviet Mickey Mouse is waving his welcoming hands at us. Forward!

At first no one understood anything. In fact, they didn't understand anything at all from first to last.

That was better both for us and for them. I moved into lower gear and we roared off. The first one to end up under our wheels was a respectable-looking gent in his Sunday best, in glasses and an astrakhan hat, an exceptionally worthy fellow; and then we hit a pair of lovers, and they flew off in different directions, in order to very soon after fly off forever; and then they all paused in confusion before they began running away, but they didn't go in the directions they should have, so it was easy to knock them over: grannies, grandpas, aunties and uncles.

They flattened themselves against the storefronts, and we flattened them into a pile next to the storefronts; they ran toward the trees, and we caught up with some of them there, those who had fallen, caught up in the folds of their nasty dark overcoats. It was particular fun toying with the young men, I suddenly felt that I was growing younger myself.

"Thirteen," counted Olympia. "Fourteen! Fifteen!"

I was growing younger. I suddenly realized that I was doing something. Something real. This is my work. I'd never worked as well as this before.

"Twenty!" shouted Olympia. The car leaped and jumped over the bodies. It seemed as if they were made of rubber.

"Don't miss that prick!" laughed Olympia. "Hurrah! Or that cunt!"

"At last you're speaking normally!" I said, overjoyed. "Fancy that!"

"Twenty-six!"

"A revolutionary number," I noted. "Forgive me, baby!" I said to a fat maiden. We squashed her and rushed on further. I saw a cop, who had swiftly thrown aside his felt boots and, wearing only socks on his feet, was dashing to head us off. Come here! I turned around, knocked him off his feet, he flew into a shop window full of dummies, bathing in an ocean spray of glass. There is no time! Forward!

"Thirty!" exulted Olympia.

It's as if they were fleeing machine-gun fire. As if it were the dispersal of the demonstration, in summer, in Petrograd, in July 1917, love of which they've had drummed into them from childhood. A machine gun fired from the roof. Mickey Mouse was ahead of us! Here's another youth—probably a technical school pupil, a rock fan, come on over, let's have a song and dance!

Teeth, beads and whole jawbones were hanging on the front of the car. And shreds of clothes. A special bonus in the form of a woman, swimming, as if in an aquarium, past the windshield with a full-frontal wound and goggled-eyed. We were just about level with the Jupiter shop.

Olympia switched on the tape recorder. A nice surprise! "The Waves of the Amur" waltz. And there's a nice-looking bit of skirt. "Look, Olympia, look and learn: that's city titty for you."

"Thirty-eight."

"Forty!"

"We've fulfilled the plan. Now it's time to earn our bonuses!"

I clipped with my left headlight a speedy chap carrying a plastic bag. A wave of milk hit us. The moisture of life.

"You ace driver!"

"Don't distract me!" I slapped her superstitiously on her knee.

"I won't say another word. Forty-six! Oh, and that one as well."

We squash a short-assed soldier. We push through toward the grocery store. There's a pile of people there. They thought: TV, some program, live transmission. And with these thoughts they fly to a better world. No sight or sound of the Keystone Kops. Where have they got to?

The crowd is in full flood. A traveling circus come to pay you a visit. On wheels. A mountain of bodies.

"Fifty-four."

"There'll be loads of wounded," I say.

"And that cunt. Oh, pretty please?"

She wants to get the tarts more, but I want to pick off the blokes. A subject for psychoanalysis.

No, I have nothing against the sluts either. All those who are slimmer, taller, prettier, come to me, my little chickens, cheep cheep cheep!

"Something hit me."

Her sleeve is ripped. Her arm is covered with blood. Her mouth is twisted. But this doesn't spoil how she looks. She looks like a teenage schoolgirl.

"Be patient. Not long now."

"Sixty-three," whispers Olympia.

We are carrying battered and bruised buns, fruit, papers, clothes, underwear, stuff that we've picked up on our travels. Oh! I hit a Mom and her stroller. The baby flies through the air! Catch the baby!

We get stuck in the pile of people. The car snarls. There is nowhere to go. Move away. We spin around on something slippery. Olympia falls on me. She is covered in blood now. The car hurls itself at the wall of the well-known bar Valdai, I haven't been there for quite some time. The engine stops. Come on, darling, start, start! A superb advertisement for our native Russian car industry.

"How many?"

"I lost count," babbles Olympia.

I stroke her on the cheek. On the Yalta promenade—in the sprayed fragments of glass and sea—a brass band plays on the prom-prom-prom.

"That's not important." Panting, eyes screwed up. "I felt good with you."

Dozens of hands thrust into the car. They grab us and yank us out. I hear her terrible howl. The crowd tore us to pieces—they didn't wait for the cops. We were torn to pieces.

Cotton Wool

OH, EVEN one with Down syndrome would have been better! Down syndrome! To go to the cafe with the camp commandant. Café, with an accent. To sink into one's memories. They all say, "Upbringing, education, education." Lies! They lie from cowardice. She sat down, wiped away the sniffles. She started coughing, a deep smoker's cough, a man's cough. Golden-headed, like a cupola. She unfolded her scarf. Eggs, with far too much salt on them. And that Symbolist lot at the Tower had lied too. She would have taken care of a Down syndrome child. Out of protest, because of the contradiction, proudly, on her own, even going as far as spitting blood. They lie that it is possible to put things right. She smiled at the concierge: forgive me, I don't subscribe to anything. Not a single journal.

Wearing their woolen pantaloons, the new mothers pushed their strollers. In the Moscow Zoo, before the divorce, they'd suddenly started talking about Marxism. Some sort of complete cretin would have been better. The toddlers played in the sand.

Serafima Myaukina left the women's consulting room. The camp commandant had taken a fancy to her. Her armpits were sweating. She somehow managed to drag herself to the meat shop to buy a chicken. She paid at the register and fainted, crashing to the floor.

Never. Serafima Myaukina will never have anyone. No children, no grandchildren, no great-grandchildren. There will be no one, only the chicken. There will be only the chicken with its hawk's span of wings. Long and fruitless will be the flight of our chicken over the plains, expanses and rivers of the Motherland, for there is no, alas, Serafima, Easter loaf... salty eggs with painted shells, Marxism, Nikolai, menagerie and the smell... here it is: the smell... her neighbor listened eagerly and in a state of disbelief... tired skin, tired smell... there is no Easter loaf... smooth strokes of hawk's wings... without a Christmas carp... little fishes! little fishes!... early Christians... oh, no, Serafima, no, there is no life without a slimy embryo, no apple without a worm, oh, Serafima, there is no slimy corpse of a drowned woman without water from melted snow, no Christ without the womb of the Mother of God, oh, no, Serafima!

It had got much warmer in town. As if on someone's order the Mommies unbuttoned their coats, took out their needlework, became softer, nicer. From the side they looked like some girls without makeup who were just happening to look after other people's children. Irreparable, primordial, only the mechanism is incomprehensible. Take for example Chagall. Vitebsk. Selling fish. Barbers' shops. Oh, well, Jews aren't representative. In fact they're bloodsuckers. But all the same one can do some sort of valuation, find the root. The girls were not yet experts in motherhood. They were slowly maturing on poor soil, growing wiser. Serafima Myaukina rushed around in their midst with her pale-faced little bastard.

He will follow the herd. He will be embittered, angry, suspicious, always clenching his fists. The entire genetic inheritance has been wasted, the gene pool has been drained dry.

Serafima Myaukina, golden-haired, with a zero level of interest in life. Hiroshima—so what? Terrorists? Fine by me.

"Mummy!"

"Whaddu you want?"

"I've pooped my pants again!"

A child? Fine by me. Without a name, without a family, makes no difference. Wish they would all just snuff it! Except for Mommy, Daddy and my brother—let them survive, I feel sorry for them.

"Shit or get off the pot!"

"Mommy, I've pooped my pants again."

Serafima Myaukina parted the damp overgrowth of her child's tights with her hands and quietly howled in the small kitchen.

To make up for it she slept a lot. Her dreams were sinless and colorless. God has punished me. Why am I so indifferent? Why don't I want anything? Why can't I love anyone?

The camp commandant summoned Serafima Myaukina. The camp commandant subjected her to a humiliating interrogation, and as she left him she was reeling from happiness.

Her neighbor couldn't wait to hear about the smell. How and where does it collect? Nikolai told me in the zoo. It just slipped off his tongue. Before the divorce. As a hint of unfaithfulness. It happens, Serafima Myaukina went over to a whisper, the first time one sleeps with a new woman. In what sense "the first time"? The neighbor was confused. Serafima thought that in actual fact she wasn't explaining it very well.

"Strictly speaking, it was my first husband's discovery."

Her neighbor asked: "But does mankind, I wonder, know about this discovery? He was, I believe, a chemist?"

As a hint at his unfaithfulness. Nikolai—he was in his twenty-first year—"a mere strip of a lad," sighed the neighbor—married Serafima Myaukina in an act of great love and didn't even notice himself how quickly he became a complete bastard, a commonplace swine, a skinflint, a clodhopper, a useless jerk, a nothing. Nikolai didn't know that you have to crush a woman's backbone if you want to live with her, slap her in the mug no less often than you fondle and fuck her; that a woman should cringe before her husband and crawl on her belly, and not give him lectures or play the orator. Nikolai, this chubby little boy with a university badge, didn't know that without all this a woman is a corpse rotting away, breaking into pieces filled with venomous juices. Serafima Myaukina's lively eyes smiled. Then, she said, they dripped juices on the carpet, and the neighbors burned it on the garbage heap. A woman needs chilling. The neighbor, having thought about this for a bit, drank her coffee. But burning would be even better, to avoid trouble.

Once upon a time she gave birth to a blue-eyed, twelve-pound, marvelous little boy with a full head of hair.

Once upon a time Serafima Myaukina went on a mission to a neighboring friendly country, with her own bare hands strangled all the satanic forces and scum, put out any fires of resistance that were still burning with her own urine, and returned, rumpled but unharmed. They erected a monument to her on Red Square, swamped it in flowers and gifts, and the statue of Minin and Pozharsky was carted off somewhere to the backwoods of Maria's Grove.

Once upon a time Serafima Myaukina had a cutlet for breakfast, felt sick and bloated and started to vomit, even though she was an excellent cook and renowned for her eclairs, Nikolai rushed home from work, and the local doctor, who managed to arrive by the evening, confirmed, somewhat slyly, that she was pregnant. With every hour the pregnancy grew and grew. In the fifth month, shocked, she understood that pregnancy and logical thinking are arguably more incompatible than genius and villainy.

Once upon a time Serafima Myaukina had a good smoke of weed and she felt a tiny bit better, and then felt better and better, more and more fantastic, like in a fairy tale.

Once upon a time Serafima Myaukina read the Constitutional Democrats' collection of essays *Signposts* and danced all night long in her nightshirt on broken glass. The nightshirt was short and semitransparent.

Once upon a time in an Intourist Hotel for Foreigners they bumped into each other quite by chance. The camp commandant had gone gray and got slimmer. "I don't regret a thing," he said. Serafima Myaukina literally came out in a sweat on hearing these penetrating words; first of all she felt frightened, then went all wet, then felt wet again, and her breasts started to ache. To the john! To the john! They got it together there. An officer's uniform is binding.

Once upon a time, in secret from Serafima Myaukina, Nikolai wrote and successfully defended a thesis in order to make her happy, and Serafima thought as she looked at all the faces present at the defense: But why are there so many ugly, crooked, mis-shapen mugs among our technical intelligentsia? Why do they look so sick and untidy? And the creative intelligentsia are no better! Another real crowd of monsters, a cesspool of vanity! And the working class, not to mention the peasants! So who's left to marry?

Serafima Myaukina invited her three best girlfriends to her birthday. They came, all dressed up to the nines. Nikolai was run off his feet: he passed the food around, carried the trays, served, tossed the salads, changed the plates, made jokes. They drank tea, praised the eclairs, praised the tea set, went red in the face, Serafima became animated and was shouting loudly. Nikolai, clearing away yet another empty bottle, said, "Put the dead soldiers under the table. Dead under the table."

"You see, Kolya," said Serafima Myaukina, and then fell silent. "In my childhood I had a nanny." "Aha," said Nikolai. He always inserted his "ahas" when he was listening to someone intently. "Incidentally, her surname was Pushkin. In their village everyone was called Pushkin, honestly!" "Aha," said Nikolai. "Now that's something!"

All the most talented and notable people of the epoch—poets, philosophers, scholars, artists, actors, sometimes even politicians—gathered every Wednesday at Vyacheslav Ivanov's Tower in the heart of Petersburg. The most refined conversations on themes literary, philosophical, mystical, occult, religious and also political would be held there.

"We won't go to see the elephants."

"As you wish."

"I want an ice cream."

"I've got enough for an ice cream, I think."

"I liked eggs, especially poached. I like them now too for that matter. My nanny used to feed me from a spoon and would dip it into salt all the time. The salt would stick to the damp spoon..." "So that's why you don't have any salt when you eat eggs!" "You don't miss a trick," laughed Serafima Myaukina.

And it was true. Nikolai sometimes astonished his friends with his powers of observation. "So which of you has noticed," Nikolai asked (as long as there weren't any girls nearby), looking lovingly at his male companions, "that when you screw a new woman, then the next morning when you have a shit, your shit will always smell of her?" "What? How?" A flicker of understanding would suddenly appear in his friend's eyes. "Moreover," Nikolai would add, "this is only when it's a new screw. After that, no matter how often you screw, it doesn't have that smell." "That's absolutely true!" his friends would say in astonishment. "Some mystic power!" Nikolai would say, shrugging his shoulders, pleased with himself. "Mystic power!"

But this was only in male company. Even Serafima Myaukina wasn't let in on the secret.

It was a religious procession, and she was singing, and walking through the puddles, Nikolai was alongside her, with the face of a bumpkin, he always had a sickly-sweet, syrupy expression on his face at moments of love. Serafima pressed tighter to her husband. "I love you."

Once upon a time Nicholas II married Serafima, and he didn't even notice himself how quickly he was crushed by her intellect, contempt and sarcasm. She had many children with Nicholas II: Kirov, Rudzutak, Rykov, Yagoda, Vernadsky, Mandelstam, Tsvetaeva, Mikhail Koltsov, Ordzhonikidze. Too many to mention. Many of them died from intellectual misfortunes and nervous exhaustion.

Once upon a time Serafima Myaukina divorced Nikolai. She thought that he would fight for her, that he wouldn't give in without a battle, but he simply retired into his shell, into his own quiet despair. Yes! He also said, "Mother said to tell you, Serafima"—he was stumbling over his words but kept going—"to give her back the wedding ring." Serafima said, calmly, "Yes, of course." She yanked it from her finger. The ring flew under the wardrobe. Nikolai started crawling after it. "Sorry, I didn't mean to," prattled Serafima Myaukina. But to herself she thought, "Oh, to hell with you, fat ass! Crawl! Crawl! You bloody Philistine!"

A peaceful land. Selling fish. The young mothers pushed their baby carriages. Dead men under the table.

"Mommy, I've pooped my pants again!"

She grabbed him and carried him, ass in the air, into the bathroom.

Fair enough.

Her neighbor called. Well, not a neighbor, exactly, not exactly a—well, what with our economy there's a shortage of symbols in this country—no, not that.

Myaukina said to her, "Nikolai told me. Had you ever heard about it?"

The neighbor was stunned.

I have made up my mind.

I'm fed up with him.

To her neighbor, "It doesn't worry me. I don't need any wunderkinds."

Her neighbor says, "The Nikitins' boy knows miles of *The Iliad* off by heart."

Myaukina made a wry face, "It's not that. He shits an awful lot." She gestures in the direction of the diaper.

"I've got something wicked in mind."

She looked more closely: not her neighbor, but the Virgin Mary. And she'd always felt attracted to religion. From her youth. She wouldn't admit it to herself, suppressed it, but the attraction was there.

Something wicked.

Mouth always half open, clouded eye, there is something of Myaukina in him, like a parody. Like a nightmare, Nikolai's face showed through.

I don't know, maybe one should accept things as they are.

But I can't.

She just started dancing. In her short nightshirt.

Shall we dance together? The neighbor looked at her suspiciously, out of the corner of her eye. Something had finally got through to her. The ruins of feminine intuition.

Serafima Myaukina stopped sharply, squatted down, her knees apart. Curls of gold, like the Kremlin bell towers.

"The Iliad!"

She started guffawing. He'd started talking at three and a half, lisping, mixing up his words and his boogers.

"Push harder, little one."

A rotten eye. A damp forehead.

They were right to hate genetics, the poisoner of dreams. Myaukina added, "The poisoner of the future."

"So you didn't know, then?"

"How would I know!"

Of course she hadn't suspected a thing. Everyone was intrigued. She looked at her knees and hurried to get away. OK, I'm off. Myaukina squatted, thinking sadly about the camp commandant and the cut soles of her feet. The child pulled the plastic bag off the hook. Like a ring. Myaukina laughed.

"Silly! That's not a toy!"

Her cotton wool was there. Silly fool! The essence of woman is cotton wool. Multicolored balls of cotton wool. I am cotton wool. You are cotton wool, fool. Don't play with it! It's not a toy.

He holds the plastic bag with one hand and punches it with the other. The genes shot up like seeds. Through Nikolai's face her mother-in-law smiled to her from the coffin. Myaukina got up quickly. Don't touch it, fool!

Touch it! Touch it!

He pulled it off the hook. Pulled it toward him. Go on, then, pull it. Try it. Abroad they have special warning messages. Plastic bags can be dangerous. Try harder! He was looking at her with the eyes of her mother-in-law. A vengeful glare. Give the ring back.

I can see it all now. In the herd, following the herd, mediocrity. Genes, genes.

They are like bullets. A fan, a spread of genes.

Well, if you really want to, you CAN play with it.

It had been a misalliance. Now it was a lifelong cross to bear. The police?

They won't work it out.

Come on come on.

Strange. But only when it's the first time.

The child gulped. He stood up.

"Are you playing games with me?"

The child sat down obediently, looking at her with a vindictive glance, her mother-in-law's. Then he went for it again. A fool's cap. An astronaut's space suit. Voyage to the Moon. Happy, he started to pull it over his head.

She was thinking: first, in some sort of East German book, when she'd been about eighteen, she'd read a warning: if he should look at you with the unloved eyes of an unloved relative, don't lose your mind, he's not to blame. Logical. The Germans are always logical, but we aren't Germans. And she smiled. Second, what's second? She'd forgotten what was second. Ah, yes, it's common. It happens. She was absorbed in doing something in the kitchen. It happens. They won't find out the truth. Even in India the bags have 'Danger!' on them. To avoid danger of suffocation keep away from children.

A gray face, not a child's face. And the eyes are prickly. If only Hitler hadn't been allowed to grow up...! The teacher asks a question, "What do you expect? All these D grades will do nicely." Bitch. Doesn't even feel embarrassed. Straight out with it. Just like in America, "You've got cancer. You're fucked."

Peek-a-boo! A spaceman's suit. He even appeared to be smiling: he understood. And then it started sticking to his face.

His little hands struggled.

Squatting, she watched.

He kept trying with his hands, his little hands!

Genes are like weights. Heavy dumbbells.

She rests her cheeks on her palms, and watches.

The potty dances. The potty grates on the tiled floor. His little legs are kicking on all sides. It's stuck to his face.

Myaukina leapt up. She rushed out of the bathroom. Fell onto the bed. Drowned out the grating of the potty with her hands. I shall count to one hundred. Slowly. She started counting.

There in the bathroom—Voyage to the Moon—the astronaut's protective space suit—his little hands—cotton wool balls—blue in the face—little fishies! little fishies—the potty tipped over—she heard it through her hands.

Myaukina lay there and continued counting. She leapt up and went straight into the bathroom. From the bathroom—back to the bedroom. From the bedroom to the bathroom.

There is a ring at the doorbell.

Myaukina goes toward the door. She stands there, listens carefully, all ears. The police. She lies in the bedroom, across the bed, and she remembers how, lying across the bed after eating that cutlet, she'd experienced an intense surge of maternal feeling.

The camp commandant: "Well, what's with you?"

A child with the nimbus of the potty on his porous bum. On the porous bum of Nikolai, on the blooming bum.

Myaukina kept saying: "Push harder! Harder!"

Her neighbor made a grand entrance, wearing light blue. Symbols are in short supply.

Myaukina squealed at her, "We are all cotton wool. You are cotton wool. I am cotton wool."

Then she thought and added: "Cotton wool in briefs."

She lies on the bed in her short nightshirt and squeals.

She parts the seaweed of the child's soiled tights and squeals. She wipes the baby's ass and mumbles, "I am cotton wool."

She lies quietly across the bed.

Dead on the table.

Sweet Fanny Adams

"Leaning against the door-frame..."
—Boris Pasternak, "Hamlet"

"YOU MAY get changed in here," said the administrator, flicking on the light switch, and in the turbid greenery of the three-leaved mirror their multiple images introduced themselves, collided and scattered: a neat, coquettish haircut, a denim suit with worn elbows and knees, an effeminate leather bag over his shoulder and a white turn-down collar, tight hair-sprayed curls, a faint, sour whiff of perfume and perplexed eyebrows. She, most probably, was puzzled how a black ironed suit, a white shirt and a tie could all fit into the bag—what's the trick? Perhaps he'd left his case in the hotel? She looked around without stepping over the threshold—this room, in which a male stranger would in the next minute or so strip down to his underpants and spread the smell of sweat, was repulsive to her in advance. She looked around, searching for the suitcase. The performer guessed the meaning of her gaze.

"I'll be dressed like this for the poetry reading," he said in a conciliatory tone, and his voice sailed through the air like a ring of sweet smoke which a relaxed smoker lets fly from his pipe as he reclines in his armchair. The administrator wanted to say something, but didn't. Her lips made the mere ghost of a movement and she looked at him mistrustfully.

"Nina Lvovna," said the performer, who had made it his rule always to memorize the name and patronymic of administrators of all hues to make life easier, "where's the men's room?"

The question, with its roots going back to Derzhavin's "Where's the john?," to an age of greater simplicity, of serfdom, of male gallantry, was ill-considered. Despite her best efforts, Nina Lvovna could not overcome her annoyance, and started to sulk.

"Second to last along the corridor," she forced herself to say, offended, and making clear with her entire being that she was not a concierge and not a cleaning lady, but a representative of the local intelligentsia working in the service of the Muses, a singing teacher, a politically active citizen who enjoyed authority and respect in the town, a member of the civic town commission ("flipping hell, what a complete birdbrain!") and you know, young man, I just don't understand you, how you could come out with such a question to a woman? Or do I look the type? Thinks he's special just because he's from the capital!

Men pee standing up—how awful!

She turned away.

But somehow a mistake had crept in. She would have to correct it.

"No, the men's is the last door along the corridor," she babbled, her face full of embarrassed distaste.

"Sorry, what was that?" The performer cupped his hand around the milky shell of his ear.

"He's making fun of me!" She quailed before such impudence.
"There are no signs there, but it's the last door."

"Aha!" said the performer. "Makes no difference to me anyway."

Nina Lvovna was simply at a complete loss for words.

The water roared. Wiping his hands with his handkerchief, the poetry performer tarried before the canvas of the toilet door. This was quite a rare example, a masterpiece of its kind, a parade of unbridled collective male thought. Inscriptions flew off in all directions, written in various-colored inks, ballpoint pen, indelible pencil, but written with the knife too and with God knows what other sharp objects. A hairy world of passions found substantiation in this tattooing of space. Genres mixed. Poems were neighbors with prose passages full of shiny aphorisms. Bellowing interjections, surrounded, as if by feathers, with exclamation marks, fluttered over the entire landscape. The door was in full bloom. Here was everything: pieces of advice, suggestions for improvement, piggish grunts, howls of flesh rearing their ugly heads, elegiac witticisms, warnings and threats, nasty and tasty invective aimed at Lenochka Salnikova (don't be angry, Lena!), quotes, toasts, autographs with dates and cities, cunning hints about bigger things to come, heartrending appeals and the most complete and utter nonsense.

> *I was naked when Mama bore me*
> *Looked and said Olya's the name for me*
> *I find blokes sweeterer than raspberries*
> *And on my birthday I'll get rat-assed.*

The last line met with an approving "Hmm" from the performer. In this promise to get rat-assed on her birthday there was some strange, Tartar-like mystery in an enigma that tugged at the heartstrings. What sort of sad cretin had composed this Olya? A choirboy from some amateur choir? A traveling artist? Some backward pioneer, forced to repeat a grade? Where did this "sweeterer," a huge, voice-straining effort, come from, if not from the bowels?

The performer suddenly felt that he too wanted to write something: something strong, something rude, something criminal. He took a ballpoint pen out of his pocket, leaned his palm against the door and started to think. Nothing decent (or indecent) came to mind. Having strained in vain, he suddenly caught himself thinking that he longed to be absolutely original, to be different in such a way that the result would be *sweeterer*. Any comparison with the other writers, who created involuntarily, from excess—they splashed themselves onto the door and exited, relieved—any comparison did not work in his favor. He didn't even dare to scratch some simple obscenity. Simplicity would have stunk of snobbery, aestheticism or, if one were to look at it from another angle, as an ingratiating attempt to slum it, to live like the common people. All of this was neither in his nature nor his nurture, but he wanted to write something for all that. Pondering what precisely he should write, he examined the door further, mechanically.

In addition to the texts there were, naturally, drawings as well. One of them stood out from all the others by virtue of its dimensions and antiquity. Making use of the whole sweep of the door, it had already pretty much worn away and was overwritten and obscured by later layers. However, one could make out the contours of a woman wearing sweet fuck-all and flying in the direction of fuck knows where, with her face in profile, her hair loose, narrow eyes, the low brow of a violator and murderer, her jaw hanging down carelessly. The implausibly dislocated pose of her trunk with its warlike wobbling bazookas could not help but make one think of a garlic-grilled chicken. One leg dangled down half eaten or else perhaps half drawn—someone had prevented it, given the artist a fright, not given him the chance to finish.

"Wild woman! Just imagine drawing one like that," thought the performer, with almost a touch of envy. "She's not scared of all these clumsy, swollen finger rolls"—cocks were present and erect in large numbers—"pointing from the thick undergrowth. She just flies onward to her heart's content and sings."

"Yes, of course, that's who she is, Sweet Fanny Adams herself!" exclaimed the artist, guessing the truth at last.

But what, then, was *he* going to write? What announcement should he make? He vetoed everything: this wasn't right and that wasn't right. Lord, but why should he be vouchsafed less than others? What about equal rights? He scratched his pen on the door. "I won't give birth to anything."

The door was in full bloom.

Once again he examined the inscriptions. Isn't it amazing how people hear words differently! Primordial chaos reigned in the orthography of blessed Russia's blessed obscene language. And the spirit moved upon the face of the waters. Perhaps energetically toss off something taken from the Bible, but with a new twist? But why from the Bible? What's the Bible got to do with it? Or perhaps he should confess to some secret vice? With a chuckle: Which? Once again it was turning out "sweeterer." Or maybe he should immortalize his act of betrayal? That's a brazen verb, "immortalize." And then, on his return to Moscow, to the rosy vomit of family relationships, to say to her, "Well, there you have it. I let the cat out of the bag. On the flower bed of some shitty toilet door, in the grand old town of . . ." At this point he stumbled. "Wait a sec, what on earth is this town called? Damn, I've forgotten. Begins with *K*, I think. What's it today, Tuesday? If it's Tuesday this must be— where? No, beginning with *K*—that's Kostroma. I've already done Kostroma. Kostroma's big. It's damp there, I think that's the one with"—wretched poseur!—"the Volga. So, immortalize my act of betrayal?" He stroked the door tenderly. "Oh, what an ass I am! Do I really owe her anything at all now? To confess to my sins . . . when I'm sick to death of it all! When everything can be fitted into

one simple little particle? 'NOT.' I shall write 'NOT.' Stupid. I shall
not write. But what *is* the name of this town?"

The performer was cheered by his own forgetfulness. He
didn't have a clue where he was. How marvelous! How wonderful!
He'd be annoyed now if the name of the town were suddenly to
come to him. Trying to be clever, he unobtrusively started placing
obstacles in the way of his memory. He said to himself, "OK, so I
arrived in the morning, I slept in my hotel until lunch. I had meat
soup and a gooey goulash, after lunch I had another nap in my hotel room. The window looks out onto a garden, wind, sun, September. I got into the car, houses flashed past, International Street,
the shop called Quality Leisure, an arch, a church... and who
knows where all this is?" The performer soared above the town
without a name.

And so, without having immortalized anything, having forced
himself not to remember the name, contented, he left the gents'.
Yes indeed, he thought, such doors should be taken off their
hinges, covered with varnish and sent off to the storerooms of the
state museums; let them be preserved there until their time comes.
As priceless documents of an epoch. Sweet Fanny Adams flying
and singing!... as perfect examples of the people's art.

A few steps along the corridor the performer looked around
furtively and opened the door of the neighboring room slightly.
Having made certain that there wasn't a soul inside, he sneaked
in. He was interested to see what the womenfolk's "knees-up"
would be like. From the experience he'd gathered while rushing
about on tour, he knew that women couldn't pull it off, well, perhaps a lonely inscription would suddenly let out a cry of lacerating
melancholy, and its sweet shamelessness makes your heart miss a
beat, and the world is turned upside down, and you long to look
into the eyes of the woman who wrote it, although disappointment is bound to follow—the laws of creativity are perverse

indeed—and the solitary inscription will cry and fade in the emptiness.

The door was a virgin. No poems. No graphics. Nothing. Just prints from fingers, patterns from the cleaner's rag. After putting the folds of their lips in order, women maintained an enigmatic, wretched silence. Click!—and out into the life of society, but their faces for some time yet preserve the traces of the triumphant self-absorption of the toilet. Each to his own: some will take travel sweets for the final journey, some will take a pure soul, but I, when I'm called to the Last Judgment, I'll grab that door from the men's crapper.

The door opened away from him.

Nina Lvovna looked at the performer with the strict tin eye of an armed guard.

"I appear to have got a bit muddled up," said the performer with a wince. In the distance all sorts of bells were ringing.

"Do you feel unwell?" asked Nina Lvovna sympathetically and fell flat on her back. The performer ascended onto her stomach and politely wiped his feet.

"How did you get such a soft stomach?" he inquired with interest.

"Oh, that's not important!"

"But still, I'd like to know."

"You're embarrassing me." Tears gushed from her eyes. Nina Lvovna turned away.

"But no, do tell me, how?"

"From enemas," she began to sob. "You are awful."

The performer thought and got off her stomach.

"We should be onstage—shall we make a dash for it?" suggested Nina Lvovna, when she'd finished weeping.

"OK, let's go," the performer agreed reluctantly.

They started running. They ran for a long time down the corridors, their steps echoing. They startled a flock of pioneers, who had sat down to rest under an old raspberry-colored poplar tree (a crappy, faded stage decoration). Then they came upon soldiers, potato fields, mushrooms at the forest's edge and a woman with a guitar. On the way they played hide-and-seek. Here I come, ready or not! Sometimes the performer pressed her to his body and spoke indistinctly to her.

"Oh, let me go, love!" said Nina Lvovna, protesting, and she rushed on as fast as she could, shouting as she ran. "You know, I gave up school, music, playing the piano. I gave up everything. I've waited for you for forty years. I would have waited another forty. My little boy! My knight in shining armor! Imagine, I only recently found out that men pee standing up! But surely not every single one of them? And even you, my dear, you *as well?*"

"Me as well," said the performer, with a sad nod of the head, scarcely managing to keep up with Nina Lvovna. "Force of habit. What can I do? Forgive me."

The bell was ringing fit to burst. Nina Lvovna concealed the performer behind the dirt-colored curtains. He wiped the sweat from his brow and tried to bring his breathing under control. When was the last time he'd been nervous before a performance? How many of them were out there—ten? a thousand? nobody? He took out his comb and combed his hair.

"What's your patronymic?" whispered Nina Lvovna lovingly.

"No need for it." He frowned. "Just give my name and surname."

His breathing was back to normal. Once again, once again the plaster bust of Lenin squinting at the back of his head would torment him all evening. The performer saw himself clearly in his mind's eye: he advances, touches his throat, says, "That hurts!," laughs, then starts to grieve, saws the air with his hand. And the sweet smell of pipe tobacco pleases the crowd, lulls them to sleep.

The performer feels nauseous. He gives a polite bow in response to the sound of applause. Two twins from Vorkuta, performers in an almost unique genre, queers, most likely, make signs to him from the wings: wind it up now, let us on, we have to catch a train at ten, forgive us bro, give us some room. He brakes. This is how an experienced driver drives a car—he forgets that he's driving it. And he stops, thinking about the white turn-down collar, about how tonight he will force the golden-toothed Nina Lvovna to sniff and suck the forbidden fruit, he stops just before the red light. Smoothly. Top Gear! A Lofty Malady!

Nina Lvovna fluttered out onto the stage and suddenly hunched up, like a sparrow, and announced: *The Love Lyrics of Russian Poets*. Her knees were clearly trembling. A huge hole on the right leg of her tights yawned. He made little attempt to listen to her. He only came alive when she pronounced Akhmatova's name wrongly. With the stress on the first *A* it sounded almost like Pakhmutova, the pop singer. He thought, "Aah, the Queen of Spades! how appropriate! how appropriate!" He thought, "I won't allow her to take off the white blouse with its white turn-down collar."

Nina Lvovna kissed him on the eyes when she returned, and she was all of a shiver, all of a shiver inside.

"Good luck. Have a good one. Break a leg!"

She tried to make the sign of the cross over him.

"My little one! My beloved!"

As though she were sending him off to war.

The performer made the traditional actor's retort, but with real feeling in the words: "Go to hell!"

Mother

Like the majority of her contemporaries, your typical Russian broads, Mother resembled, both in face and body, both in her astral body and even in her ears with their small earrings, the type of peasant-woman material which, in the old days, in hamlets along the River Vyatka, at fairs and sometimes even in gentry houses, in response to the call of our shared pantheistic family womb (the theme to which Tolstoy devoted his best pages) went by the name of daughters, no less, even though peasants from the Kostroma area would still persist in calling them: sows! sows! not suspecting the Ugro-Finnish roots of this somewhat strong word.

Oh, those Russians!

At night Mother dreamed dreams full of hostilities.

In parts of the country outside the Black Earth region such a type was called by even less mellifluous names, which yet again bore witness to the historical coarseness of the vulgar male peasant masses, who were for no good reason hailed as the future, and for this reason collectivization was undoubtedly a tool of Divine Providence and not simply some cheapo Bolshevik diaboliad.

In any event, that's precisely what Mother thought, seeing in Bolshevism the heavenly battalions of our everlasting God, Who in the autumn of that memorable year preferred self-immolation to the prospect of national destruction by means of universal exploitation.

It is possible that such a subtle mystical self-cloning remained the best-kept secret in the story of the Son's duplicate, as indeed of Russian history in general, inasmuch as the average Kostroma peasant stubbornly persisted in calling them sows, while the sought-for act of Resurrection was postponed for an indefinite period, alongside any decision to permit various political fractions and deviations.

In any event, thus, and only thus, was how Mother saw it, who at night had prophetic dreams filled with hostilities and who not without some cause supposed that the Communists were extremely close to their final goal at the beginning of the 1950s, in that divine incarnation would have taken place as a result of fusion and hybridization, which would have resulted in not only the Great Leader becoming immortal, but all his forced victims too, including Lenin's comrades-in-arms, who would have been once again called back to living life, and, repenting this time completely, and, most importantly, sincerely, the Bolshevik apostles would have sung a Hosannah to preventative campaigns of terror.

This all had its very own All-Soviet, all-unifying, universal meaning.

Oh, Mother tossed and turned at night, thinking how slow-witted those people are who have swapped the Kingdom of God for all sorts of Western and Baltic rubbish, for all that chewing gum and other pap! How tightly their stupid trousers cling to their thighs! Inside us! Inside us! I love working lads who are able to kill simply at the call of a hating heart.

"Nothing hurts, but everything is groaning," she would say about herself, in the dark nights of her sufferings.

In her youth she'd had the reputation of being a virgin. Did it last long? She was so shy that shyly, during the initial bloody outpourings, she had broken her hymen with an indelible pencil, having wrapped a piece of yellow cotton wool around it first. All her life she loved military men, for their bearing, their quick reactions, the shine of their boots and eyes, but never has she been able to touch a uniform.

Her mystical insights, the by-product of a proud poverty and bashfulness, would have turned her into a saint, if only saintliness had not been in Soviet Russia the sacred secret routine of every true Party member, all of whom possessed, in addition to their Party membership cards, another mandate certifying Russian divinity, preserved in special priest holes in the depths of their bodies in the event of unexpected Resurrection.

Alive!

And with a hole inside!

At the Meat Factory the intelligentsia used syringes to inject rat poison into the sausages. Haydn was playing quietly in the background.

"Whose music is this?"

She pretended to be deaf and dumb.

"Your handwriting is too easy to read, unintellectual," said the intellectuals.

"This is women's writing." Mother decided to be sly.

"Well done!" Pavel stroked his Mother on her head. She just melted inside and went all wet and juicy. Then she felt herself being shaken violently, as if she were riding on a cart.

"At the weaving mill," said Pavel, "the lasses had their eyes poked out, and then they were replaced with computers."

"Their eyes were replaced?" The elderly worker Petrov pricked up his ears and, embarrassed by his lack of native wit, directed a tender gaze at his comrade.

"Not the eyes, the women, you stupid prick!" said her son, not really angry. He secretly considered Petrov to be his gofer, but never gave this away, hiding it behind gentle ragging. Mother liked this immensely, and she also started to boss Petrov around, but he just kept on smiling and smiling regardless. On the whole he was a nice chap.

"And in the Collective Farm certain agronomists impale all those who have had less than seven years' schooling," Petrov informed them.

"How have you come by this information?" inquired Pavel.

Petrov smiled slyly, but didn't confess. He had a small wart beneath his eye. It should have ruined his looks, but somehow it didn't.

Mother pretended to be a pig, it worked out well, and trotted off to the Meat Factory. The murderers in dirty white overalls were guarding the sausage bastion. Mother picked a banner off the ground and walked through the checkpoint.

"What sort of banner is that?" asked the guard, sympathizing with the creature.

"Winner's prize in the Best Worker Competition," answered Mother.

"Well, come on through, then," decided the old soldier.

Young bum-fluffed bastards were terrorizing the streets, setting fire to what the French call *poubelles* and beating up completely innocent workers. Mother went to the bathhouse for a soak.

"Go to the grave."

"Let's have a wake in Father's memory."

Potatoes. Mother rushed into the kitchen to get potatoes.

"We have to mark the primed sausages with crosses," mused Pavel.

"With an indelible pencil so that it won't rub off," prompted Petrov. Mother remembered her youth and grew sad.

Mironov, the captain of the local militia, also turned out to be an intellectual in disguise.

The immature girl workers at the weaving mill, with heavily forested pubes down to their knees, smirked secretly as Mother slowly reached orgasm.

"They're looking at us!" said Mother, ashamed.

Then Yegor, alias Pavel, started to flog everyone in turn with birch twigs; Mother rushed to cover up, slipped, Yegor swooped down on her like a kite, Mother was surprised that she wasn't embarrassed, but, on the contrary, that it was fun and she enjoyed the fact that they were being watched, and that's how she realized that she'd lived wrongly.

"A real brainteaser for you. Who is to blame: Stalin or Lenin?"

"Communism," said Mother.

"You may pass," said the delighted intellectual.

Mother exhausted herself putting crosses on the sausages, and instead she started eating them, to save people from being poisoned. She was choking on them, but kept eating patiently. The thought never occurred to her that she had already become a martyr, and that henceforth she had a place in the mid-Russian Pantheon.

"It's hard to be a Russian nowadays, so hard," sighed Mother, having filled herself with sausages.

The same one on the wall as at the cemetery, only larger.

Mother waited for the dream, but the dream didn't repeat itself. Her dead husband used to be a Buddhist before they called him into the army. And all this got her hot to trot, got the juices flowing all through her meat, her breasts, womb, legs and ass.

Yegor was flying along the spring road, flapping his wings.

"Mother, look here, life is beautiful! Let me in!"

She let him in.

"That's an idea," approved Yegor.

"Who's there?" she asked ungraciously.

There was no reply.

"Open the door, oldie," she heard a dear voice say.

The intellectuals flavored the sausages with rat poison, but the population ate them, because their stomachs were stronger than the poison.

The dream wasn't recurring. Mother decided to entice her son for the Day of Remembrance.

"You're not looking after yourself at all."

"That's the underground for you," her son joked sternly in reply.

"Ninka won't be coming. She hates you," he said gloomily.

Toward morning Mother had a vision: the intellectuals were spraying the sausages at the Meat Factory with rat poison, in order to exterminate their own people. Mother turned into a pig and rushed to the police. At the Meat Factory meat was lying here, there and everywhere; some of the pieces of flesh were human.

Everybody was rushed off their feet in Ignatiev's headquarters. They were decorating the Christmas tree. When Yegor got drunk, Mother loaded him onto her back, carried him to her bedroom and impatiently but slowly undressed him. Petrov, drunk, had fallen asleep on the chair. Mother took her clothes off too, think-ing of her son's father, can't be much fun for him there, under the snowdrift. The gravestone needs washing, she thought, scratch-ing herself. Mother started sucking her son's breast. Slowly his cock started to rise. Then she started sucking her son's cock. The cock expanded to fill the universe. Then Mother mounted her son and carefully turned her cunt inside out. Sweet saliva drooled from the corner of her son's mouth. He started to purr some old revolutionary song. She greedily wiped herself with the edge of the sheets and stretched herself out, holding her satis-fied legs apart. Soon, completely drunk, her son woke up, saw Mother, guessed exactly what had happened and started to re-proach her.

Pavel suddenly wanted to know all about certain details. Mo-ther candidly answered all the questions put to her. She admitted that her life had been wrong, because of Father. His balls, she sighed, were too long and saggy. Her son suggested that they should change the subject, to talk instead about issues of food pro-duction. Mother agreed, but didn't cover up her cunt.

"In the countryside the semiliterate are being impaled," she complained.

"I know," said Pavel gloomily.

"Avenge them, please," asked Mother.

She thought that if worse comes to worst she could murder her son and put the blame on the war all around them. She was slightly frightened about killing him. She was a shy girl alto-gether. She had put cotton wool on the indelible pencil and there you were. She had never told anyone about this, but this time she just couldn't stop herself.

"What do you mean, cotton wool?" said Yegor in astonish-ment.

Then it got through to him. He thought for a while and burst out laughing. It was interesting after all. Tomorrow we'll go to the cemetery together. We'll wash the tombstone, with soap. This was Mother's suggestion. Definitely. This was her son's response. But tell me about you and Nina.

Her son was very annoyed when he found out what Mother had done with him during the night of Father's anniversary. At long last she made up her mind. She invited her son to come on the Day of Remembrance. They sat there and remembered him. They clinked glasses with the photograph that hangs on the wall, the same photograph that is on the gravestone, heavily retouched to the point of being unrecognizable, except it's bigger than the one on the tombstone.

As a theoretician, Klavdiya Vasilevna explained the historical inevitability of terror. Her son started to get his words mixed up. And Petrov had long since got everything muddled. Mother put Yegor to bed and starting beating his meat.

The son wheezes: "Why are you doing that, Mother?" And she says: "It's nothing, nothing. I'll be gentle."

"Gentle what?" the son doesn't understand.

The image of the Mother lifts up her dress, takes out her tit.

"Here you are, suck it, as you used to when you were a baby."

He sucks it in languorous sadness. Klavdiya Vasilevna's cunt has grown bald and old. She turns over onto her back.

During the fuck Mother farts in exultation, but both of them are so carried away that they don't even hear.

It takes them less than two and half minutes to reach simultaneous orgasm. Mother sinks slowly into some blessed realm, with a towel clamped between her legs. She wants to preserve it all within herself. As deep as possible. Deeper. Forever. Somewhere deep inside her a thought was starting to stir: that she hadn't lived her life properly, that she'd wasted it on the wrong things.

They lie there and chat. Klavdiya Vasilevna complains about Father, she says he was never normal, his cock was sort of genitally challenged and he had no balls.

"How can that be, no balls?" her son wonders.

"How the hell should I know?!" answered a disgruntled Klavdiya Vasilevna. "Somehow I could never understand why, and I was too shy to ask. I even went to the museum just to see them, to compare notes. Like Hemingway with that, what d'you call him, yeah, Fitzgerald."

"But how could you have me, if he had no balls?" asked her son in astonishment.

"Well, somehow or other."

"Perhaps I'm not his at all?"

"Well, who else's could you be other than his?"

"You didn't sleep with anyone else, I suppose?"

"Did once, but didn't like being unfaithful. It's a sin after all."

"Tell me how the two of you used to fuck."

"Some other time." She stroked his head.

And then they had another one, and then he fell asleep, but Mother was lying there, restless. At first her thoughts took a pessimistic turn. She thought about what she had lost, what kinds of pleasures. She even thought that she had devoted too much time and energy to Party matters. Then she fantasized about how her son would come to her, twice a week, and they would keep it in the family, and, the main thing is, no one would be able to make a fuss.

But then she gradually came to see that her son would wake up, would evaluate with fresh morning eyes what had happened, and then, what would happen then?

They almost came to blows over it. But afterward he raped her. In punishment. Fair enough. Mother took this in a different way. And they had almost made up, although her son kept on reproaching her, kept calling her an ignorant creature. Nevertheless, out of curiosity he questioned her about Father's habits. Mother didn't dare to hide a single detail. The nitty-gritty offered little comfort. Mother burst into tears and told her son about her dream. I felt ashamed. Not the right ideals, and that she fears for herself. Her son assured her that he understood her, but that this is an obstacle. He is in favor of the Soviets, but without intellectuals. He told of how in the Collective Farms the agronomists impale everyone who does not have at least a seven-year education. The people turned out to be greater than the poison. Their stomachs coped with the provocation. Mother repented, but kept her own counsel, naturally.

When her son fell asleep she, weighed down by pangs of conscience, killed him with an axe, and then killed the aged Petrov, and she carried the corpses off to the intellectuals as booty.

"In the end you're still better," she said with tears in her eyes. "Better, more educated and more humane."

This led to some awkwardness.

Mother recalled that her son at one time had dreamed of becoming a Muslim, but instead of this dear Petrov had, with embarrassment, pulled a small bouquet of carnations from under his jacket. "Well, you know, that," he said. Congratulations, so to speak.

Yegor, the leader of the town's underground movement, entered the hallway. Mother started dragging down his trousers, and something missed a beat in her spleen when in all its splendor a young strong cock appeared before her eyes. His biography turned out to be very ordinary. Mother got scared, asked,

"What do you need that for?"

She took him in hand and started to jerk him off gently, with love, crooning as she did so.

"Once I gave birth to all this myself," she thought, not without pride.

Memories surged upon her. "Tell me how you fuck with Ninka," she whispered hotly in his ear. "Tell me what her *pussy's* like."

"A cunt like any other," said Yegor, knitting his brow, but one could feel that he was aroused by the straightforward conversation.

Quick—ride to the Meat Factory and put marks on the poisoned sausages! The intellectuals were standing guard, smoking sweet foreign cigarettes. Mother picked up the red banner and set off. With an indelible pencil. The intellectuals greeted her with looks of contempt.

"Where do you think you're off to?" they asked her. "You're one of those who pisses without squatting and without taking your pants off."

"How is it you know everything?" said Mother in astonishment and looked at them with respect.

"Take off your pants, bitch!"

"Gentlemen, where does that quote come from?"

Mother wore such awful underwear that her pubis had turned cornflower blue in color. In the police station Captain Mironov heard the agitated lady out, but he was in no rush to respond to the signal. "But why are you saying nothing? Speak again!" said Mother in astonishment. Captain Mironov was silent as he looked through the barred window.

There wasn't enough psychological plausibility. Like the majority of Russian women of her generation, Klavdiya Vasilevna resembled a pig.

"They were against you," she said to the intellectuals, as she dumped the still-warm corpses on the ground; and then she went to the Meat Factory and said that she and her son had come to a parting of the ways, because he is for the radiant future, but such a thing does not exist.

The intellectuals accepted her into their ranks as a comrade-in-arms and decadent. The murderers in white overalls made the underground warrior, her son, into first-class sausages, which then poisoned the entire population.

Petrov's corpse was used for "Sausage Supreme."

THE GIRLFRIENDS

LISTEN, I'LL tell you a story, perhaps you won't like it, I don't care for it much myself either, but I'll tell it to you anyway. You can't make heads or tails of it, but let's try together. On the whole, I think, both girls were in the wrong, that is, both *ours* and *theirs*, as one says, only, of course, both of them were not typical, indeed almost the precise opposite, they were exceptional, completely unique, and that's the reason why, in essence, they are both so attractive. Still, when one is dealing with extremes, no doubt somewhere even in that which is most particular, an element of the national character shows through, only you shouldn't think that by this I have in mind some arithmetical mean.

Well, of course, the fact that life in the final analysis would in any event have dragged them off in different directions was something they understood only too well themselves, even though they didn't even permit themselves to think about that fact: that one would return to America (because after all it's impossible to be settled *here* forever), whereas life would keep the other here, and on our spit of land she wouldn't have such a bad time at all, except that, of course, she'd be without her girlfriend. But it is impossible to imagine that they could have lived in the same city and not seen each other, or that if they were suddenly to bump into each other somewhere, I don't know where, at an exhibition perhaps or at the traffic lights on the Moscow North Circular, waiting next to each other—and even their cars were of the same make, provided that Suzie hadn't taken her husband's car, which was a bit longer—so yes, that they could be waiting next to each other at a red light and yet not yell out hello is simply inconceivable! And if one compares them at this moment as they are in their cars, tapping out a beat with their fingers on the steering wheels, their free-flowing clothes flapping in the wind, scarves around their necks, they look very much like each other, women who stand out, who catch the eye, *theirs*—with darkish, slightly curly hair, with a clean complexion which looks as if it has been washed by the dew and with plucked eyebrows that make her facial features seem fragile, somewhat like porcelain, and *ours* (afraid we can't escape the stereotypes)—with light brown hair, the Russian color, though at least there's no Slavic plait. Both are jolly, fond of a good laugh, boisterous girls, I'd even say girls ready to laugh in the face of danger, ours, it is true, is a bit healthier, a bit more sculptural. I saw her once in her nightshirt, at the dacha, she was coming downstairs to put out the light, and I was sitting under the lamp, reading an American magazine, almost the latest issue, Suzie's, naturally, and I caught sight of her and immediately thought: If you were to put a nightshirt on a statue, then that's how it would look—a statue in a nightshirt. The bronze breasts tear the delicate cotton, the bronze hips sway as she comes down the stairs, looking at me quizzically—I'd lost track of time as I read, my bed had been made up long since in her late husband's study, amid his photographs, she and I were very good friends without any innuendo, but night is not the truest of times, and I'm not blind, I could see how hot and cramped she felt in this nightshirt. She was thirsty, her mouth had gone dry, she'd had a terrible dream: it's his memorial service again, in the restaurant, there's the tasty aroma of garlic-grilled chicken and beefsteak, and on that very table where we had often dined together lies his coffin, indeed where I first made his acquaintance, but this time she suddenly felt—she doesn't know how to explain this—that there is some kind of hope, but everyone around is stuffing their faces as if nothing has happened, she downs in one gulp a glass of white wine, licks her lips, looks at me (tonight I am her sole defender, who cares what tomorrow will bring), they toast his memory, a group of five well-groomed, harsh-looking men is sitting behind a small table in a corner, sharing one bottle of vodka between them, theirs, it seems, is genuine grief, an antenna pokes out discreetly from the pocket of one of them, they drink without clinking glasses. Suzie suddenly feels unwell, this American girl finds such a wake indecent, for the first time in her life she starts to think about the fact that God's presence is desirable at funerals, this is roughly how she puts it to her long-legged, well-proportioned husband, a former literary scholar who under the pressures of capitalist circumstances swapped literary studies for fur-trading, the husband agrees with Suzie, but one senses that his interest in what is going on is stronger than any metaphysical unease, he looks around the hall with curiosity, his face shows respect for local customs—if they are eating then that must be the way things are done here; there is an element of the ethnologist Miklukho-Maklai in this former literary scholar, his benevolent gaze stops on those five, the bottle of vodka is already dead and hidden behind the leg of the table, the antenna doesn't protrude anymore, something's about to happen. She plays with the chain, she pulls the golden cross from her bosom, I know that the cross is warm, we look at each other as if we're seeing each other for the first time, as if we're sizing each other up, and at the very moment when this mutual eye examination is about to resolve itself, I pusillanimously lower my eyes.

After the wake Suzie stays with Liza for the night. When she takes the black mourning shoes off Liza's feet, Suzie finds swollen soles, blisters on the heels. The shoes had rubbed. Suzie's head spins slightly from the smell from Liza's feet. Liza weeps. Life is over. No one needs her. The wake is the last time interesting people will visit her. Liza weeps. She feels sorry for herself and her dead husband. But Suzie finds a way of comforting her friend. Suzie learned this method in her college, when she was sixteen years old. American girls often comfort one another in this way. Suzie takes Liza's big toe in her mouth and starts to suck it.

I play with the American magazine in my hands. My respect for Liza's husband knows no bounds. She has every reason to despise me. Our relations will not deteriorate, but they will lose warmth. She will never again pat me on the head, for no particular reason, in a friendly manner. Nevermore will she share her dreams with me: she has Suzie. And she turns around regally and walks up the narrow staircase. I observe from below how the fabric tightens once again, I want to compare her buttocks (out of Maillol's sculptures) to the constantly moving jaws of a glutton, I see her antique head and the worker-peasant soles of a work by Mukhina—three epochs of sculpture, gathered into one form together, move away slowly, forward, upward, forevermore.

Suzie was a Slavist. She also wrote poems and had published in such journals as *Paris Review, Poetry Now, Newport Review*. With a gap of eight years between publication Suzie had published two tiny books of texts with titles easily lost in translation. The books, from a microscopic publishing house named after a famous line by an English poet whose name Suzie can't remember, were printed on beautiful paper and smelled marvelous. Suzie had tried to fuse poetry and Slavic studies. One poem, for example, though I didn't get it straightaway, was written about that very same watermelon which Chekhov's Gurov ate after he, in the poet's terminology, had enjoyed the lady with the lapdog. To be fair, other texts, whose refined humor resembled a hallucination, developed un-Russian themes of female rebellion and husband hatred. There was an amusing prose poem there about little old men who, wrapped up in their plaids, look from their chaise longues at nuns who, lifting up their long habits, walk barefoot by the ocean shore; after this came a poem about Bakhtin who, as it turned out, during the Great Patriotic War used the entire manuscript of his book on the German novel of the eighteenth century for cigarette paper. In other words, a Russian theme again. Among these poems there was also some "found" poetry: the texts of ads for some sort of washing powder or cream for shaving one's legs copied out verbatim. Suzie, naturally, shaved her legs. In imitation of Suzie her favorite Russian girlfriend Liza also shaved her legs once, but then stopped doing it, I don't really know why, to be honest. Among the "found" poems I was pleased to see an English translation of the slogan on packets of Georgian tea: "Tea is good for you" and so on. I liked Suzie's poetry. I understood that her verses were true to life when I realized that the hatred toward the husband which ran throughout her cycle of poems *The Abduction and Rebellion of Saint Teresa* possessed a real-life addressee. This was Suzie's first husband, who was, according to her, a rather rude and pedantic man, also a literary scholar, who had studied German literature. For some reason I take pleasure from the thought that he might have written and published that very book on the eighteenth-century German novel whose manuscript turned to cigarette ash in Bakhtin's hands, but my surmise left Suzie unmoved. Having quarreled with her Germanist, she went off on a study visit to Moscow for a whole academic year, where she very soon took up with a representative of an American company which purchased Russian fur. Both of them, but he in particular, with his mink and ermine, were among the hottest tickets out of town and country to be found anywhere in Moscow, but these egoists did not make anyone else happy other than themselves.

I remember them when they were still in love: on Liza's recommendation they came to visit me, at the stroke of midnight. I had already given up hope that they would show. Grievously offended and quarreling bitterly, my wife and I ate half of the apple pie which she had baked in honor of our planned acquaintanceship. I was sitting in the bath when the doorbell rang. They brought with them three bottles of French champagne and some sort of fresh fruit from Latin America, which spread the smell of wild forest strawberry throughout the whole apartment. As they talked they held hands, their fingers entwined.

After the death of her husband Liza returned to translation work. Liza translated a Kalmyk detective story. Some Kalmyk or other stole watermelons from a Collective Farm, took them to the Collective Farm market and started selling them off as if they were his own. No big deal, you might think, but three corpses were the result: the main bookkeeper of the Collective Farm, the vet and also one twelve-year-old Young Pioneer.

A year and a half have passed since the day of the funeral. The burial service for Liza's husband had taken place in the restaurant of the Creative Union. In view of the tireless honesty of his work they couldn't put him in the main concert hall, but they felt awkward about putting him in the small hall. So that left the restaurant. The tables and chairs were moved, the place ventilated, speeches were made. Then they lifted up the coffin and carried it out of the restaurant. And it really did smell of garlic-grilled chicken there, and it is true that the coffin lay on that very same table at which we had become acquainted. He had said, laughing, that to such a young man as me he probably resembled a mastodon. I said that it was my dream to write a long article about him. In Liza's dream the tables hadn't been moved, the people ate and drank and the coffin with her husband's body, which was placed on a separate table, looked like some intricate dish decorated with all sorts of salads.

Standing next to the coffin, Steve recalled how the four of them had very recently gone to a movie theater in Sokolniki to see a lyrical Georgian comedy. The movie theater was packed, men and woman sat in heavy overcoats on creaking, uncomfortable seats, their fur hats on their laps. Steve loved Russians, but not with all his heart. He had thought up a definition for them: a people with dirty teeth and boots, but he hadn't plucked up the courage to tell this to Suzie. It transpired that two of their four places in the seventh row were taken. Sitting in them were a Soviet major and his unattractive wife.

Steve speaks good Russian. He asked the major to show his tickets. "No chance," answered the major, somewhat rudely. Liza's husband, so pale now—in the morgue Liza had been given a coffin containing a ruddy husband, his cheeks had had rouge applied to them, and Liza had screamed in despair, "Lord, they've made him all dirty!," which made everyone felt uneasy, so that the coffin was removed and then a pale husband was returned to her—but back then in the movie theater his face had turned blood-red and he had yelled, "These are our places!" The major said, "You can yell as much as you like." Liza's husband went to fetch the manager. In the meantime Steve said to the major, "You shouldn't get so angry." The major said, "And just who are you, boy, to reprimand me?" Steve said, "I am an American businessman." The major guffawed. His wife, however, didn't even turn her head in Steve's direction once during the entire conversation. Steve was flustered by the major's guffaws. And then Suzie said, "Here you are, then," and showed her American passport. Then the major stopped laughing immediately.

Suzie loved Italian cooking and was an excellent cook. One evening when they were entertaining us Liza and I ate lasagna, helping it down with wine from Piedmont. Steve showed on the video a made-for-TV movie about the Academician—as they kept on calling him in the film—Zakharov. This Zakharov spent the whole film coming up against some sort of red and white barriers, which he was permitted to pass through at first, but then wasn't, and he kept lifting on outstretched arms his homemade placards, which would immediately be torn from his arms by policemen wearing bright navy greatcoats not known in these parts. We literally laughed until we cried at such a sham, at such blatant misrepresentation. For dessert Suzie offered us her own homemade ice cream. Suzie looked at Liza with tenderness. Steve smoked a cigar.

In the yard outside, a policeman who guarded the foreigners gave us a dirty look, a wolflike snarl—he seemed about to pounce, he'd tear us to shreds. Steve shooed him away, took us to the taxi. "I'm scared of them," Liza admitted to me, "for I'm a widow now, I'm nothing."

Liza is typing on her typewriter a translation of the Kalmyk detective story, but her thoughts are far from the problems facing the experienced police investigator. She is thinking about her dream. Beyond the gates she hears the noise of an approaching car. It's Suzie! Liza pushes the typewriter away from her and like a little girl rushes to open the gates for her friend. It is autumn, but Suzie is dressed for winter, her cheeks are rosy, she kisses Liza on the corner of her mouth.

With a sporty step, hands thrust into the pockets of their light sheepskin coats, they emerge on the high bank of a river. There they are met by wind and a Russian landscape. Liza tells her girlfriend about her dream. She is standing before the coffin and in some strange way has a presentiment of something good. In other words, she is not completely certain that this isn't all some sort of masquerade. "Wait!" Suzie interrupts her. "What's with you?" says Liza, amazed. "I think we're being followed." "Where? Who?" Liza's face is a picture of horror. She looks around.

About thirty meters behind them trails some scrawny bloke wearing a worn fur hat with long flaps and a long overcoat of an uncertain shade. An iron tooth glints in his mouth. "Let's speed up a bit!" says Liza. They are almost running now. After some time it is Suzie's turn to glance behind them. Their stalker keeps up with them. Liza starts to pant from this quickened pace. "He's been following us since the dacha," says Suzie. "So why didn't you tell me earlier?" says Liza in amazement. "I wanted to make absolutely certain," replies Suzie. Liza is astonished that the American is so composed. Everything is shaking inside her. She wishes she had some medicine to calm her heart. The friends run down a slope. Now they are walking over the damp sand at the river's edge. In summer this is the beach area of the Union Rest Home for workers in the food industry. A bit further on is a boathouse. An old lifeboat lies on the bank, belly-up. The man keeps up. As he walks he keeps on adjusting his hat, which is constantly slipping down onto his forehead. "I can't go on!" whispers Liza. She's not as fit as Suzie. After all, she is a statue. "Now here's the deal," decides Suzie. "Let's turn around now and walk toward him." "But what if he shoots?" says Liza, scared. "Well, he's driven us into a dead end anyway," says Suzie. And indeed, further on the bushes are impenetrable. The women turn around courageously. Their faces show a mixed expression of hatred, fear and entreaty. In their light sheepskins, tightly holding hands, they march toward the enemy. The enemy stops, hands in his overcoat pockets. He stands, his head resting slightly to one side, waiting for something.

Suddenly, with the swiftest of movements, his coat flashes open. The girls do not have time to react before he thrusts his stomach forward and shoots his thick white load at them.

Suzie and Liza laugh loudly in his face, continuing to hold each other's hand and feeling incredibly relieved. The scrawny Russian bloke is offended by such a lighthearted response. He shakes his fist at them, bares his teeth, buttons up his coat and flees the scene of battle.

On the way back Suzie tells how there are lots of people *like that* in the States. "They beg you, 'Hey, look at me. Hey, please, pretty please. That's all I'm asking.' I sometimes look out of humanitarian considerations." Liza laughs, but Suzie, for whom the idea of the rights of man isn't simply an abstract one, sighs. She doesn't understand how Russians can laugh at cripples, Eskimos, the Chinese and retards. She sometimes thinks that yes, the Russians are just that bit inhuman, but she doesn't share this opinion with her husband.

At the dacha the girlfriends, feet frozen, slide into the marital bed and until evening falls drink coffee with cognac and eat chocolates. By evening their faces are completely covered in chocolate.

During the night Liza wakes up with a start, as if she'd been struck. She remembers where she'd seen that scrawny little bloke before. Why hadn't she realized straightaway! She tries to wake Suzie. Suzie mutters something sweetly in her sleep. "Wake up! Suzie! Wake up!" Liza shakes her. "That was no regular guy! Wake up, Suzie! He's the shortest one of the five who were sitting there in the corner, the one with the antenna poking out of the pocket."

At last Suzie wakes. Liza is still shaking her, and she is trembling herself. "Suzie! He *was* following us! We're doomed! We shouldn't have laughed at him!" Suzie doesn't want to believe this. Suzie yells at Liza. "No!" she shouts. "No, I don't believe it!" Liza has a fit. Suzie hits her friend across the cheeks: slap! slap!

Instead of calming down, Liza gets madder. She starts choking Suzie. Liza has a heavy hand. Suzie doesn't give in. Two large female bodies, Russian and American, intertwine and struggle in a sweaty fight. During the summer Suzie had sunbathed in Puerto Rico, Liza had been on vacation in Pitsunda on the Black Sea. Their bodies are still suntanned, with narrow pale stripes left by their bikini bottoms. Sweat pours from their tanned faces. At last Suzie somehow frees herself, leaps up, sees herself in a large mirror. Liza is weeping amid the torn sheets. There are marks on Suzie's neck. They're just the sort of marks, it seems, that Steve left with his kisses when they were a couple in love, when they visited me at midnight with their champagne and fruit smelling of wild strawberries. Suzie tries to tidy her hair and doesn't quite know what to do next. There are three red furrows on Liza's brow from Suzie's fingernails. Whimpering, Liza says, "I know...I know...you're also a spy!"

You have to know Suzie. She was brought up in the best liberal traditions, the sixties mean something to her, she adores long-haired Vietnam deserters. Both she and Steve hate the American Establishment. Steve can speak calmly about anything other than U.S. policy. Only then does he start to get agitated, his voice grows harsh. How Suzie hates crossing the threshold of the American Embassy on Tchaikovsky Street! There she finds herself surrounded by an atmosphere of insincerity, pseudo-democracy, hypocritical nice smiles. She's a free-flying spirit. She cannot endure such an insult.

Suzie pulls her jeans directly onto her naked body, grabs her sheepskin coat and runs outside. One hears her starting the car's engine. The windshield wipers start working. Suzie gazes long and hard at the damp empty road. Deepest darkest night and thick fog have enveloped the Moscow suburbs. On her face—chocolate, tears, blood.

Liza sits in the very same hall of the restaurant where her husband's burial service was held. She had vowed not to visit this place, but then had somehow forgotten about this. I walk past her. She greets me in a friendly enough way, but there is a certain stiffness in her words and voice. She clearly does not want me to approach her table. She is not alone. Next to her sits the actor Tatarinov, a nasty piece of work who is, one is assured, a not insignificant player in the Mosfilm studios. Liza tells him her dream from long ago, the one about this restaurant: "And suddenly, just imagine, he gets up from his coffin. And at this point I realize that I'd never fully believed in his death." "That's very symbolic," says Tatarinov. "He gets up, shakes the carnations off him, walks toward me, holds out his hand. To tell you the truth, I was in fact terrified of touching his hand, I expected it to be cold, like a frog's. But no, the hand is warm, alive!" "And how did the five in the corner react?" "God only knows," she says, "I didn't notice. All I remember is that there was applause all around." "The five probably applauded more than anyone else," laughs the actor Tatarinov. "What do you mean by that?" asks Liza. "Well, because," says Tatarinov enigmatically. "No, come on, what are you saying?" "Well precisely because," laughs Tatarinov with his rather stupid eyes. Liza bites her lip. She is on the verge of slapping his ugly face. She says, "So why then did they hold the funeral service here, and not in the main hall?" "But what about the conspiracy?" answers Tatarinov instantly. "Oh, to hell with you." Liza hauls up her cross by its chain and twirls it in her fingers. "So what have I said now?" says Tatarinov, trying to justify himself. "It's just that when he went abroad...A casual contact, I think it's called." "Hey, look, hot buns!" exclaims Liza. The waiter Edik is walking through the hall with a tray of hot buns.

In her spacious apartment on Kutuzov Prospect Suzie is packing her things into open suitcases. First of all she packs her things, and then with evident distaste starts to pack Steve's sweaters and shirts.

The week before Steve had gone to a fur auction in Helsinki. There he was notified that his presence was no longer desirable in our country. Steve immediately phoned Suzie in Moscow. He said that he was completely innocent, that he had already issued a denial via the United Press Agency. Steve's voice was agitated. Suzie listened to Steve in silence. Before she left Moscow Suzie phoned me. We met at the Patriarch's Ponds. Heads turned to look at her. She was very beautiful. "No," she said, "not to New York. I'll try and get fixed up in some modest little university. I don't know whether it will work out. Slavists have a tough time of it in America."

As a parting gift she gives me an expensive cashmere scarf. I look mockingly into her gray, sad eyes. "Don't want to leave?" She smiles. I want to yell out, "Suzie, don't leave!" All heads are turning to look at us. I loved Suzie.

ocket Apocalypse

I LOVE working at night, like Stalin. In the last gasp of youth I sit and I write. I feel sick, feverish. Wrapped in a blanket, feathers puffed up, overcoming my spinning head, I turn my quill.

The breasts of my female coevals are already drooping.

Toward morning I allow myself not to clean my teeth. In the bathroom my head spins in a particularly unbearable way. The bright towels fly off in all directions. The toothpaste makes me want to vomit. But most of all I fear bridges and tunnels.

I am frightened of losing consciousness, but that is only the half of the matter, a source of embarrassment before passersby. Sweeping up all this trash into a pile, I see something different: a coffin in a church on Novokuznetskaya Street, and in it a familiar corpse, not resembling himself, swollen, as if he'd been put behind the thick glass of an aquarium. The victim of the stifling heat on the streets and passions harmful for both parties.

I am not ready for such a transport. This auto-psychoanalytic conclusion does not bring me relief, but gives birth to a limp tenderness toward the process of life. Paranoia, I whisper, is simply another name for a pathological form of watchfulness. And once again: neither smiles nor relief. Words have lost their power.

Such is the nature of my complaint.

In the last gasp of youth I realize that Russia is far from being in its worst-ever state and condition, I cherish dreams, I place my hopes on the distant future, on dormant powers, on et cetera.

My Biryukov shares the same sort of thoughts. However, he was so much more radical than I was, up until the events which took place here at any rate, that is, he was so much more of a philosopher, more of a Chaadaev than his author. I am uneasy with such a black-and-white attitude toward imperialism. I fear that, even if I were living in the Polish city of Danzig, in that corridor open to the winds of change and freedom, I would have been as good as dead for putting it all in such terms. So what could one say about my chances here, then? I think about Pushkin and about what he might have written if the Emperor had not been his main censor, and I come to the conclusion that he wouldn't have written anything worthwhile.

Except for a few poems, quite ignoble in essence, he fitted into the vessel which his time had blown for him.

But everything is different now.

Girls enter. They are not skinheads, but their hair is cropped short. They smile as they look at the dead Biryukov.

The finale: announcements in the papers about his suicide.

A photograph of his weeping wife Martha. Let's call her Kristina instead. Weeping Kristina. An interview by an honest journalist.

The honest journalist says that he doesn't believe it was a suicide, he makes transparent hints, although he does not deny that the handwriting is genuine.

He was kidnapped!

But who did it?

He predicted the fall of the Empire.

That's why they killed him.

A malodorous Joseph describes how they used to sit together on the veranda.

Kristina will marry the honest journalist.

"Let me see how the land lies first!"

"One would think that you didn't follow events while you were over there!"

"Honestly, I didn't."

They don't believe him, naturally. But he isn't lying. And it will always be like that.

"How are you feeling? Sorry if the violence was somewhat excessive."

Everyone has his or her own Moscow, Moscows swarm, like springs and stars, and suddenly he embarks upon a normal life, and everything is fine, but he worries, because so many years, so many decades have been lost so pointlessly, everything has crashed in ruins, and it has all crashed on his head. He arrives in his own Moscow, and the tears! the hot, bitter tears!—he never realized that it was possible to cry like that. But, walking through this city, looking closely at the street names, he meets a friend who has left, and that friend warns him about the danger, and he knows himself that there is some invisible boundary, that you must not cross it, and if you do, you're dead, and he crosses this line and he knows that he is doomed; and the surveillance starts; he jumps into a taxi and sees that he's being followed, and suddenly mugs from a past life appear, and it's hard to say whether the new capital has faded away or whether he's already in the old capital once more.

"I'm going to Petersburg first."

"Back, that is?"

"More sideways, I'd say. From there by sea. It'll be cheaper. They'll kill you."

"But for what?"

No, that can't be right, after all I myself have always argued for tolerance. But nevertheless they have lost everything... Yet what have they lost? They've gained everything!

"Look here," said Joseph, "you were there at the source."

Biryukov merely waved him away and asked the driver, "Surely it wasn't better before?"

"Before it was a mess, but now we have inflation," said the driver gloomily.

At this point he suddenly remembered that he didn't actually have any money, only the old ten ruble.

The West had miscalculated again. We cannot live by Pepsi-Cola alone. We are above that. Scratch a Russian and you'll find a Tartar. But no one even scratched the surface.

"Your personal responsibility is considerable. You mocked Russia. Our boys don't like you. They're ready to squash you like a fly. I'm trying to hold them back, and it's not easy."

Redemption is needed.

"So where were you, then, sir, all this time?"

"I was ill," I said. "Once... in brief, I had some local difficulties with the authorities."

"Everyone had troubles with the authorities then," said the taxi driver, "but then on the other hand..."

He looked disapprovingly at the hat which contained Biryukov, looking like an idiot.

"Throat spasms," explained Biryukov. "It became impossible to breathe. Nausea in the mornings, a nervous shiver, bouts of vertigo."

He walked toward the open-wide doors of the clinic. The gravel crunched under his feet. It was fall. Women in light-blue uniforms slid through the park.

His wife walked alongside him and was joyfully saying something, and kept on talking, as she lived through the end of being

Penelope, very stormily, emotionally and joyfully. He remembered her former nervousness, the glint in her eyes, and felt nostalgic.

"I have different intentions. I was never involved in politics."

"Well, well. It all depends on what you understand by, in a word..."

"My dear friend, a healthy national religious spirit is reviving. Dostoevsky. You don't, I think, have anything against Dostoevsky?"

Russia, oh! The more you think about her, the less you feel life.

"Everything's available! Everything's for sale! But the prices! Have you bought gas? Do you know how much a gallon of gas costs?"

"Your wife, Aleksandr Nikolaevich, sleeps with that journalist, with that very Jew who wrote a book about you. Have you read it? An amusing and harmful kike piece of work."

Aleksandr Nikolaevich winced.

"Ah, forgive me, my primitive anti-—as it were—Semitism grates with you! The Jews always supported you."

"Not always," corrected Biryukov.

"Wait. What about the Baltic states?"

Joseph gave a whistle,

"Phew-wee!"

"And what about the Ukraine?" he asked, worried.

"And Ukraine has also gone 'phew-wee.'"

He was walking out of the clinic. It was autumn. His wife suggested that he put his hat on. He was amazed. "You see, British elegance is now in fashion, none of those vagabondish things—put your hat on, Sasha!" "But I haven't worn a hat in my life!"

They got into the car. "So where did you get such a car?" "I wrote a book about you." "About me? You?"

He doubted her abilities. In his presence she had always felt herself to be a nonentity.

"Well, with the assistance of a journalist."

"And what journalist is this?"

"He's a very nice person."

"Really?"

"Why do you say that?"

"It's nothing."

"I've always known that you don't care. We shall spend this evening together, the two of us." "And our son? Where's our son?" "He's in a camp." "What do you mean, in a camp?" "Here, near Moscow. A very nice sort of sports camp it is too. He's excellent at soccer."

"Soccer?"

"It's the in thing."

"But soccer?!"

On the way they stop off at a French shop to buy a bottle of white wine.

"And for supper your favorite."

"Ravioli?" asked Biryukov.

"No," said his wife, offended. "Langoustines."

"Ah, langoustines!" said Biryukov, playing up.

She entered the shop—he saw her through the shop window—he saw rows of shelves with wine—he saw her fluttering there, and he slipped out of the car and tiptoed away.

Peeping is far more interesting than simply looking. Voyeurism is in fact the very essence of true writing; looking is the essence of works written with prior permission. Though, in fact, it's not like that at all.

She waits for him, writes a book about him, prepares to meet him again, look how well she's dressed, she has so many merits, except that she's no longer in her first youth, and her legs are a bit fat, but all he does is just knit his brow. Bastard. She gave her whole life to him, so that he could work in peace, she gave him her life—she's a Decembrist's wife—but what about him? What is he? He's just a bastard.

In a newspaper kiosk Biryukov noticed a magazine whose dubious cover had Russian letters written all over it. One of my Polish acquaintances said that Russian letters look like small chairs. On these chairs sit the apostles of Russian literature. Some of these chairs turned out to be electric.

He carried on walking, onto the square, and where one of the city's rare equine monuments had been there now stood something constructivist, vaguely familiar from old photographs. And there, on the corner, was a bookstore.

The store was empty. There were books on the shelves. He started to cry. He looked at the books and started to cry hot, bitter tears.

"You see," said Biryukov, "I was never a Westernizer in the sense that I wanted to turn a collective farmer into a Dutch miller. I was thinking about the Europeanization of the country only on the level of things, and not of ideas."

How quickly you can get used to a normal life! How quickly you stop being surprised! A mere two minutes ago there'd been the naughty magazine in Palashovskii Alley, the pile of books . . . Now he didn't even give them a second glance. No, that's not quite true. He was rapidly getting used to it, but nevertheless the novelty didn't wear off for some time, or the feeling of triumph, or the astonishment: why did we suffer so? The city was out on the streets. It was as if previously all the people of the city had barricaded themselves in their apartments and laid low, and now the city had burst open and blossomed, it had transformed itself into a southern resort and started singing long-drawn-out, joyful songs.

Russia had bored everyone stiff with her problems. Suddenly a moment arrived in which she simply vanished into thin air. And all of a sudden one felt sorry for her.

No, not quite like that.

At the end of the day, we suffered more than anyone else, ergo, we are right. More than that, the truth is with us. Moreover, suffering brings enlightenment. However, while it is only artists who need suffering, suffering as the foundation of public life makes our lives picturesque.

And so, Moscow is becoming a perfectly civilized capital. But the people are unhappy. It is only now that it is becoming clear that this people is by no means European. But what type is it, then? It can't be of no type at all, surely? On the other hand, why not?

And so for some time now Catholicism has been tempting me. I am resisting its charms, Kristina, but in my soul I have already made a series of concessions. I began with minor things. That Roman Catholic church in the backyard of that government building is so much like Notre Dame, as much as—well, any comparison will do, I can't be bothered with comparisons—and I was thinking, Why is it that Chaadaev is so cold? He writes Pushkin such friendly letters, but his flame is cold. Later I learned that Chaadaev had been born with an atrophied sexual drive. How Freud would have livened up at the sight of this gray-eyed patient with his jibing lips! Pushkin's letter to him holds far less intelligence. At times Pushkin is even prone to simplistic explanations. For example, the clergy are bad because they have to wear beards, and because they are not admitted into high society. It sounds almost stupid. But this is precisely where Pushkin's strength lies: he could allow himself to be stupid and to get drunk with his nanny, who then ended up in the school textbooks alongside Pavel Korchagin, the hero of How the Steel Was Tempered. Once at Christmas we came to the church—no, it was at Easter—to bless the Easter loaf and the eggs. And I was attracted by certain minor details: the women with their hair loose, and girls in long boots (it was early April, time of puddles) and with corduroy trousers tucked into their boots, party, tarty girls, their hair thick and curling with health. And I thought, "In the Orthodox churches everyone is poorer, there they disapprove of health. There they ask lots of things, but, having asked, they forget, and even less often do they correspond to . . . " And I also liked that here they sit on benches and read the Gospel as if they're in a village library. And every old woman sits alone, not all in one pile, and every old woman was in her time a bit of a tart with thick curls, bangs and conceit, and there's no scrum, although it still stinks, but in a different way, it's not them stinking, and even before all this I'd had a tourist's liking for the churches which Napoleon had threatened to carry away with him, whereas he'd only goggled his eyes at the others, and another, less-great Frenchman, for example, wrote some choice insults about St. Basil's Cathedral, but nonetheless I could not bring myself to make some sort of decisive step and hang a simple Catholic cross without a border around my neck and swear allegiance to Catholicism, Kristina. And generally speaking, everything was so cultured inside the Catholic church, there was no feeling of tension, no sense of a threshold, unlike in a Russian church. And after all this orthodoxy, well, it's Asia nonetheless, and Moscow is also Asia, and we ourselves are too. And why should I—a Muscovite Asian—become a European? And the thought came to me, well, not exactly that it's a betrayal of my ancestors, no . . . I don't know what precisely, but I didn't go again.

But I see here the possibility of embraces and welcoming cries apropos.

But I don't like.

No, Catholicism is closer to me.

And then he realizes that he is not meant for public work. After all, that means having to think all the time about the good of the people.

There is a certain difference between Chaadaev and me. For starters, I don't suffer from constipation, or at least I haven't up to this point in time, whereas he suffered from it and spent a long time sitting out his notorious letter. Second, I'm not so extravagantly neurotic. Third, I scarcely recognize the immanent role of God in the historical fate of Russia or indeed any other countries. Finally, my sexual drive is not atrophied. But as far as dizziness goes he and I are similar. Persecution mania bore down on me like a wave. I could have been seen for all sorts of different diagnoses simultaneously.

My fate is inevitable. No one will like me. Neither side. In this there is something of Chaadaev, but Pushkin didn't become Chaadaev precisely because he is Pushkin, and not simply a clever and vain man with no sexual feeling, a patient of Freud, who should be caught in a trap and examined until he starts to bore and repel one. But I, Kristina, love screwing women. Moreover, when I'm pissed I can fuck the sort of shit that even the mechanic who mends my car or the hairdresser who cuts my hair wouldn't touch with a ten-foot barge pole.

All this Biryukov takes upon himself and, like a bedbug, fills up with blood. He understands too late that he's got involved in somebody else's business. And they will kill him.

And the murder will take place, as is the custom, in a bathhouse. He will be boiled alive.

Russian life was such a one-off that it all went into a dimension where there is in fact no life, nothing was left, only a fiction, and I did not enjoy such a substitution, but instead sank slowly into horror.

The Ukrainians will spit the Crimea out in our face like a cherry stone, and we shall once again have a Russian flowering sakura.

In short, Biryukov, in case someone still hasn't got it, will simply "disappear."

The weakness of man in general, divided by the weakness of the Russian man in particular and multiplied by the immortality of the soul—that's her, that's what our motherland is, Kristina!

Rozanov kept on hassling the dying Strakhov with a mass of vile questions. Strakhov for the most part said nothing, because he was dying of mouth cancer and because he didn't trust Rozanov very much; but Rozanov kept insisting, and when Strakhov turned his face to the wall, Rozanov rudely turned the dying man toward him and asked what epitaph Strakhov would wish for himself. Strakhov, fearing that Rozanov would hurt him, even though his pain was already unbearable, thought, and said, "I wanted to be a sober man among drunkards."

These are remarkable words.

On hearing them, Rozanov burst into tears, and Strakhov died.

"Well, and what solution do you see, dear Aleksandr Nikolae-vich?"

"No solution," replied Biryukov anxiously.

They boiled him alive.

Why did they boil him? The reader will think that they boiled him because he was considered a threat by one of the parties, but in fact he was considered a threat by them both, and they agreed to remove him, so that he could no longer get in the way of their quarrels. But it's not quite like that.

"And so, boundaries by Kursk?"

"But is that really where they are set, by Kursk?"

"But surely you know?"

In the meantime, Biryukov was being treated in a psychiatric clinic and didn't know. He was there not because he was mad, but because he was neurotic, and when it was announced that Brezh-nev had died he once again fell ill for several years. His whole nervous system came to the surface and looked like his intestines or like the world tree that holds all things. And all this came to light.

His nerves grew so sensitive that he remembered everything about himself, every last detail from his earliest childhood years, and he realized that he'd lived in spurts and thought in fits and starts. He remembered how his parents had conceived him, on that very Wednesday, in the morning, because his father worked in the evenings, and sometimes slept in the mornings, and when he woke up that morning they conceived him, and his mother was rosy that morning, and he remembered that rosiness, he recalled everything and ended up in the clinic for nervous disorders, because he needed to be treated; and at first the clinic was like a clinic, that is, real crap and not what a clinic should be at all, and he lay in a ward for seven in stifling conditions, and the nurses' uniforms were ripped and the smell of fish came from under their smocks; and they conceived him on that very Wednesday, he remembered everything, and fell very ill.

"So what do you suggest?" asked Biryukov.

I don't know what they will do with me. Chaadaev got scared. When it all blew up he informed on Nadezhdin, on everyone. Pushkin wrote him a letter. Vyzaemsky also behaved dishonorably.

"To consolidate Russia within her historical boundaries," was the answer.

But one day everything changed in the clinic: the nurses no longer wore ripped uniforms and no longer stank. They had all been kicked out, and were replaced by nice young girls in light-blue smocks and large tinted glasses. They resembled owls.

At that particular time Biryukov couldn't have cared less. He only wanted to know what awaited him after death. No matter who he asked, nobody was able to give him a reassuring answer. But one day the new director of the clinic, a Dane called Karl Stif (with one f) came into his ward, and said that he knew what would happen to Biryukov after death and, winking, offered Biryukov a tight rubber toy. Biryukov refused angrily.

On what basis can one unite Russia? On the basis of the impossibility of living without her?

"No," said Biryukov. "I don't want a rubber doll. Give me the real thing."

"Leave it out! Finland manages perfectly well without us!"

"We're the ones who won't get by without them all. But no, we will manage too!"

"To become a second- or third-rate country, like France."

"But who will trust us again? We'll bear-hug them and then trick them."

Toward evening they gave him the real thing. It took the form of a sweet young girl, and Biryukov decided that she was in love with him. But she wasn't in love with him, as she admitted to him, she was simply earning money to pay for her university course, and she would be paid out of his account at the clinic, which by now had been handed over to Stif, just as everything seemed to have been handed over to someone; the houses were sprouting new signboards, at last everyone had obtained sheepskin coats and jeans, and prices had soared, like a patient's temperature during pneumonia, and the people frowned. In general the people didn't like any of this one little bit. Then unattractive young men started going around the apartments and asking, "What is it you want?" and a referendum was held, but nobody really knew what they wanted.

"The idea itself was not a bad one and was quite national."

"As far as national is concerned—that's exactly right," agreed Biryukov.

"Economically inefficient, that's the problem."

"But why?"

"Well, who knows? Inefficient and that's that."

"But was much blood spilled?" inquired Biryukov delicately.

A brief silence. A few coughs.

"So what, let it be second-rate!" said Biryukov. "We've already lived in a first-rate one. People manage to live their lives in all sorts of countries!"

As he is crying over the books a man comes up to him in the empty bookstore, and he recognized him: "Jo!"

Jo is old. He is bearded and his appearance is hardly of the freshest. They go to a restaurant, sit on the veranda. Yes, I'll have something, meat loaf or something like that.

"To drink?"

"What drinks do you have?"

"We have everything!" grinned the waiter.

Biryukov looked at him suspiciously. "Bring us some beer."

"Two beers!" shouted Joseph. "I'll pay for the apertif, and go halves on the lunch, OK?"

"I'm not hungry," said Biryukov.

"I certainly wasn't expecting to meet you. I knew that you were supposed to come out, but I didn't know."

"Did you return a long time ago?"

"I'm already planning to go back."

"Back?"

"But what is to be done here?"

"Really?" said Biryukov vaguely, somewhat surprised.

A coup is on the way. The Western democracies have washed their hands of everything. Russia will once again become a mighty state. The young are shaving their heads as a sign of mourning for great Russia. No, we shall preserve something, of course. But we'll certainly stop the Yid revival. Tell us, Biryukov, was this what you wanted? You, the cheap corrupter of a great nation!

You have been found guilty by our court, Biryukov. You are sentenced to death. I shall tell you what it will be. You are submerged in a cauldron of icy water. It is heated up slowly. You experience hellish cold at first, then you begin to warm up, then you will feel splendid, like in a bath or a swimming pool; but the temperature will creep up steadily, higher and higher. The first little bubbles rise to the surface. Finally, you are boiling at a hundred degrees Celsius. You are boiled right through. Your flesh will come away from your bones. Now that's what I call an execution. How do you like it?

Biryukov wanted to go back to the clinic, under the wing of the old man Karl Stif. His wife was rushing around about the city somewhere, phoning the police. Biryukov dreamed of going to the clinic so that he could at some time in the future leave it once again, but leave it for somewhere different next time, not for this transitional dimension, but for a less mocking plane of being, or, even better, to go home, home, into the close-knit circle of whatever good friends had been preserved.

The ending is botched, a real potboiler. Of course, Biryukov took fright, messed up, went back on everything. That is, he had planned on tricking the skinheads and slipping away in time to South Africa, where Apartheid still ruled.

"Fair enough," he said in a spirit of conciliation. "Let me have a think! But where are the guarantees?"

They gave guarantees and left politely.

He thinks. When they enter he says: I agree.

He writes, to all appearances not even under dictation:

WHAT I HAVE SEEN HAS SHOCKED ME. THIS WAS NOT WHAT I HAD DREAMED OF. I RENOUNCE MY FORMER VIEWS. LONG LIVE MIGHTY RUSSIA! LONG LIVE THE VOLUNTARY UNION OF PEOPLES!

"Well, that's wonderful!" He smiles and smiles broadly and smiles in utter joy, and adds, almost kindly, "Oh yes, you forgot to sign, right here, Aleksandr Nikolaevich!"

Aleksandr Nikolaevich signs and wipes away the sweat with his handkerchief. A shot rings out. The room immediately fills with people.

"We shall be treating this as suicide. Put his suicide note in his jacket pocket. Fingerprints on the gun. I want no slipups."

He taps Biryukov with the tip of his boot.

"Quiet now, the bastard."

"It's a shame we couldn't torture him. Would have left traces."

Biryukov lay on the floor, so cute, with an open mouth.

LIFE WITH AN IDIOT

As mentioned in the Introduction, "Life with an Idiot" may be viewed as an allegory of life under Communism, but its richness as a parable about the relationship between totalitarianism, barbarism and culture becomes more apparent if we understand why the narrator chooses the punishment he does. If the story's wider message is that every individual and every nation has his or her idiot, an idiot who may be described in political or existential or psychological terms, the narrator's choice of a "holy fool," a key figure from Russian culture, reflects tendencies within, and choices made by, the Russians themselves.

Although the Russian word for a holy fool, *yurodivy* (or "holy fool for the sake of Christ"—*yurodivy radi Khrista*) can be used loosely to refer to any crazy person, its primary meaning refers not simply to one whose madness reflects God's love and provides prophetic insights into and contact with a higher reality, but to a man or woman who *feigns* madness, puts on an antic disposition, in order to acquire greater humility. Whether the majority of such fools were simply mad, or charlatans, or genuine holy fools is open to debate, but what is clear is that Russians came to view the holy fools' offensive behavior as a deliberate provocation. Only the true saint, the argument ran, would be able to love those who had insulted him—even if he had to insult them first in order to provoke such a reaction. The saintly fools took on the sufferings of a Job and risked rejection by society in order to perfect themselves, a self-sacrifice that embodies a central feature of Russian religion and culture: its kenoticism, its imitation of Christ's humbling of Himself by becoming mortal. It is the positive aspect of the verbal and physical assaults committed by the holy fools that has been stressed in Russian culture, the ways in which the fools challenge the powerful. Two of the most famous examples, Vasily the Blessed and Nikolka of Pskov, fearlessly condemned the atrocities committed by Ivan the Terrible, and the holy fool in Pushkin's *Boris Godunov* is another such figure. Moreover, many Russian writers have been viewed as holy fools: Stalin's sometimes lenient treatment of Mandelstam, Pasternak and Bulgakov may reflect a fear that these writers were shamans, with the power to see into his soul or even cast a spell on him.

Many aspects of Vova's behavior connect him to this tradition: holy fools often went around naked, even in winter, or dressed strangely; they loved metal objects; and though usually chaste, some (such as Rasputin) were highly promiscuous. Often the holy fools made no coherent sounds or their sentences were nonsensical, so that others took on the role of interpreting their prophecies. The narrator's attempts to learn the truth from his "holy fool" therefore parody the idealization of this figure in Russian literature. The most important "modern" holy fool in Russian literature, Dostoevsky's Prince Lev Myshkin, is the subject of the main parody, as the title suggests. It may seem strange to compare the Christ-like Myshkin, Dostoevsky's attempt to create "a positively good man," with Erofeyev's idiot, but there are significant similarities between the works, especially from a Freudian viewpoint. Erofeyev may be said to parody both Dostoevsky and Freudian readings of Dostoevsky, by making explicit what psychoanalytical literary criticism would argue is implicit in the Oedipal triangle of Myshkin–Nastasiya Filippovna–Rogozhin: primal scenes, castration anxieties, repressed homosexuality, sadomasochism and so on. Yet by doing so Erofeyev is also acknowledging that Freudian theory may help to make sense not only of *The Idiot* and Dostoevsky's work as a whole, but of wider issues of the Russian psyche.

"Life with an Idiot" suggests that to understand the holy fool may be to understand the Russians. For it would be possible to view acts of violence or even murder committed by holy fools as being free of sin if the saint had sinned deliberately in order to increase his humility. The broader applicability of this notion to any ideology weighing up ends and means is painfully obvious. Dostoevsky is typical of Russian writers in ultimately justifying intellectual and emotional extremism in the name of an ideal or idea; at least the Russian feels guilty when he does wrong and knows he is doing wrong. Moreover, such acts merely serve as proof of the Russian's more extreme, more authentic, more human, more divine character. The words from Revelation, quoted in *The Possessed*, summarize the Russian belief that one can be sinner or saint, cold or hot, but one must not be lukewarm. Dostoevsky may be the most extreme representative of the phenomenon that D. H. Lawrence termed "sinning one's way to Jesus"; but at least Dostoevsky's novels honestly show all sides of this idealism. Unfortunately, Russian culture has on the whole followed Dostoevsky the publicist: writers, philosophers and politicians of all political persuasions have made a cult of the idea that both extremes, good and evil, are ultimately positive. They have also failed to see how, for example, meekness and submissiveness are questionable virtues if they allow aggressive impulses to triumph. Fortunately for many apologists for the Russian way, there have been convenient solutions to hand: the chief aggressors can't have been native Russians, or if they were, the baneful (and centuries-old) influence of the Mongol yoke or Russia's geographical vulnerability can be blamed for present repressions.

Also implicit in "Life with an Idiot" is the question whether an analogous idealization of culture was responsible in part for the triumph of barbarism in the twentieth century. It is strange that Russian literature, certainly one of the strongest and certainly the most didactic of modern literatures, and one whose summons to the reader to change both his own and the nation's life has been so eloquent, a literature well placed to offer proof that the humanities can humanize, belongs to the country where the claims of the ideal have produced the most terrible of realities. Russian literature from Pushkin to the present has provided many heroic defenses of poetry; but that absolute faith in the power of literature which shaped not merely so many literary masterpieces, but also their authors' very lives, is in painful contrast to the overall failure of the intelligentsia and culture as a whole to resist barbarism in the Soviet period.

Yet the political and cultural allegories in "Life with an Idiot" may also apply to Western society. Although he is less convinced than most Russian writers of the advantages of living dangerously, Erofeyev avoids a simplistic endorsement of the advantages of a quiet life, and even asks whether such a life is possible. Vova may symbolize not only political dictatorship, but also various impulses of sex and violence, of the unconscious, of war, of the uneasy relationships between Eros and Thanatos. Do the narrator and his wife welcome their sexual liberation? Must ennui erupt into barbarism? The story may reflect Erofeyev's literary anxieties as well as his realization that the writer always runs the risk (needs to run the risk, some Russian writers might say) of letting idiocy and existential terror into his life, with or without the help of the KGB. Consequently another of the story's aims is to question culture's inability to resist tyranny, or culture's complicity in tyranny, to investigate the benefits allegedly gained by artists in a repressive society, and to ask whether or not art makes anything happen.

Although Freud believed that Russians were exceptional in their degree of psychic ambivalence, what is true of Russians is also true of other peoples. Vova represents some primordial and largely evil force. Certainly he shares some features with Lenin: Vova is a short form of the name Vladimir; his physical appearance recalls Lenin's; there is a reference to the Lena River, from which Lenin took his name, and so on. But these allusions are partly tongue-in-cheek, and even on the political level the work aims to be a broader allegory of Russian submissiveness and aggression, idealism and messianism. The story certainly betrays Erofeyev's fear that Lenin, Stalin and their heirs are always seeking to escape from the Mausoleum, but it may also suggest that it is another building on Red Square, the Cathedral of the Blessed Vasily, St. Basil's Cathedral, which better symbolizes Russia's unique destiny. The impulses which Lenin and Vasily embody—materialism and idealism, rationalism and irrationalism, humanism and religion, Westernizing and Russophile beliefs, but all underwritten by a very Russian maximalism—interact in an analysis of the tragic choices faced by man in his attempts to escape the conclusion that life is a tale told by an idiot, signifying nothing. In having the courage to work in this dangerous area of metaphysical *pro* and *contra* and in searching for "the truth" rather than staying with idealized notions of beauty, humility and art, Erofeyev's cruel talent is simply being cruel to be kind.

3   some imbecile suffering from oligophrenia

Soviet medicine distinguished three main categories of "oligophrenia": debils (mild retardation), imbeciles (moderate) and idiots (profound). Incompetent or false diagnoses of oligophrenia were used against dissidents in the USSR, and there continues to be an overuse of the categories in the treatment of many children placed in orphanages and institutions in the former Soviet Union to this day.

3   blessed, holy fool type of abnormality, national in both form and content

"Blessed" is the epithet applied to Vasily the Blessed, the saint after whom St. Basil's Cathedral (The Cathedral of Basil the Blessed in Russian) is named, and has the connotations of holiness and foolishness.

"National in both form and content" refers to the idea that Socialist Realist writing was, according to the official definition adopted in 1934 by the First Congress of the Writers' Union, "realist in form and socialist in content."

3   starets

In the Russian Orthodox church, an elder or spiritual father; a spiritual leader.

3   the parvis of a Zagorsk monastery

Zagorsk—now Sergius-Possad—is one of Russia's most holy places. It was the headquarters of the Orthodox church for much of the Soviet period.

3   the sake of diversion (in the Pascalian sense of the word, of course)

See in particular Section I, VIII of the *Pensées*.

3 *For life is a tale told by an idiot, gentlemen!*

The original has a variation on a famous quotation, the last line of Gogol's "The Story of How Ivan Ivanovich Quarreled with Ivan Nikiforovich": *"Skuchno na etom svete, gospoda!"* ("What a dreary world we live in, Gentlemen!") Erofeyev changes this to "It's a terrifying world we live in, Gentlemen!"

4 *He says his name is Kraig Benson*

Possible that this name combines the names of two of Erofeyev's American friends (at the time of the *Metropol* affair) with a pun on the KGB.

6 *So my holy peasant Marei Mareich had to suffer as well.*

Presumably a reference to Dostoevsky's "Peasant Marei" ("Muzhik Marei"), from his *Diary of a Writer*. The significance of this section is that it describes Dostoevsky recollecting how, in his Siberian prison camp, he had been feeling a deep hatred of the common Russian people, when he suddenly remembered a kind, loving peasant from his past. This memory rekindled his faith in the ultimate goodness of, or at the least the hope of redemption for, the Russian peasant. Here it would also seem to suggest Dostoevsky's tendency to overidealize and sentimentalize the broad Russian character, and as such is representative of a wider impulse toward the justification of maximalism within the Russians themselves. (See the entry for February 1876 in *A Writer's Diary, Volume 1, 1873–1876*, translated and annotated by Kenneth Lantz, with an Introductory Study by Gary Saul Morson [Evanston, Ill.: Northwestern University Press, 1994] pp. 351–355.)

7 zakuski

Russian hors d'oeuvres.

7 *"Will I ever," I say, "see my beloved wife Masha again?"*

On April 15, 1864, Dostoevsky's first wife, Maria Dmitrievna, died. The following day Dostoevsky wrote in his notebook:

> Masha is lying on the table. Will I see Masha again? To love a person as one's own self, as Christ commanded, is impossible, On earth the law of personality binds us; the I *stands in the way... Christ was able, but Christ was eternal, from all ages the ideal* toward which man strives and according to the law of nature must strive. After Christ's appearance, it became clear that the highest development of personality must attain to that point where man annihilates his own "I," surrenders it

completely to all and everyone without division or reserve . . . And this is the greatest happiness . . . This is Christ's paradise . . . And so, on earth man strives toward an ideal contrary to his nature. When man has not fulfilled the law of striving toward the ideal, i.e., has not *by love* offered his "I" in sacrifice to people or to another being (*Masha and I*), he experiences suffering and has called this condition sin.

(Quoted from Konstantin Mochulsky: *Dostoevsky, His Life and Art*, translated by Michael A. Minihan [Princeton University Press, 1973].)

11 *A birch was standing in a field*

A very popular Russian folk song.

12 *"His skull's rather Socratic, I'm sure."*

Gorky wrote about the Socratic appearance of Lenin's head.

14 *I loved you, people. Report from the gallows—it's happened before.*

"People, I have loved you. Be on your guard" is the last entry from the prison journal (*Notes From the Gallows*) of the Czech Communist journalist and writer Julius Fuchik, who was executed by the Nazis in 1943 at the age of forty.

14 *The blood-dimmed tide is loosed, Vova, the ceremony of innocence drowned.*

The original is a quote from Akhmatova's 1921 poem "Everything has been looted, betrayed, sold."

15 *I even spread out a map of the USSR before him*

A possible echo of the map scene in Pushkin's *Boris Godunov*.

26 *I am Renoir.*

Although the direct reference appears to be to Auguste Renoir, it is also worth noting that Erofeyev's story seems to be a reworking of Jean Renoir's classic film *Boudu sauvé des eaux* (*Boudu Saved from Drowning*) (1932).

A WHITE NEUTERED TOMCAT WITH THE EYES OF A BEAUTIFUL WOMAN

31 *Perhaps they'll only give me a fright, like Dostoevsky, and exile me.*

In 1849 Dostoevsky, along with his fellow members of the Petrashevsky circle, was led out to be executed. At the very last moment the sentence was commuted to a prison labor camp in Siberia. Apart from the obvious links with Dostoevsky's life and works, this story has echoes of works on this theme by Hugo and Nabokov, among others.

31 *"He would have become Chernyshevsky, got it?"*

Nikolai Chernyshevsky, author of *What Is to Be Done?* (1863), for many one of the worst novels of all time (somewhat unfair). Certainly one of the most influential novels of all time. Martin Amis writes:

> It fills you with extraordinary torpor to learn that Lenin read Nikolai Chernyshevsky's insuperably talentless novel *What Is to Be Done?* (1863) *five times* in one summer. To read this book once in five summers would defeat most of us; but Lenin persisted, "It completely reshaped me," he said in 1904. "This is a book that changes one for a whole lifetime." Its greatest merit, he stressed, was that it showed you "what a revolutionary *must be like*." Humiliating though it may feel, we are obliged to conclude that *What Is to Be Done?* is the most influential novel of all time. With its didactic portrait of the revolutionary New man, its "russification" of current radical themes, and its contempt for ordinary people, "Chernyshevsky's novel, far more than Marx's *Capital*, supplied the emotional dynamic that eventually went to make the Russian Revolution" (Joseph Frank).

(Martin Amis, *Koba the Dread. Laughter and the Twenty Million* [New York: Miramax Books 2002], p. 27.)

32 *Khlebnikov has a poem about laughers.*

"Incantation by laughter" (1910), one of the most famous works by Velimir Khlebnikov, the great Futurist poet (1885–1922), begins with the lines given here.

> Man is born happy and free,
> But is everywhere enchained.

The original has the words "Man is created for happiness like a bird is for flight." In his article "Russia's *Fleurs du mal*" Erofeyev comments on nineteenth-century Russian literature's "philosophy of hope":

However, Russian literature did not wish to part with its optimistic illusions. It followed in the footsteps of the Russian Populist belletrist Vladimir Korolenko (1853–1921), whose famous phrase stated that "Man is created for happiness like a bird is for flight," and of Gorky with his proclamation "Man—that has a proud ring!" Both utterances became part of the foundation of Socialist Realism.

As Korolenko's words are not quite as famous as Rousseau's, the slight misquotation in my translation seems appropriate.

SHIT-SUCKER

35 Herzen

Aleksandr Ivanovich Herzen (1812–1870), leading Russian writer, journalist, editor and increasingly recognized as one of Russia's greatest political and moral philosophers. Herzen was the son of a Russian noble, I. A. Yakovlev, and his German common-law wife, hence the reference here to his bastardy. In 1847 he emigrated to Paris, and from 1852 to 1864 lived in London, where he established a Russian printing press. Copies of the annual *Polar Star* and the fortnightly newspaper *Kolokol (The Bell)* (1857–1867) were smuggled into Russia (and sometimes mailed) and played a major role in the intellectual life of the nation. Herzen's masterpiece is his memoir, *My Past and Thoughts*; other important works include *From the Other Shore* and *Who Is to Blame?*

36 Yeah, they're just the sort that shot down the Korean airliner!

On September 1, 1983, the Soviet air force shot down the South Korean jet KAL 007 over Sakhalin, killing all 269 people on board, an event that brought relations between the Soviets and the Reagan administration to a new low.

38 Gorky Street

Now Tverskaya—one of the main streets in the very heart of Moscow.

40 If Gogol's Chichikov had had a fling with a domestic serf

Chichikov—the hero/anti-hero of *Dead Souls*.

41–42 Having been demobilized four years ago, Vladimir Sorokin, member of the Young Communists' League

The Communist Youth League or Komsomol, or, to give it its full title, the All-Union Leninist Union of Communist Youth, the organization for would-be

Communists aged fourteen to twenty-eight. There is also a playful allusion here to Vladimir Sorokin, one of Russia's leading postmodernists (but not widely known at the time this story was written).

43 *all the marshals with Zhukov at their head, and the culture vulture*
Zhdanov, and old man Kalinin, and Malenkov, and Molotov, and
Mikhail Andreevich Suslov, chief ideologist. And in the doorway to the
Main Cabinet lies a huge frozen idol, the fiery comrade-in-arms Klim
Voroshilov, ready for anything...

Georgy Zhukov (1896–1974) was one of Russia's greatest military heroes, and one of the men most responsible for Allied victory in the Second World War. Deputy Supreme Commander-in-Chief from 1942, he played a major role in the planning and execution of most of the major battles of the war, including the defense of both Leningrad and Moscow, the eventual victory at Stalingrad and the final assault on Berlin. Removed from his posts by Stalin after 1945, but was appointed Defense Minister by Khrushchev later (only to be dismissed again shortly afterward).

Andrei Zhdanov (1896–1948) was a close ally of Stalin and a member of the Politburo from 1939. Played an important role in the defense of Leningrad from 1941 to 1944, but is perhaps best known for the harsh ideological and culture policies in the immediate postwar period (Zhdanovism), for example, the attacks on Anna Akhmatova and Mikhail Zoshchenko and their expulsion from the Writers' Union in 1946.

Georgy Malenkov (1902–1984) was a powerful ally of Stalin and for a short period after Stalin's death the most powerful politician in the USSR. Out-maneuvered by Khrushchev in the subsequent power struggle and sent into virtual (internal) exile in 1957.

Vyacheslav Molotov (1890–1986; real name Vyacheslav Mikhailovich Skriabin—the pseudonym Molotov means "the hammer") was Stalin's virtual deputy for many years, Molotov is best known in the West as the Soviet Minister for Foreign Affairs during the Second World War and for crucial periods of the Cold War (1939–1949 and 1953–1956).

Mikhail Suslov (1902–1982) was the leading Party ideologist, a notoriously cautious gray cardinal who was one of those most responsible for Soviet foreign policy in the post-Stalin period.

Kliment Voroshilov (1881–1969) was a loyal associate of Stalin from the Civil War, who held a number of prominent political and military posts under both Stalin and Khrushchev (People's Commissar of Military and Naval Affairs from 1925 to 1940, Deputy Chairman of the Council of Ministers from 1946 to 1953 and President of the Supreme Soviet from 1953 to 1960 without ever showing any particular competence or aptitude for these tasks. Removed from power by Khrushchev in 1961.

Lavrenty Beria (1899–1953) was head of the Soviet Secret Police from 1938. Executed after Stalin's death.

HOW WE MURDERED THE FRENCHMAN

50 Voluntary Society for Collaboration with the Armed Forces

A mass organization responsible for training citizens in civil defense, but also for organizing sports events and other activities.

51 Trust, but verify.

A Russian saying often quoted by President Ronald Reagan in his negotiations with the Soviet Union's leaders.

THE MAIDEN AND DEATH

56 Sklifosovsky Accident and Emergency Hospital

The main casualty hospital in Moscow.

58 "Do you think that love conquers death?"

In 1931 Gorky read his poem (which he called a "fairy tale") "The Maiden and Death" to Stalin and Voroshilov, and the Soviet press reported that Stalin wrote on the margin of the manuscript: "This thing is more powerful than Goethe's *Faust*. Love conquers death."
    In Gorky's overly sentimental and frankly not very good poem, Death grants a young maiden one extra day of life so she may experience the joys of love. The power of love so impresses Death that she (death is female in Russian) takes pity on the maiden, and from that day, Gorky tells us, love and death go hand in hand.

63 I thought that she would wink at me, like the Countess in **The Queen of Spades.**

A number of aspects of this scene parallel the funeral service held for the Countess in Pushkin's *The Queen of Spades.*

68 Man—that has a proud ring.

Quote from Gorky's play *The Lower Depths*. See also note above, pages 227–28.

68 Love conquers death.

In the story's last line the Russian reader is likely to wonder whether in fact the "free word order" of Russian is being exploited here to suggest that in fact

"Death conquers love." One can argue the case for the triumph of either love or death in this story, especially as it is not clear which reading is a more unsettling summary of the plot, or indeed of the joint triumph (and/or defeat) of both; but presumably the ambiguity is the main point here.

ANNA'S BODY, OR THE END OF THE RUSSIAN AVANT-GARDE

70–71   *Sometimes Anna felt that she was Anna Karenina, sometimes Anna Akhmatova, sometimes simply Chekhov's burdensome Anna-round-the-neck.*

In Chekhov's story "Anna Round the Neck," the title is both an allusion to "The Order of St Anne's" desired by Anna's older, unpleasant husband, and to the way in which she becomes a burden to him by turning the tables on him. There is a mild polemic here with *Anna Karenina* (as there is in Chekhov's story of another Anna, "The Lady with the Little Dog"), in that Anna refuses to be a victim, though at the cost of losing her former good nature.

71   *"I'll get rid of it by March, before Women's Day"*

International Women's Day, March 8, in the Soviet Union and in Russia is a favorite celebration, similar to, but obviously broader than, Mother's Day.

THE PARAKEET

76   *world culture, my right honorable Spiridon Ermolaevich, as I most humbly understand it, thinks predominantly in symbols*

World culture—a very Russian concept. Compare, for example, Osip Mandelstam's definition of his poetic school of Acmeism as being a "longing for world culture (*toska po mirovi kul'ture*)."

76   *albeit the humblest goldfinch*

One of the most symbolic of birds, usually associated with Christ's passion.

PERSIAN LILAC

93   *something uncomplicated, of course, naturally, some musical phrase or other from* Moscow Nights

A very popular Russian song (often translated, somewhat more accurately, if not very poetically for such a romantic song, as "Moscow Suburb Nights").

BERDYAEV

Nikolai Aleksandrovich Berdyaev (1874–1948) was a leading Russian religious existentialist philosopher. Originally a Marxist, in his youth Berdyaev was exiled to Vologda for three years for his membership in the Social Democratic party. Professor of Philosophy at Moscow University after the 1917 revolution, he was sent into exile in 1922 because of his religious views, and settled in France. His works include *The Russian Idea*.

98 *the animals from Grandfather Krylov's* Fables

Ivan Andreevich Krylov (1769–1844) was a journalist, a playwright and author of Russia's best fables. His early fables were translations and reworkings of La Fontaine's, but his later works deal convincingly with issues in the Russia of his day.

99 *if one thinks of Rozanov*

Vasily Vasilevich Rozanov (1856–1919) was a writer, philosopher and literary critic. In 1880 he married Apollonariya Suslova, fourteen years his senior, who had been at one time Dostoevsky's mistress. His most famous works include *Dostoevsky and the Legend of the Grand Inquisitor* (1894), *Solitaria* (1912) and *The Apocalypse of Our Times* (1917–1918).

101 *a certain scumbag like Nestor Kukolnik*

Nestor Vasilevich Kukolnik (1808–1868) was a dominant figure in the Russian literary scene under Nicholas I, and one of the leading sycophants and least talented writers of his age.

106–107 *I asked Kruglitsky what had become of Michel ... "He still nicked his best line from Bestuzhev!" snorted Julia. "He never got rid of that Scottish sediment," said Kruglitsky angrily, "that Scottish smell of cheap whiskey on his breath."*

This would appear to be an idiosyncratic reference to Mikhail Lermontov, given his Scottish ancestry and the fact that the first line of one of his most famous poems, *"Beleet parus odinokii"* ("A sail shows white"), was indeed borrowed from a Bestuzhev poem.

Aleksandr Aleksandrovich Bestuzhev (1797–1837; pseudonym Marlinsky) was a Romantic poet and prose writer and Decembrist revolutionary.

107 *The conversation, as is always the case, turned to the Marquis de Custine.*

Astolphe Louis Léonor, Marquis de Custine (1790–1857), was a diplomat and a writer whose journey to Russia in 1839 was described in a four-volume work

La Russie en 1839, published in Paris in 1843. In a review of Custine's work Erofeyev, referring to Herzen's statement that *La Russie en 1839* was "unquestionably the most diverting and intelligent book written about Russia by a foreigner," states that "Herzen's words are still true today, despite the thousands of books written about Russia since that time."

Custine ends his work with this provocative observation:

> Whenever your son is discontented in France, I have a simple remedy: tell him to go to Russia. The journey is beneficial for any foreigner, for whoever has properly experienced that country will be happy to live anywhere else. It is always good to know that there exists a society in which no happiness is possible, because, by reason of his nature, man cannot be happy unless he is free.

(Marquis de Custine, *Letters from Russia*, translated by Robin Buss [Penguin Classics, 1991], p. 241.)

107 *"I'm just so fed up with all those obsolete letters, those Yats and Yers." "And Izhitsa's even worse!"*

In 1918 some of the letters from the pre-Revolutionary Russian alphabet, such as Yats and Izhitsa, were abolished to simplify spelling.

107–108 *"The Erfurt Program doesn't forbid it!"*

The program adopted by the German Social-Democratic party at the Congress in Erfurt in October 1891.

109 *"You look like Pugachev"*

Yemelyan Pugachev (c. 1742–1775), a Don Cossack, led a major Cossack and peasant rebellion in Russia (Pugachev Rebellion, 1773–1775). One of Russian history's many Pretenders, he claimed to be Peter III (who had in fact been deposed and assassinated by his wife, Catherine the Great). Pugachev was eventually defeated, captured and executed. Pushkin wrote about Pugachev in his 1836 novel *The Captain's Daughter* and also in his nonfictional *The History of Pugachev* (1834).

115 *Everything about her was just as one would expect: thirty-something*

In the Russian original, the reference is to "the Balzacian age." This is a lighthearted reference to women between thirty and forty, and became popular after the publication in Russian of Honoré de Balzac's novel *La femme de trente ans*.

117   *the namesake of the wonderful painter Filonov*

Pavel Nikolaevich Filonov (1883–1941) was one of the outstanding Russian avant-garde artists of the twentieth century.

118   *Korolenko wrote to her*

See third note on "A White Neutered Tomcat with the Eyes of a Beautiful Woman," above.

118   *Countess Rostopchina*

Evdokiia Petrovna Rostopchina (1811–1858) was a poet and a playwright and Moscow socialite, one of the most popular and best nineteenth-century Russian women writers. Many of her poems were set to music by leading composers.

THE END OF EVERYTHING

123   *Blinova*

Blin is the Russian word for "pancake."

124   *"The sun has got his hat on," said Skaftymov*

The Russian original is somewhat more poetic: he quotes the well-known poem by Afanasy Fet:

> I have come to greet you,
> To tell you that the sun has risen.

The point of the allusion, however, is merely to convey a clichéd, recognizable quote for the morning. "Here comes the sun, little darling," "Morning has broken" or "Sunrise, early in the morning" would all do just as well.

124   *At the very height of the notorious campaign against cosmopolitanism*

Stalin's campaign against cosmopolitanism was first and foremost a campaign against the Jewish intelligentsia.

126   *Meister Eckehart*

Eckehart (c. 1260–1327) was a German mystic philosopher.

BOLDINO AUTUMN

In the fall of 1830 and again in 1833 at his Boldino estate Pushkin experienced two of the most productive periods of writing of his life. More generally, the phrase is used about any exceptional creative period of an artist's life.

131 Sisin was staring out

As in the previous story, the surname here is not very serious, as it implies "Mr. Tits" in Russian. The antihero of Erofeyev's second novel, *The Last Judgment*, is also called Sisin.

LETTER TO MOTHER

The title alludes to a much-loved poem by Sergei Esenin (1895–1925), one of the best and most popular of twentieth-century Russian poets. Esenin was a "peasant" poet, and his melancholy verse and bohemian lifestyle have always struck a chord with the mass Russian reader. He married Isadora Duncan in 1923, but they divorced in 1924. He hanged himself in 1925.

135 No retreat, no surrender!

The original has the phrase "Not one step back!" a popular slogan in Soviet war propaganda from 1942 onward.

138 Are our pitiful wannabe members of the Signposts group right?

The *Vekhi* (*Signposts* or *Landmarks*) group refers to the authors whose collection of essays under this title formed a damning critique of the radical Russian intelligentsia. The authors were Berdyaev, S. N. Bulgakov, M. O. Gershenzon, A. S. Izgoev, B. A. Kistyakovsky, P. B. Struve and S. L. Frank.

138 I have read an interesting book, one of the banned ones.

Alludes to the subject matter of Gogol's *Dead Souls*.

138 The book is sharp, useful, I would even say timely

Lenin's characterization of Gorky's novel *Mother* (as expressed to the author himself): "A very timely book." (See the notes on the story "Mother" for further details of this work.)

138 "Herzen! Herzen!" he shouts, "is coming back. Starting tomorrow The Bell will be on sale!"

On Herzen and *The Bell*, see the first entry for the story "Shit-sucker."

139 "'The world's great page begins anew.'"

In the original Zotov misquotes (by changing one letter) the first line of a famous Pushkin poem of 1823 (*"Svobody seiatel' pustynnyi"*), changing it from "The sower of freedom in the desert" to "the leader (or doer) of freedom in the desert." Pushkin described his poem as an imitation of a "parable of that moderate democrat, Jesus Christ."

142 monument to Ivan Susanin

Ivan Susanin was a peasant from Kostroma who in 1613 tricked Polish insurgents by leading them into a wilderness, thereby helping the Russian resistance to the Poles. Susanin was tortured to death for his efforts, and became the hero of Glinka's opera *A Life for the Tsar* (renamed *Ivan Susanin* in Soviet times).

143 "So I suppose Suvorov didn't exist either, then?"

Count Aleksandr Vasilevich Suvorov (1729–1800) was one of Russia's greatest generals, famous for commanding the Russian army during the Russo-Turkish War of 1787–1791 and in the French Revolutionary Wars.

146 We shall build a new world on these foundations, and we who were naught, we shall be all!

Lines from "The Internationale." "The Internationale" was written in Paris, in June 1871 by Eugène Pottier. A member of the International and of the Central Committee of the Commune, he escaped the death sentence in 1873 by going to America. "The Internationale" was the Soviet Union's official anthem from 1917 until 1944.

THREE MEETINGS

The title alludes to a work by Vladimir Sergeevich Soloviev (1853–1900), the leading Russian theologican, philosopher and poet. This poem of 1898 describes Soloviev's three encounters with Sophia, Divine Wisdom, the second of which "occurred" in the reading room of the British Museum in London. (The final meeting took place in the Egyptian desert.)

147 Stalin's Little Helper Kalinin

Mikhail Ivanovich Kalinin (1875–1946) was a close ally of Stalin (their acquaintanceship may date from 1900), sufficiently adaptable and unimpressive to be one of the few "Old Bolsheviks" not to be executed by Stalin.

148 Your Mayakovsky

Vladimir Mayakovsky (1893–1930) was one of the leading Russian poets of the twentieth century. Increasingly disillusioned with the Revolution he had served so faithfully, he shot himself in 1930.

149 this Siberian Rastignac

Rastignac, hero of Balzac's *Le Père Goriot* (1835) and other works, here would appear to allude to the theme of an ambitious young person from the provinces hoping to make good in the capital. The allusion would also appear to be to the fact that fashionable trousers may be no less important in twentieth-century Moscow than Rastignac believed they were in nineteenth-century Paris!

150 Lobnoe Mesto

A small, circular stone dias on Red Square, originally the platform from where Tsars and patriarchs would address the crowds, but also known as a place of execution. The body of the first False Dmitry was left here in 1606.

152 "I love Vrubel"

Mikhail Aleksandrovich Vrubel (1856–1910) was the leading Russian Symbolist painter, most famous for his works on the theme of Lermontov's *Demon*, and a very popular painter in Russia.

154 stretching her Ingres neck

Jean-Auguste-Dominique Ingres (1780–1867) was a leading French Neoclassical painter, famous for his nudes and portraits.

154 On this point the poet Joseph Brodsky and I part company.

Alludes to the closing lines of Joseph Brodsky's poem on the occasion of his fortieth birthday: *"Ia vknodil vmesto dikogo zveria v kletku"*—"I have braved, for want of wild beasts, steel cages." The poem concludes by saying that, despite everything, until his throat is stuffed with clay, "only gratitude will be gushing from it."

155 I brake by the Arbat Restaurant

On Kalinin Prospect, one of the main streets in central Moscow.

156 "Twenty-six!"

A revolutionary number in a number of ways, perhaps—primarily, the number of Baku commissars shot by the British in August 1918, but maybe also hinting at Gorky's story "Twenty-six Men and a Girl" and perhaps also at the date of the 1917 Russian Revolution.

COTTON WOOL

159 *And that Symbolist lot at the Tower had lied too.*

From 1905 the Russian symbolist writer Vyacheslav Ivanov and his wife Lidia Dmitrievna held gatherings in their St. Petersburg apartment (known as "the Tower"), which became a major feature of Russian cultural life.

162 *the statue of Minin and Pozharsky was carted off somewhere to the backwoods of Maria's Grove*

Dmitry Pozharsky and Kuzma Minin, heroes of the war against the Poles in the early seventeenth century. Only after the Poles (with a second "False Dmitry" or Pretender to the Russian throne) had captured Moscow did the Russians unite under the leadership of Pozharsky and Minin. The statue erected in their honor in 1818 now stands in front of St. Basil's Cathedral.

165 *She had many children with Nicholas II: Kirov, Rudzutak, Rykov, Yagoda, Vernadsky, Mandelstam, Tsvetaeva, Mikhail Koltsov, Ordzhonikidze.*

Sergey Mironovich Kirov (1886–1934; original surname Kostrikov) was a prominent Russian Communist whose death by assassination heralded the start of the Great Terror in the Soviet Union. Head of the Leningrad Party organization from 1926 and at first a loyal supporter of Stalin, Kirov gradually built up his own power base and began to be seen as some (and no doubt by Stalin above all) as a potential rival to Stalin. Whether or not Kirov's murder in December 1934 was arranged by Stalin is still a mystery; what is not in doubt is that it suited Stalin's purposes and served as a convenient pretext for mass arrests and executions.

Yan Ernestovich Rudzutak (1887–1938) was born in Latvia, took part in October Revolution in Moscow, full member of the Politburo from 1926 to 1937. Arrested in 1937, and died in prison.

Aleksei Ivanovich Rykov (1881–1938) was, after Lenin's death in 1924, chairman of the Council of People's Commissars (that is, Soviet premier). Became associated with Right Opposition and had to give up all his posts in 1930. Arrested in 1937 and executed after a show trial.

Genrikh Grigor'evich Yagoda (1891–1938) was head of the NKVD (Security Organs) in 1934, but replaced by Yezhov in 1936. Arrested in 1937, and executed after a show trial.

Vladimir Ivanovich Vernadsky (1862–1945) was an outstanding Soviet scientist, one of the founders of modern geochemistry.

Osip Emilievich Mandelstam (1891–1938) was one of the outstanding Russian writers of the twentieth century. Sent into internal exile to Voronezh in 1934 for writing an epigram attacking Stalin, he was rearrested in 1938 and died in a transit camp near Vladivostok.

Marina Ivanovna Tsvetaeva (1892–1941) was one of the oustanding Russian poets of the twentieth century. Emigrated in 1922, but returned to the USSR in 1938, and hanged herself in 1941.

Mikhail Koltsov (1898–1940) was a Russian writer, one of countless writers whose biography reads "repressed, rehabilitated posthumously."

Grigory Konstantinovich Ordzhonikidze (1886–1937) was a Georgian revolutionary and Commissar for Heavy Industry from 1932. Took his own life in 1937.

SWEET FANNY ADAMS

This story "Yadrena Fenya" involves a complex play on the title itself and the young lady portrayed on the toilet door, combining as it does a euphemism for "Fuck your Mother," an allusion to the broader category of thieves' cant or prison slang, and the person of a somewhat questionable lady. However, I believe most of these connotations can be rendered by the British slang phrase "Sweet Fanny Adams." (An earlier translation of this story rendered the title as "Humping Hannah.") The source of the English phrase is the name of a young girl who was murdered in 1867, and the term was soon picked up as navy slang for tinned meat. Nowadays it is more commonly used (usually preceded by "sweet") to mean "nothing of any good at all," and the general sense is that this is a euphemism for "sweet fuck-all." But, like Erofeyev, I did not wish to offend readers' sensibilities by having this sort of phrase on the contents page, and Sweet F.A. would have been better, though even less familiar to American readers.

170 "Leaning against the door-frame..."

The second line of Boris Pasternak's poem "Hamlet," the first of the "poems of Doctor Zhivago" that form the final chapter of the novel.

171 The question, with its roots going back to Derzhavin's "Where's the john?"

Gavrila Romanovich Derzhavin (1743–1816) was the leading Russian poet of the eighteenth century. In 1815 he attended a graduation ceremony at Pushkin's school and heard the fifteen-year-old poet recite a poem which honored, in part,

Derzhavin's political and poetic legacy. In *Eugene Onegin* Pushkin describes this passing of the poetic baton as the aging Derzhavin "noticing him" and "blessing him as he descended into the grave." It is to Pushkin that we owe the information that, on arriving at the school (the Tsarskoye Selo Lyceum), Derzhavin had asked Pushkin's friend Baron Delvig the unpoetic question, "Tell me, sonny, where's the john here?"

178   A Lofty Malady!

Title of a long poem (1923–1928) by Pasternak.

MOTHER

Gorky's novel *Mother* (1906), for all its artistic weakness and lack of psychological profundity, has been one of the most influential novels of all times in both literary and political terms. Lenin referred to it as a "very timely book," and it has inspired revolutionaries, writers and ordinary readers in Russia and beyond. It was later canonized as one of the precursor texts of Socialist Realism and became a model for emulation. Broadly based on real-life characters and events, it tells the story of the political growth of a young revolutionary, Pavel, and his uneducated, illiterate mother. A number of the elements in Erofeyev's story are a blasphemous reworking of Gorky's novel.

183   Mironov, the captain of the local militia

The name of one of the leading characters in Pushkin's *The Captain's Daughter*.

THE GIRLFRIENDS

193   there is an element of . . . Miklukho-Maklai in this former literary scholar

Nikolai Nikolaevich Miklukho-Maklai (1846–1888) was a famous Russian ethnographer.

194   her buttocks (out of Maillol's sculptures)

Aristide Maillol (1861–1944) was a French painter and sculptor, best known for his statues of female nudes.

Vera Ignatevna Mukhina (1889–1953), one of the Soviet Union's greatest sculptresses, was best known for her monumental sculpture *Rabochyi i Kolkhoznitsa (The Worker and Collective-Farm Girl)*, first exhibited at the Paris World Fair in 1937.

195 *after this came a poem about Bakhtin*

Mikhail Mikhailovich Bakhtin (1895–1975) was one of the twentieth century's most influential literary theorists and philosophers of language, perhaps best known for his study of Dostoevsky's poetics.

196 *Both of them, but he in particular, with his mink and ermine, were among the hottest tickets out of town and country to be found anywhere in Moscow, but these egoists did not make anyone else happy other than themselves.*

Egoists because they married each other instead of marrying Russians and giving them an exit (visa).

POCKET APOCALYPSE

205 *My Biryukov shares the same sort of thoughts.*

The story deliberately blurs the identities of the narrator, Biryukov, and, in a certain sense, the real-life author as well as other potential prototypes.

205 *more of a Chaadaev than his author*

Pyotr Yakovlevich Chaadaev (1774–1856) was a Russian philosopher whose "First Philosophical Letter" (published in 1836) was deeply critical of the Russia of his time, in particular of its (spiritual) isolation and cultural isolation from the West. Publication of the letter resulted in Chaadaev's being declared insane and being placed under house arrest for a year.

207 *Scratch a Russian and you'll find a Tartar.*

Saying usually attributed to Napoleon, but also attributed to Joseph de Maistre and to Prince de Ligne.

210 *she's a Decembrist's wife*

After the failure of their revolt in 1825, many of the ringleaders of the Decembrists were sent to Siberia. A number of their wives freely chose to share with them the harsh conditions of exile.

211 *Pavel Korchagin, the hero of* How the Steel Was Tempered

Nikolai Alekseevich Ostrovsky's (1904–1936) novel, largely autobiographical in nature, was one of the canonical texts of Socialist Realism. Blind from 1928, Ostrovsky decided to serve the Communist cause by writing the uplifting story of his life. Its most famous lines are: "Man's dearest possession is life. It is given to him but once, and he must live it so as to feel no tormenting regrets for wasted years, never know the burning shame of a mean and petty past" (translated by Rosa Prokofieva). These lines appear to be echoed in one of Biryukov's thoughts.

212   *and another, less-great Frenchman, for example, wrote some choice insults about St. Basil's Cathedral*

Namely, de Custine—see fifth note for the story "Berdyaev."

214   *Rozanov kept on hassling the dying Strakhov*

Nikolai Nikolaevich Strakhov (1828–1896), a philosopher and critic, worked for the Dostoevsky brothers on their journal *Vremia (Time)*, and was a friend and supporter of both Dostoevsky and Tolstoy. One of the leading *pochvenniki* ("men of the soil"), who argued that Russians had lost touch with the "soil," that is, with the people.

Rozanov—see second note for the story "Berdyaev."

215   *Chaadaev got scared. When it all blew up he informed on Nadezhdin, on everyone. Pushkin wrote him a letter. Vyazemsky also behaved dishonorably.*

Nikolai Ivanovich Nadezhdin (1804–1856) was a publicist, literary critic and ethnographer. In 1831 founded the monthly *Teleskop*, which was closed down in 1836 for publishing Chaadaev's "Philosophical Letter." Nadezhdin was exiled to Siberia for two years. Chaadaev claimed (falsely, it appears) that Nadezhdin had published it without his consent.

Prince Pyotr Andreevich Vyazemsky (1792–1878) was a poet and critic.

FOR THE BEST IN PAPERBACKS, LOOK FOR THE

In every corner of the world, on every subject under the sun, Penguin represents quality and variety—the very best in publishing today.

For complete information about books available from Penguin—including Penguin Classics, Penguin Compass, and Puffins—and how to order them, write to us at the appropriate address below. Please note that for copyright reasons the selection of books varies from country to country.

In the United States: Please write to *Penguin Group (USA), P.O. Box 12289 Dept. B, Newark, New Jersey 07101-5289* or call 1-800-788-6262.

In the United Kingdom: Please write to *Dept. EP, Penguin Books Ltd, Bath Road, Harmondsworth, West Drayton, Middlesex UB7 0DA.*

In Canada: Please write to *Penguin Books Canada Ltd, 10 Alcorn Avenue, Suite 300, Toronto, Ontario M4V 3B2.*

In Australia: Please write to *Penguin Books Australia Ltd, P.O. Box 257, Ringwood, Victoria 3134.*

In New Zealand: Please write to *Penguin Books (NZ) Ltd, Private Bag 102902, North Shore Mail Centre, Auckland 10.*

In India: Please write to *Penguin Books India Pvt Ltd, 11 Panchsheel Shopping Centre, Panchsheel Park, New Delhi 110 017.*

In the Netherlands: Please write to *Penguin Books Netherlands bv, Postbus 3507, NL-1001 AH Amsterdam.*

In Germany: Please write to *Penguin Books Deutschland GmbH, Metzlerstrasse 26, 60594 Frankfurt am Main.*

In Spain: Please write to *Penguin Books S. A., Bravo Murillo 19, 1° B, 28015 Madrid.*

In Italy: Please write to *Penguin Italia s.r.l., Via Benedetto Croce 2, 20094 Corsico, Milano.*

In France: Please write to *Penguin France, Le Carré Wilson, 62 rue Benjamin Baillaud, 31500 Toulouse.*

In Japan: Please write to *Penguin Books Japan Ltd, Kaneko Building, 2-3-25 Koraku, Bunkyo-Ku, Tokyo 112.*

In South Africa: Please write to *Penguin Books South Africa (Pty) Ltd, Private Bag X14, Parkview, 2122 Johannesburg.*